I0535372

The Benefits of Line Dancing

by

Edward Shull

Moai
Press

The Benefits of Line Dancing

Copyright © 2013 by Edward Shull

ISBN: 978-0-9891827-0-6

Cover design by Damonza www.damonza.com

For Gail.

Prologue

The horizon shifted and the earth jostled, skipping and accelerating. The sky stole her sight, and the lights above brightened in a sudden flare, leaving only darkness. She reached out, but there was no one. She crashed, and the pain swelled.

*

"I told you not to wear those heels," cackled her roommate Marlee. "You're not even drinking yet and you're on your ass!"

Grabbing her sore ankle, Amanda felt the cool sensation of a scratch on her forearm. She looked at the trickling blood, brushing off the dirt and hiding the wound as best she could.

"You okay?" asked a voice from above.

At first, she saw only white Nike's and jeans. The man crouched down in front of her, bringing his black shirt and big smile down to her level.

"That was a bad fall, you okay?" he asked again.

"Fine," she said, embarrassed and now a little nervous.

The man took her hand and placed his other palm on her elbow, helping her stand.

"Ankle okay?" he asked.

"Yeah," Amanda said. "I'm okay."

"She's like this all the time," Marlee insisted, pushing passed Amanda toward the club door. "She's always leaving a trail of disaster in her wake."

Amanda rolled her eyes, embarrassment shining in her cheeks.

"Nothing wrong with a little disaster every now and then," the man said, picking up Amanda's purse. "It's sometimes what brings people together."

Marlee reached back and grabbed Amanda, dragging her to the front of the line. Amanda tried to push her hand off, but Marlee held tight.

"Ignore that guy," Marlee said. "We're hot, and if we're alone, we don't have to wait in line."

Amanda couldn't pull her eyes from the guy in the black shirt, and when he started to walk towards them, she grew anxious trying to think of what to say.

He smiled as he walked up next to her, and then stepped in front of Marlee. "I need to see your ID," he told Marlee as he took his place on the bouncer's wooden stool.

"Everything okay out there, Jim?" a man hollered from inside the club.

"It's fine," Jim replied.

"Oh," Marlee said, a little embarrassed, handing Jim an ID.

Jim admired the card and looked over at Amanda.

"And yours," he insisted, holding on to Marlee's ID.

Amanda reached out and handed her ID to Jim, who looked at the two cards together.

"At least you bought them from the same guy," Jim said, handing them back their fake IDs.

"What the hell does that mean?" Marlee said. "These are real, we come here all the time."

"Really?" Jim asked, still smiling at Amanda, making her smile grow.

"Yes, you must be new," Marlee insisted.

"What's the color of the ladies' room door?" he asked.

Marlee stood back and considered for a moment, knowing she would have to guess. "Black," she said.

"Nope," Jim smirked.

"Then it's been painted," Marlee argued.

"There is no door on the ladies' room," he admitted, making Amanda giggle.

Marlee threw up her hands. "Fuck you," she said, "this place sounds like a shit hole anyway." She grabbed Amanda's sore arm, turning to leave.

"Wait a second!" he said. "She didn't try to convince me," Jim added, nodding his head towards Amanda.

Marlee spun Amanda around into Jim.

"Hi," Amanda said nervously.

"Hi," Jim said, giving her a mischievous smile.

"May we please go in?" she asked.

Jim rocked back on the stool. "I have to admit I'm tempted, you asking so sweet and all." He waggled his eyebrows suggestively. "But I'm afraid I'm drunk with power and need a bit more coaxing."

Amanda laughed and reached for a button on her already cleavage-displaying shirt, popping it open.

Jim looked and nodded towards the next button. Amanda smiled and popped the next, exposing the new bra she'd purchased for the night.

"I'll look at your cleavage, just so you know you've done all you can," he said, a boyish grin curving his cheeks.

"Hey, asshole, just let us in," Marlee said.

Jim ignored Marlee, leaning over to Amanda. "For you, I'd break any law," he said. "Have fun in there, ladies."

"Let's go," Marlee huffed, pushing Amanda backwards into the club.

The club was packed and the music was barely decipherable above the screech of the poorly set up amps and the sound of the drunken crowd. Within five minutes, Marlee had a pair of engineering students buying them drinks.

Amanda danced with one of the students, and then with Marlee. But she kept thinking about the cute guy at the door and felt stupid for not making more of their encounter.

At some point a fight broke out, and a few bouncers came through breaking up the melee, but she didn't see her doorman. She had another drink and ended up getting into an argument with Marlee over her desire to leave with the engineering students.

As she walked toward the door with Marlee, Amanda felt someone running his hand up her skirt. She turned around to some guy in a Limp Bizkit tee leering at her. She slapped his hand away and he tried again. The crowd pushed her into him, and this time his grasping fingers made it passed her underwear.

She shoved back and kicked him in the knee, then pushed him again to gain distance, but the crowd was too tight. The music was too loud, and Marlee was too drunk to notice. The guy grabbed her crotch hard and laughed, removing his hands and throwing a triumphant salute to his friends.

Like a snapped glow stick, Amanda felt a neon fury replace her fear, and she lunged at the guy, knocking him onto his back amidst a tower of guitar amps. He yelped as the amps began to topple. Amanda grabbed a pitcher of beer and threw it at the perv, barely missing him as he leapt off the boxes. The beer hit the amps and they sparked brightly. There was a large hum and the lights dimmed in and out.

The sound stopped and the club fell silent, everyone looking at Amanda.

"Holy shit! You almost fried that guy!" Marlee covered her mouth in glee.

Amanda felt two sets of hands grab her and pull her towards

the door.

"I got her," she heard the familiar voice say, and Amanda turned to see her doorman. "You are a handful, aren't you?" he mused, releasing his grip on her shoulders.

"Sorry," she said, unable to control her smile at seeing him again.

"She blew out the fuses!" a club worker with tools in his hands fumed, walking by indignantly.

Jim smiled back at her. "Some girls are high maintenance, but you're high voltage."

Amanda was sorting out a response when a hand grabbed her, yanking her down the street. "I think they called the cops!" Marlee gasped as she tried to hail a passing cab.

"Wait a minute," Jim said, walking in front of Marlee.

"What?" she asked.

"I'm Jim," he said, holding out his hand to Amanda.

"Amanda," she replied, slowly reaching out and filling his hand with hers.

"Want to have coffee tomorrow?" he asked.

"Yes," Amanda immediately agreed.

"The Starbucks on the corner here, at eleven?" he asked.

"I'll be there," she said.

"Let's go, I'm not going to jail for your crap," Marlee said, dragging Amanda off. "And the bathroom doors are black, asshole!" Marlee added as she stormed off, a giddy Amanda in tow.

*

Jim arrived at Starbucks early the next day, hoping to see the girl who had been on his mind all night. When she finally arrived, they sat together and talked about the rest of her evening, which had thankfully been less eventful. They moved on to the topic of their pasts, as he tried to squeeze in as many questions as socially acceptable.

He learned she was from Greenbush, a small town up north in Sheboygan County, not much different from Jim's suburban background in Illinois. Her grandmother, a school teacher set to retire next year, had raised her from the time she was four years old, when Amanda's mother had finally lost a protracted battle with cancer that had begun before Amanda was even born.

Jim, who had no equivalent story to share, returned the conversation to the safety of the present.

"You're an art student?" Jim asked upon hearing she attended MIAD, the local design school.

"Yeah," she laughed, "can't you tell?"

Art student did seem to fit her personality, he decided.

"What are you majoring in at UWM?" she asked.

"Business right now, but I'm thinking of going to law school," he admitted.

"Going to defend the down trodden against the oppressive powers that be?"

"More, squash the dreams of the common person on behalf of big banks and corporations," he said. "Pays better, and I want a BMW."

"You strike me more as the save the world type," Amanda mused. "We'll have to work on that."

Before they knew it, three hours had passed and they made plans for the next day. Three days later, she spent the night in his dorm, and three weeks later they were having dinner together for the tenth night in a row.

*

As time progressed Jim became more fascinated with Amanda. He was happy to find he wasn't the only one disarmed by her charms. Everyone who met Amanda seemed to fall in love with her, confirming to Jim that she was someone truly special.

When he brought Amanda home for Christmas a few months later, he was surprised to find his parents completely immune to her smile. They viewed Amanda's free-spirited nature as a distraction for Jim, and it was clear they hoped this would be a short-lived romance.

Fortunately, his sister and her children took to Amanda right away. And, as he watched Amanda hold his three-month-old niece, he felt the pieces of his imagined future clicking smoothly into place, locking into the pattern of love and success he had always pictured.

On New Year's Eve, Jim asked Amanda to move in with him, in spite of his parents' whispered warnings for caution. Two months later, they moved what little furniture they had into a cozy one bedroom on the sixth floor of an old brick building near the lake.

Amanda had never seen herself moving in with someone. She knew it might be inevitable someday, but certainly not at nineteen. But that's how in love with Jim she was. He made her feel safe.

*

Six months after moving in, she learned her grandmother was dying of cancer, and three months later Amanda said goodbye to the only family she had left, giving her a simultaneous look at her past, and her future.

Through all the misery of that time, Jim kept her sane, and most importantly constantly reminded her she wasn't alone. She hated being alone.

Trips to the doctor confirmed what Amanda had always suspected. It wasn't the possibility of meeting the fate of her mother and grandmother that bothered her; she was too young to consider those types of things. It was the current reality which weighed on her, keeping her from sharing the burden with her love. She simply wouldn't be able to provide Jim with something he so clearly wanted, no matter how hard they tried.

Amanda knew Jim would tell her it didn't matter. She knew he would hold her and tell her it was okay. But she didn't want to have that conversation. She didn't want to be weak and pitied and forever feel guilty.

She made the decision to push it out of her mind. They were young and playing house while in college. It wasn't as if they were going to get married anytime soon.

*

Few traumatic experiences can match a Milwaukee January. The cold wind struck Jim's face like a thousand needles, and the blackened sleet of the parking lot cracked and skidded under his brisk steps, doing its best to slip him up. Inside, the building provided little comfort, as a sharp cold draft whipped through the lobby, filling it with a bone-shivering chill. He really had to piss, but was determined to check the mail before heading up.

The mailbox's lock was rarely cooperative on cold days, and today was no exception. Nearing the point of abandoning the effort and leaving his keys in the lock for a chance to flee upstairs and take a quick leak, he was finally able to open the small door and grab a group of envelopes. Focused on his bladder control, Jim wouldn't bother to examine the mail until he was relieved.

Standing in the poorly lit elevator, Jim was now succumbing to the dance he had reverted to since childhood, whenever the need to pee was upon him. Left leg up and bent, a slight bounce on the right, then reverse and repeat.

He was on his second switch up when the doors finally opened to the sixth floor and he ran to his front door. With any luck, the door would be open since Amanda was already home. But it was not Jim's lucky day. He started fumbling for his keys and ringing the doorbell.

He dropped his keychain and nearly resigned himself to losing the battle when the door miraculously opened. Jim dodged passed Amanda, throwing the envelopes in her direction as he ran to the bathroom.

"You have the bladder of a four year old, you know that?" Amanda said, scooping to pick the envelopes off the floor.

"It's not the size of the bladder, but the hose that matters!" Jim rhymed over the sound of a gushing stream.

"When did we agree that leaving the door open for that activity was acceptable?" Amanda asked as she walked passed the bathroom.

"Desperate times, babe," Jim said as he neared the end of his event, "desperate times." "That was a close one," he called as he exited the bathroom, zipping his fly and assuming an air of comical relief.

"Yeah, you almost looked retarded," she said. "And for god's sake, wash you hands!"

"Did you check the mail I gave you?" he asked, returning to the bathroom to run his hands under the faucet.

"You mean the pile of envelopes you so graciously tossed at me?" she asked sweetly, beginning to thumb through them.

"Can you check them, please?" he pleaded, walking out of the bathroom again and drying his hands on the side of his jeans. "It's been over a month and I still haven't heard shit from them."

Jim came round the corner to see Amanda quietly holding a single, thick envelope.

"Is that it?" Jim asked, stopping in his tracks.

Amanda turned the envelope over, showing Jim the Harvard emblem on the front.

Jim stepped back and took a breath. "You open it," he said.

Amanda looked back at him, wide-eyed and frightened.

"Go ahead," he said. "I already know what the answer is. I'd rather hear it from you than them. I can't stand the whole 'thank you for your interest' bullshit. Please."

Amanda looked at the envelope, inserted her finger into the seam and forced it along the edge, ripping it open. She pulled out the folded letter and began reading to herself. She knew she lacked a poker face and when she met Jim's eyes she could already see the cautious excitement on his face.

"You're in," she whispered as she started to cry.

Jim took a second and laughed to himself. "Shit!" he said as he ran his fingers through his hair.

"You're in!" she yelled, sparking Jim to grab Amanda in excitement and spin her around.

"Holy shit, you're fucking going to Harvard Law!" she said as he squeezed her. "You're really going ..."

Jim pulled Amanda's head to him, pressing his lips against hers like a conquering warrior. Amanda returned the kiss and started loosening Jim's belt. Within a minute, they were having congratulatory sex on the couch, lasting only slightly longer than it took to initiate.

Lying silently together on the couch, Jim kissed Amanda's head. "I love you," he said.

Amanda pulled in closer to Jim. "You should call your parents," she said, "they'll be thrilled."

Jim knew this was a double-edged comment. His parents were never fond of Amanda, a fact they were too stupid to hide and she was too smart to miss.

Jim got up and walked over to the phone. "You know, we need to talk about how we're going to do this," he said. "I know you like Milwaukee, but I bet you'll love Boston."

Amanda got up and pulled her pants on. "We'll talk about it later," she said. "Your parents aren't going to be happy if you don't tell them right away."

Jim dialed his parents' number and waited for his mom to pick up, as she always did. "Mom, I got the letter. I'm in!" he announced.

Amanda could hear the shouting over the line as she passed by. She slapped Jim on his bare ass as she slipped from the room.

"Yeah, it's official, I start in the fall," she heard him say as she closed the door.

Amanda sat on the bed and looked at the wall for a short time, trying not to cry. Jim's treasured BMW poster seemed designed to make her efforts ridiculous. She finally gave in to the tears, knowing they were coming sooner or later, and figuring it was better to get this out of the way now, before Jim finished his call and discovered her weakness.

Beyond the hurt, she also felt relieved. She had been feeling guilty for hoping he didn't get in. She had convinced herself the term 'wait listed' was a polite way of telling a prospect "we should see other people."

She could hear him laughing with his parents. That's the way she knew it should be. She didn't have a family, not like Jim's. Her grandmother was gone, just like her mother. She was on her own now, Jim being the closest thing she had to a family.

His family never liked her much, and she understood why. Jim's last girlfriend was a saint in their eyes. They met her while visiting Jim at UWM, and she was his first college sweetheart. Sarah was cute and smart and nice and everything you'd want your son to date while in college.

Jim sparred his parents the reality of the break up, omitting the burning sensation he had while peeing, and his knowledge it could have only come from one source. When Sarah admitted screwing around with some guy while home for Christmas, he ended it. Jim would tolerate a lot, but infidelity was the one thing sure to drive him away.

Amanda did her best to compose herself and headed back to the living room.

"Mom, we're going to figure it out," Jim was saying on the phone. "It's our business, and I love her."

Amanda pretended to be oblivious to the fact she was the topic of yet another argument, and Jim rushed the end of his call and circled his arms around Amanda's waist.

"I'm going to call off of work," he said. "We'll hang out here tonight and order in."

"No, go to work," she said. "I'll have something for you when you get home."

"Really?" he asked. "You're not cooking, right?"

"Don't worry, I know my limitations," she laughed. "Just go get ready for work."

Jim walked into the bedroom and changed into his black jeans and mock neck shirt, the default uniform for the door guy. He didn't like the term 'bouncer' as it seemed a cartoonish name for a man who spent most of his shift calling bullshit on college girls' badly faked IDs.

He kissed Amanda as he walked out the door and strode quickly to Shank Hall, the little club where he worked. He manned the door with Chris, who was about twice Jim's size and took the lead when they were faced with groups of prowling douchebags. Jim shared his good news as they leaned against the frigid wall, staring down nervous teenagers and patting down the occasional creepers.

"When do you go?" Chris asked. "To Boston?"

"Probably the end of July," Jim said, "so I can get Amanda settled in before classes start."

"She excited?" Chris asked.

"Not really," Jim admitted. "I mean, we'd talked about it, but she was always saying we would discuss it more seriously if I got in."

"She's probably just nervous," Chris said. "I mean she's what, twenty-one?"

"Yeah," Jim said. "I know it seems like a rush, but we've been together for two years, and I love her. I can't leave without her."

"Still, a long way to go for a boyfriend," Chris cautioned.

"I know," Jim said. "That's why I'm going to ask her to marry me."

Chris stood still and stopped the line, pushing his hand into the chest of a young guy wearing a Kermit the Frog beanie.

"You serious?" Chris asked.

"Yeah," Jim responded.

Chris reached over and lifted Jim off the ground in a giant bear hug. "Congratulations, my friend."

"Thanks, man," Jim wheezed. "But she hasn't said yes yet."

Chris released Jim, allowing him to take a breath. "Look at you: young, good looking, Harvard-bound. Who could turn you down?"

"Hey, can you talk to your gay lover after you let me in?" the beanie wearer asked in a snarky tone.

Jim shook his head, knowing Chris had a problem with gay bashing.

"I'm sorry," he growled, "did you say something?"

The young man stood silent, regretting his interruption.

"What's with the hat?" Jim asked, pointing to the green beanie.

"I'm peacocking," the hipster replied. "This way I'll get noticed."

"They'll notice you look like an idiot," Chris snapped, as he grabbed the guy's ID from his hands.

"You know Kermit dates a pig, right?" Jim asked.

"Kind of a hot pig, though." the guy replied.

"Go on in, but you're not wearing this," Chris said, snatching the beanie off the hipster's head as he walked by.

The cold kept most people indoors, so Chris was cool about letting Jim take off early. Jim walked back to the apartment, hoping to surprise Amanda.

Walking in, he noticed a jacket on the floor, a man's jacket, still wet from the snow. From the jacket, his eyes followed a trail of black slush prints, leading to a pair of men's shoes that had been kicked off before the bedroom door.

The man's voice was audible through the half-opened door, and Jim watched as the stranger's ass moved rhythmically, accompanied by odd noises coming from beneath him. Jim didn't know what sound he made to startle the two of them, but soon bed sheets were scrambling and excuses were coming out of the stranger's mouth.

The man's voice went silent in Jim's ears, his presence forgotten, as Jim focused on Amanda, who wouldn't meet his eyes. He finally remembered the half-naked stranger only when he attempted to push passed to get to the door. Jim grabbed him by the throat and threw him against the wall.

"I'm sorry, man!" the guy squeaked. "We just met at the bar across the street and she brought me here. I didn't know!"

Jim released his grip and let the worm slither out.

As much as she didn't want to, Amanda eventually had no choice but to look Jim in the face. She was never physically afraid of Jim, despite his 6'3" height and sometimes looming presence. But, she had never done anything like this to him before.

"Are you going to say something?" he asked.

"What's there to say?"

"You can start with why," he said.

"I guess I'm just bored with you, and he looked like a decent alternative for a couple of hours," she said.

Jim stood in silent shock.

Amanda got up and grabbed her bag, already packed.

"Enjoy Harvard and everything," she said as she retrieved her clothes and dressed. "But I have no intention of going with you."

She looked up at Jim, but he was still trying to compose himself.

"He's not the first, Jim, you should know that," she said. "It's nice having a bit of freedom while you're working nights. I've actually been seeing someone else."

"That guy?" Jim asked.

"Oh, hell no," she said. "He's just some prick I picked up across the street for a quick fuck. The funny part is, I felt guiltier about cheating on my other boyfriend than on you. I guess the timing works out."

"You're leaving?" he asked.

"I am." She lifted her bag. "I'd say I would send somebody by for my stuff, but there's nothing here I want."

Amanda opened the front door, doing her best to steady her breathing. "Goodbye, Jim," she said, closing the door firmly behind her.

Chapter 1

Jim strolled away from his BMW, tapping the keychain to roll up the convertible top and windows. The sun was shinning and his schedule was relatively light, except for lunch with a TV star he wanted to represent, and meeting Emily to preview wedding cakes. It'd been over eight years since Jim had seen or heard from Amanda, and he was finally to the point where he didn't think about her more than once a day.

He had heard she actually left Milwaukee before him. He dated a few girls at Harvard, but his dedication to school killed any chance of a social life, in spite of the fact his shoulders had broadened as his frame finally caught up to his height. After graduation, he surprised everyone by not taking a position in New York as he had always planned, and instead put his contract law specialty to use with a full service firm in Los Angeles. McInerney, Strickland & Ellis handled everything: mergers & acquisitions, entertainment law, personal injury, and criminal law.

Jim found a mentor in Charles Strickland, a legend in the entertainment law space, and had been moving in that direction, mostly preparing and reviewing contracts for film studios and talent. The back and forth of contracts between lawyers was fun for Jim. Like playing Battleship, the real skill was setting up your ships so they wouldn't get hit. It was all about protecting yourself by limiting exposure.

His phone lit up with Emily's picture, an image of a fresh-faced young woman whose light eyes shimmered with intelligence and intensity, while her dark hair framed a delicate face.

"Hey. Let me guess, you're calling to remind me about the cake," he said as he entered his office lobby.

"Yes, and now you have no excuse to pull a no show," Emily replied.

"Eliminating reasonable expectation for delay ... Remind me again why I'm marrying another lawyer?" he asked.

"Because together we'll make a buttload of cash," she said.

"That's vulgar, don't talk like that!" he heard her mother say in the background.

"I see you're with the Evil Queen," he said.

"Yes, I'm going for a fitting after the cake and she insisted on going with," Emily sighed.

"So she'll be joining us for cake?" Jim said, trying his best not to sound put out.

"Oh, you know her, never misses a chance for free food," she replied, trying to lighten the situation.

"Excuse me, but I do not go around snuffling for food like an animal," her mother interjected in the background.

"I'm going to let you deal with that," Jim said, "I'll meet you there at two."

"Love you," Emily said.

"Love you too," Jim said before hanging up.

Before proposing to Emily, Jim had made a list of pros and cons for the decision. Out of the eight cons he came up with, seven revolved around Emily's two sisters and their mother, Katherine.

Emily's parents came from money, but her father, despite being a nice enough guy, had made several bad financial choices which, after his death, left the family in what they felt was a bad way.

Though they still had more passive income than most dual income families, their unwillingness to scale down their lifestyle, including the expenses of maintaining a monstrous home, put them in constant financial jeopardy.

The youngest sister had eloped and moved to Florida, while the eldest, who was always a little crazy, still lived with their mother. Visiting them was like entering a west coast version of Grey Gardens. They walked around their mini-mansion in elaborate evening wear as if they were about to be summoned to a grand ball, and treated most visitors like they had come to steal the silver. The whole scene freaked Jim out, and he could only handle it with Emily reassuring him they were harmless.

Emily was somehow unaffected by the weirdness of her family. She stood out like Marilyn on *The Munsters*, a perfect, demure beauty surrounded by scary creatures and ghosts.

Jim's decision to marry Emily was an easy one, despite the weird family. She was beautiful, smart, and had a big heart. The best part was she seemed somehow unaware of these things, which made her even more desirable. And, even better, she honestly seemed to love Jim, despite his own, not unremarkable, luggage.

Jim walked into his office and called good morning to Jane, his assistant. Jane was a long-time employee at the firm, having worked there for a decade before Jim's arrival, and he was lucky to have her. When it came to the daily business of law, Jane had Jim beat by a mile.

"Mr. Strickland won't be in today and wanted to know if you could handle his 2:30 with Mr. Combs," she said.

"Shit, I have a cake thing with Em," he said.

"I know, so I rescheduled the 2:30 for an 11:30 tomorrow," she said. "Does that work for you?"

"You know my schedule better than I do."

"It works fine." She turned back to her computer.

"Thanks, Jane," he said.

"Of course, Mr. Morgan," she said.

Jim had given up on getting Jane to call him by his first name, and he had since realized there was logic to the formality.

He sat down and began going through his email, which always contained at least a dozen new contract edits to review. He began at the bottom of the list, and the next thing he knew Jane was reminding him of his lunch appointment with a new client.

*

Pulling up to the trendy restaurant, Jim valeted his car and discovered his new client, Kyle Hill, already seated. Jim was used to working with talent, and hadn't expected Kyle to even be on time, never mind early. A young television actor who had become a popular teenage heartthrob, Kyle had recently experienced some success in a small independent film that was now garnering him better offers for bigger roles, including the lead in a big budget franchise. As a client, he was potentially worth millions to Jim, and most actors took that fact as an excuse to ignore the most basic manners such as punctuality.

"Mr. Hill?" Jim said, walking up to the young man whose face he recognized from billboard after billboard.

"Oh, hey," he replied, offering him his hand. "Call me Kyle."

"Nice to meet you, Kyle." The handshake, firm but not aggressive, surprised Jim. Usually, a client would offer his hand as if expecting Jim to kiss his ring, or would shake with such force Jim was thankful to get his hand back intact.

Kyle, looking even younger than his seventeen years, explained his agent had recommended another attorney, but Kyle enjoyed doing his own research and found several blog posts Jim had written about how an actor can protect himself from potential legal issues unique to their lifestyle.

"I was really impressed with what you wrote," Kyle said. "I feel like you're already looking out for my needs, even before I know what they are."

"Thanks," Jim said. "I'm glad they connected with you. Anything specific you're worried about?"

Kyle looked down for a moment and it was clear he wanted to discuss something personal.

"If it's a private issue, we can take this back to my office," Jim offered.

"No, it's cool," Kyle said. "It's just difficult to talk about, and a little embarrassing. I don't want to come off as a bad guy, or ungrateful. I just need some help."

Jim could see Kyle had something heavy on his mind, not the usual desire to insist on having the right brand of water in his dressing room. Jim watched as Kyle toyed with his pricey watch, moved as if he was about to ask a sudden question, and then slowly pulled back. Of course, if Kyle's problem was embarrassingly personal, that would explain why he was talking to Jim, and not his current lawyer. Jim was several steps removed from Kyle's orbit.

"Kyle, the thing about being a lawyer is I'll never judge you," Jim explained. "I'm always on your side, no matter what. Others may betray you, but it's my job to not only have your back, but to protect you against those who don't. Your agent, manager, publicist, girlfriend, whoever. None of them are under any legal obligation to put your needs first. I am. What ever the issue, you can tell me and I'll walk you through every obstacle."

Kyle smiled and took a breath. He seemed relieved.

"Wow, very cool." Kyle took another breath, then clapped his hands closed and exhaled. "I'm turning eighteen in a few months," he began, "and I feel like my parents, more specifically, my dad, is trying to grab some of my money before then. Is there anything I can do to stop him?"

Jim leaned back and thought for a moment. "If you were younger, and this was an ongoing concern, we could set up a trust. But since we're talking about money already in your control, and therefore in your father's control, our options are limited."

"That's what I was afraid of," Kyle said, deflating.

"Cheer up, I said limited, not nonexistent," Jim said. "How much are we talking?"

"A little under half a million," Kyle said.

Jim had to laugh at the idea that only in Los Angeles could a seventeen year old boy be trying to figure out how to hide half a million dollars in earnings from his father.

"May I suggest you hire my firm?" Jim said.

"Well, yeah," Kyle said, "but I'm trying to figure out how you're going to help me first."

"Easy. You're going to give us half a million as a retainer to investigate your account."

"Wait, you want me to pay you the money I'm asking you to protect?" Kyle asked.

"Kinda," Jim said, smiling. "It's a retainer. We charge four hundred and fifty per hour. We'll spend a couple hours looking over your bank statements. If we don't find anything after a few hours, we'll just refund your retainer. Although that may take a few months."

Kyle smiled, quick to catch on. "Perfect," he said. "How do we get started?"

Jim called Jane and had her put the contract together and forward it through the studio to Kyle's parents. He quickly worded the first paragraph to make it seem like Kyle was to receive a bonus, and then made the rest of the document over eighty pages long, virtually assuring Kyle's parents would simply sign on his behalf without reading it through.

Leaving Kyle a happy customer, Jim proceeded to the bakery to meet up with Emily and the Evil Queen.

Chapter 2

"Are you sure eating before a fitting is a good idea?" her mother asked. "I mean, you already need to drop at least another ten pounds."

"I'm not dropping any weight before my wedding," Emily snapped back, trying not to get angry.

"Well, you do realize everyone will be staring right at you?" her mother explained. "You want them to think you look fat?"

"No, mother," Emily replied, "since my wedding guests are supposed to be made up of my family and friends, I was hoping they would think I look beautiful, and be happy for me."

"You don't know shit about weddings," her mother replied, lighting another cigarette.

Emily had scheduled the day off to take care of those wedding items that were difficult to tackle on weekends, but she had not planned on the addition of her mother. She had spared Jim the florists, figuring him staring blankly at flowers would not help anyone. But she did want him to have some input on the cake.

Her phone rang as she pulled into the bakery parking lot; she could see it was work.

"Mom, it's work, so please be quiet," she said.

"You don't have to shush me, I'm not a child," her mother

huffed.

"Hello?" Emily said.

"Ms. Perkins?" the voice said.

"Yes?"

"Sorry to bother you, I know you're on a personal day. This is Jamie at the office." Jamie, a new paralegal at the firm, had only been assigned to the criminal department last month.

"No problem, Jamie, what's going on?" Emily asked.

"I was filing an emergency motion for Mr. Straub, and noticed he mentioned a Detective Wilkes was arrested for soliciting narcotics last night," Jamie said. "You also have a Detective Wilkes on the Cynthia Roberts case."

"Oh, wow!" Emily said, calculating the effect of this fact on her case. Wilkes was the arresting officer on one of Emily's cases, and his testimony was crucial. If he had been compromised … Emily was a big believer in what one of her law professors at Stanford called 'factory law,' which meant she looked at the criminal legal system as a big machine. It processes cases all day long, and most go as planned. But if you disrupt the system, with something like declaring a cop's testimony unreliable, the system kicks you out. The squeaky wheel gets the grease, but the broken cog gets tossed out quickly, so the machine can go back to its mass processing. Emily specialized in being the most annoying cog imaginable to prosecutors, which encouraged them to make exceedingly quick, exceedingly generous plea deals.

"Good catch, Jamie," she said. "Straub really should have alerted everyone in the office when he found out. Can you please post this to our internal system to let everyone know?"

"Absolutely." Jamie said.

"And on the Roberts' case, prepare the motion to strike Wilkes' testimony and try to get me a hearing tomorrow," Emily said. "But first, let's cross reference the badge number to double check it's the same guy, and get me a copy of his arrest report."

"Got it," Jamie said.

"Thanks, Jamie. Excellent, excellent catch," she said.

Emily grabbed her bag and walked with her mother to the bakery.

"What was that about?" her mother asked.

"The arresting detective in a theft case I have, just got arrested for drugs," Emily said.

"So?" her mother asked.

"So, if he's a drug addicted criminal, why should the court take his word?" Emily said.

"So this thief is just going to walk away?" her mother asked.

"Alleged thief," Emily corrected out of habit.

"I didn't hear 'allegedly' about the drug addicted criminal detective," her mother shot back.

"It's not the same," Emily said. "I'm not throwing him in jail without a trial, I'm simply questioning the veracity of his word in my client's defense."

"Just like your father," her mother said, "defending a bunch of thieves and rapists while your family goes hungry."

"No one is going hungry, mom." Emily said, already exhausted with the effort of coddling her mother. "Look, we're getting cake right now."

Emily hated when her mother bashed her father. She often felt guilty about wishing it was her father who was still alive, instead of her mother. But her father was, for most of her life, her best friend.

She would sit for hours and listen to him talk about his cases when he worked for the Public Defender's Office. He would pour himself a drink, sometimes a few, and talk about how they would catch a police officer lying, or how the system was trying to force blame on someone due to their skin color. She was proud of his belief in the system, and in people. When it came time for her to choose a career path, she chose the one of which she thought he would be most proud, even though he was no longer alive to see her do it.

It was her older sister who found him that morning. Emily had been just sixteen years old, and had never been able to fill the hole in her heart his departure created. She and her mother were never close, and rarely did she have anything nice to say about Emily, or her father. Lately, Emily was starting to admit to herself what she felt for her mother was more obligation than love, and even then, she felt the debt was not so much owed to her mother as to her father, who Emily knew would have wanted his wife cared for.

The bakery was not like any bakery to which Emily had ever been. It was set up into two sections: one a traditional bakery, with display cases for the cakes, and the other half styled like a well-appointed home, with four sets of plush love seats arranged around delicate coffee tables. There were four silver serving stations, each on rolling wheels, equipped with china cake plates and an elaborate coffee service.

Her mother moved straight toward a woman positioned like a hostess in a restaurant.

"We are the Perkins party, and we expect to be seated immediately," her mother said in the tone she specially reserved for servants, and for Emily. "Someplace quiet. We'll take those seats in the corner."

"Of course, Mrs. Perkins," the woman obliged.

Despite being accustomed to her mother's abrasive nature, Emily was never comfortable with the idea of ordering people around, at least in a social context. When it came to work, she was perfectly willing to brow beat (on the behalf of her client, of course) anyone standing in her way. But that was the job; she never used those skills in her personal matters.

The hostess sat them at the requested table and said the cake specialist would be out shortly.

"Where's your boyfriend?" her mother asked.

"He's on his way." Emily replied. "And he has a name."

"Has he begun the dance classes yet?" her mother asked. "You don't want to look like a fool on the dance floor."

"No," Emily said. "He's a little self-conscious about the dancing thing. I'll have to work with him on it."

The dancing bothered Emily more than she let on. Jim had explained early on how he was shy about dancing, and she could understand why. He was a big guy and probably felt like he would be highly scrutinized. But she *would* be dancing at her wedding, and with her husband.

Her phone buzzed, but this time it was a text from Jim. "On my way, ten minutes."

"That him?" her mother asked.

"Yes, he'll be here in ten," Emily said.

"He's late. Again."

"He's busy," Emily said. "I scheduled this in the middle of a work day. It's understandable."

"I only hope he appreciates what we're paying for this wedding," her mother sighed.

This was a subject her mother enjoyed, the idea she was paying for Emily's wedding. In fact, however, it was the result of one of the only actions Emily's father had taken when he realized he was dying. He stashed away eighty-five grand, exclusively earmarked for each of his daughters' weddings. The youngest Perkins daughter had eloped, and it had taken all of Emily's skill to figure out how to get the money released to her. In all honesty, Emily would have preferred a small, inexpensive ceremony, although not as hasty as her little sister's event. Jim and she made more than enough to cover something quaint. But Emily felt she owed an elaborate wedding to her father, since he had wanted them for his girls, and it didn't seem likely her older sister would ever leave to start a family of her own.

Jim swept in, joining Emily on her love seat.

"Sorry I'm late," he said, punctuating the sentiment with a

chaste peck on her cheek. "Lunch with a new client."

"How'd it go?" Emily asked.

"Good," Jim said, smiling. "I think we're going to be a good fit. The blog writing really paid off on this one, that's how he found me."

"That's great," Emily said.

"I'm fine, by the way," Emily's mother injected.

"I can see that!" Jim said over enthusiastically. "You look fantastic, Katherine. Have you been using some new moisturizer?"

Katherine stilled her face, puzzled. She was cynical enough to understand sarcasm, but also vain enough to wonder if her new moisturizer had been working as advertised.

The head baker came out and described in graphic detail the variety of potential cakes, which seemed near endless. Recognizing Emily and Jim's lost expressions, he began to ask questions to trim down the options.

"Most women prefer the traditional multi-tier white cake, with the surprise being more within," the baker explained. "Does that sound like you?"

Emily looked to Jim, who confirmed she likely wanted the cake to appear more traditional, and she nodded.

"Do you have your dress yet?" the baker asked.

"Yes," Emily said, grabbing photos from her briefcase. "It's a Vera Wang."

"We're not sure of the size yet," her mother interjected. "We're hoping to get down at least one notch before."

Emily shot a look at her mother, who as usual appeared oblivious to the problematic nature of her statement.

Jim's phone rang and he looked at the screen.

"We're in the middle of something here," Katherine chided.

"I know," Jim said, turning the ringer off.

"I love the dress," the baker said, examining the pictures. "The accents are beautiful, and I think we can carry some of this over to the cake, which will look fantastic in the wedding photos."

"Oh, I like that!" Emily said.

Jim's phone vibrated, and Emily could see the text from Jane: "911".

"Sweetheart, go ahead and take it," she said, nodding when Jim looked at her to confirm she was serious. "It's a cake, babe. Work is more important," she reassured him. "Go ahead."

"Be right back," Jim said, and kissed her forehead gratefully, glad for the escape.

Chapter 3

Amanda turned the radio up. That was the problem with convertibles, she thought. Sure, they're a blast to drive, but you really have to crank the stereo, and she loved this .38 Special song too much to miss a single word. She was in Georgia, at least she was fairly sure she was, and the song's southern rock style blended perfectly with her belief.

Passing a sign for gas, she instinctually checked the fuel gauge only to see she was on empty. She slammed the breaks and swerved into the exit lane, crossing the white line to hit the off ramp. A chorus of honking sounded behind and to her left, and she responded with as high and proud a middle finger as she could manage. Yet another good thing about convertibles, she thought: ease of communication through hand signals. Only then did she hear the siren approaching on her tail.

Amanda pulled over on the first surface street after the off ramp, hoping the police car would somehow just flash by on its way to a real emergency. Her heart sank when she saw the car settle in behind hers.

A tall, older officer stepped out of the car, blessedly male. Amanda checked herself in the mirror, tugging her shirt lower on her ample chest. She was not above flirting, and possibly a little more, to get out of a ticket.

"Ma'am, can you please turn off the music?" the officer asked.

"Oh, sure," she said, stroking the volume knob of the radio down a bit.

"Can you please turn it off?" he asked again.

"Oh, you mean all the way?" she confirmed as she turned the volume down more.

"Yes, all the way, please," he said, showing little sense of humor.

"Okay," she said, as cutesy as she could. "I'm always willing to comply, officer."

"Ma'am, do you know why I pulled you over?" he asked.

She hated this question. It was a waste of time. He knew why, she knew why; let's just get on with it, she thought.

"Was I going a little fast?" she asked. "It's so hard to keep up with the different speed signs on a long trip."

"Well, you were," he said, "But I was going to let that slide, until you nearly caused a pile up back there by swerving into the exit lane."

"Oh, sorry about that!" she said. "I just realized I needed gas," she added, leaning over to give him a good look at the gauge, and her cleavage. "See?"

"I do see, ma'am," he said, again showing no sense of humor. "I also saw you raise your middle finger in responses to the drivers who honked. Can you guess who one of those drivers was?"

"I'm going to guess it was you," she said, "But you totally misunderstood. I was waiving an apology, I wasn't flipping you off or anything!" she lied with an apologetic smile.

"I see," he said nodding along. "Misunderstandings happen, I guess."

"They do," she said. "I would never flip off a policeman, especially not such a good looking one."

"Well, I appreciate that," he said. "I'm going to write you up on reckless driving. I'll let the speeding go. License, registration, and proof of insurance, please."

"Wait, wait, wait," she pleaded. "I'm sorry that I screwed up. The truth is, it's been a long trip and I'm not familiar with the roads. I was freaking out about running out of gas, and I just jumped when I saw the chance to get some."

The officer nodded along.

"I'm really sorry," she pleaded. "If you let me go, I promise to be more careful."

"I'm afraid I can't do that, Ma'am," he said. "If you could get me your driver's license, vehicle registration, and proof of insurance, I'll get this done as quickly as possible so you can get on your way."

She gripped the wheel, nervous Bobby may have already reported the car stolen. The last thing she needed was to be busted by some hick cop and locked up in a southern jail.

"Listen, Officer...?" she asked.

"Morris," he said. "It's actually Chief Morris."

"Oh, sorry. Chief Morris," she said, smiling with the best flirting smile she could pull off, "I really hate the idea of getting a ticket so far from home and having my insurance go up. Maybe you and I could go somewhere alone and talk more. Maybe get to know each other a bit more, you know as people. You'll see I'm really a sweet girl."

Chief Morris smiled and looked around. "You know, I do think I would like to get to know more about you," he said.

Amanda smiled back. He was actually kind of good looking, she thought, in an older, tough guy kind of way.

"That sounds great," she said.

"How about we start with your driver's license," he said, "and then we'll slip into something more comfortable, like your registration."

Amanda dropped the smile and glared at the chief.

"And when we're really getting into it, you can let me have me your insurance information," he said, smiling.

"You get off on this, don't you?" she demanded as she reached for her purse.

"Some days are better than others," he said, clearly proud of himself.

She handed him her driver's license and pulled the registration and insurance info from the glove department.

"Nevada license," he said. "On your way back to Las Vegas?"

"Yeah," she said.

"Coming from Florida?" he asked.

"Yes," she replied, getting nervous about the number of questions.

"It sure was gracious of Robert Calloway to loan you this nice Mustang here," he said, examining the registration. "He does know you have it, correct?"

"Of course," she lied. "He's my fiancé."

"Oh, congratulations," he said.

"Thank you," she replied.

"Hold tight for a second, please," Chief Morris said as he turned towards his car with the documents.

"I'm kinda in a hurry," she said.

"I understand," he said, "give me two minutes and you'll be on your way."

Amanda sat helplessly while the chief walked back to his car and called in the license plate. She watched him fill out the ticket while he waited for a response from the other end of his CB radio.

Her hands started shaking and she could feel the sweat trickling down her hairline. She knew it was more than the anxiety. The pain was coming back.

The chief stepped out of this car and sauntered back to the Mustang.

"See, less than two minutes," he said, handing her documents back. "This is a ticket for reckless driving. It's carries a five hundred dollar fine, which you can pay by mailing a cashier's check or money order to this address."

"Fine," she said.

"And, of course you have the right to come back for a court date to dispute the ticket in front of a magistrate," he added.

"Got it. Thanks. Wait! I'm in Alabama?" she asked, looking at the ticket. "I thought I was still in Georgia."

"Nope, Alabama," he corrected. "Ashford, to be exact," he added, pointing to the patch on his shirt.

"Like there's a difference anyway," she huffed as she started her car.

"Oh, I think in Georgia they may have hit you with the speeding ticket, too," he said. "They're not as understanding as I am."

"Or maybe they are more into women," she said, glaring at him.

"That could be, too," he said. "Just try to make it home to your people safe, Ms. Jeffries."

She didn't like that he remembered her name.

"I don't have 'people,'" she said dismissively, adding a mocking accent.

"Yeah, that is sadly all too clear," he said. "Still, drive safe."

She put the car in gear and pulled out before he turned away. She knew she was pushing her luck with this guy, but screw him.

She still had to deal with the gas issue, and now the pain was kicking in. Her hands were shaking and sweat was soaking through her shirt. Her was heart pounding, which was a new thing, and not something she liked.

She pulled into the small gas station and maneuvered around the big truck refilling the tanks. She parked in front of a pump, and tried to swipe her card.

"They're off for a minute," a voice shouted from inside.

Amanda looked up and saw a short bald man waiving.

"We're refilling, it will only be a minute or two," he explained.

She slammed the nozzle back into place and marched towards the door, bringing a handful of pills with her. Inside the little store, a young policeman with the same patch on his shirt as the chief was sipping coffee. He noticed her immediately, straightening his posture and running his hand through his sandy hair. "Ma'am," he said tipping his hat.

The southern bit amused Amanda. They're all such cowboys.

She grabbed a beer on her way back to the bathroom and held it above her head. "I'll pay for this before I leave," she promised without looking back.

"Of course," the bald man agreed, "No problem."

Amanda closed the door behind her and splashed water on her face. She opened the beer and took three of the pills, which was three times more than that quack had told her, but the pain was nearly as bad as it had ever been. Sitting on the toilet while she tried to collect herself, she let several minutes pass before deciding she felt well enough to walk back into the store. She immediately tripped over a rack she didn't see, knocking several bags of potato chips to the floor.

"Sorry," she said as she bent down to pick them up, rattling into another display.

"Are you okay?" the bald man asked.

"Sorry!" she said, laughing. "I guess I spilled the potatoes," she quipped, finding the comment quite clever. "No beans, just potatoes, so it's cool!"

She had a hard time finding her feet.

"Ma'am, you all right?" the young policeman asked as he tried to steady her.

She dropped her bag, spilling out her makeup and brush. "Ah, shit," she said.

"It's okay," the policeman said, "I'll get it for you."

As he bent over to gather her things, Amanda noticed the shiny, steely revolver at his waist. She reached over and unbuttoned the holster, pulling the gun out.

"Why do you have a cowboy gun?" she asked, looking down the barrel.

"Whoa!" he said, ducking as she spun the gun towards him. "Ma'am, give me that back!"

Amanda could see her reflection in the gun, but it was all distorted and made her look as ugly as she felt.

"Everywhere else, cops have army guns, but you have a cowboy gun," she stated. "Are you a cowboy?"

"No Ma'am, I'm a police officer, and you need to hand my gun back over," he said, maneuvering to her side and raising his hand slowly. Just as the policeman lunged for the gun, Amanda jerked away, pulling the trigger and sending a bullet through the window and directly into the fueling hose of the tanker truck. The tank exploded with a bright flash, followed by three equal explosions that blew in the windows and scorched the front aisle of the store.

Amanda and the policeman were knocked backward into the beer aisle, smashing into the glass and sending bottles crashing down upon them. Slowly, she pushed herself to her feet and watched the lazy collapse of the awning above the pumps. She still had the gun in her hand, and she looked at it, awed by its power.

"Holy shit," she said, as she stood in the middle of the devastation. She didn't even feel it when the policeman tackled her from behind.

Chapter 4

"I'm sorry, what was that name again?" Jim asked, certain his mind had just played a cruel trick on him.

"Amanda Jeffries," Jane repeated. "Should I tell her you're unreachable? I tried already, but she was quite insistent it was an emergency."

Jim's mind scattered. He found himself intentionally pulling back from being excited and firmly made his disposition apathetic, maybe even a little angry. But he still didn't know if he should take the call.

"Mr. Morgan?" Jane asked

"Yeah, sorry," he said. "Go ahead and put her through."

Jim took a breath and remembered he was not that college kid anymore. "I am a high priced, L.A. lawyer," he told himself. "I am an adult." And the adult thing to do was to take the call, get as much info about Amanda as possible, and then nail her with a quick emotional jab to finally even the score, right before hanging up on her sorry ass.

"Ms. Jeffries, I'm transferring you now," he heard Jane say. He thought about hanging up the phone. But then he heard the familiar voice he used to cherish.

"About time," Amanda said.

"This is Jim Morgan," he said, realizing his voice cracked half way through his own name.

"Hey, sweetheart, it's Amanda," she said. "How are you?"

He wasn't prepared for the greeting. He wasn't sure what he was prepared for, or had expected, but this wasn't it.

"I'm good," he said, pausing to breath. "How are you?"

This was not the conversation he wanted to have. She should ask for money, he thought. That would be great. Then he could call her a loser, and a leech, and hang up.

"I'm doing okay," she said. "Well, … to be honest, I'm not. I'm in trouble and I need help. You remember how I hate asking for help, right?"

"Yeah, I remember," he said, quickly chastising himself for agreeing with her and being dragged into a polite conversation.

"Well, I'm asking for help," she said.

Settling on the idea this was definitely a money call, he was able to revert to his professional nature.

"What do you need help with, Amanda?" he said in his chilly lawyer voice, a tone many found intimidating.

"I've been arrested and I need a lawyer," she said. "A good one."

This was an easy request to turn down, he thought. "I'm not that kind of lawyer," he said, "I don't handle criminal cases."

"Yeah, I know," she said, "but I don't trust anyone else, and I also need someone to post bail for me."

He lost track after "I know." How did she know what kind of lawyer he was?

"Are you in L.A.?" he asked, trying to not sound hopeful.

"No, I'm in … hold on …," she seemed to cover the phone and then came back, "I'm in Ashford. Ashford, Alabama."

His laugh was involuntary. She always seemed an odd fit for the Midwest, but the thought of Amanda being in the South was too funny. And clearly he couldn't do anything to help her there.

"Well, I'm in California," he said. "I'm not licensed there, so there's nothing I can do."

"I know it's a pain, but I need your help," she said. "I really need to be bailed out."

He was now finding it easier to get angry, "I haven't heard from you in over eight years, and we didn't exactly part on the best terms. Why would I possibly go out of my way to bail you out?" he asked.

"I know you're probably still mad," she said, "but I wouldn't be calling you unless there really was no one else. I'm in a lot of trouble, Jim."

"Well, that's a shame," he said, "because there's nothing in Ashford, Alabama I'm interested in." He hung up, gratified to get the last word, but then looked at his phone and regretted cutting her off. He noticed his hand shaking and he focused on pulling himself together.

Amanda looked at the receiver and tried not to let it get to her. He sounded different now, she thought.

"I'm sorry," Sam said. "That didn't sound like it went too well. Not that I was listening, but I couldn't help but hear."

Sam was the young policeman who had tackled her, and the owner of the shiny gun that helped her destroy an entire building, three vehicles, and injure four people. Yet, somehow, he was still being sweet. It's good to be pretty, she thought.

He was also the son of Chief Morris, although Amanda was confident Sam took more after his mother.

Sam lead her back to the cell to which she was confined, although he left the barred door open so she could use the normal bathroom, and not the semi-private metal pot protruding from the wall.

"I'm going to be ordering dinner soon," Sam said. "Got any preference?"

Amanda sat quietly on the bench in her cell, trying to not cry.

"Lucky Panda isn't half bad for Chinese," he said, obviously trying to take her mind off the call. "And they serve American food, which is pretty good if you want to mix up your order a bit,"

"I'm not really hungry," she said.

Sam walked over and took a knee in front of her. "I'm sorry your friend isn't coming," he said. "But we have a good lawyer here in town that will do his best to help you."

She looked at Sam, realizing he mistook the reason for her sadness. "No, he'll be here in the morning," she said. She forced a smiled and wiped the sole tear coming from her eye. "Just a couple egg rolls and a Diet Coke," she said.

Sam smiled and stood up. "I'm going to get some pot stickers for us to share, too. I think you'll like them."

Chapter 5

Jim walked back into the bakery as causally as possible and re-claimed his seat next to Emily, who now had three different plates in front of her, each with a small piece of a unique type of cake.

"Everything okay?" she asked.

"Yeah, fine," he replied. "It was Jane."

"Yeah, I saw," she said. "Everything all right? What was up with the 911?"

"Someone having a legal issue," he said, trying not to lie.

"Well, I would hope so," chimed in Katherine. "You're a lawyer. What else would they call you for, brain surgery?"

He hated that woman.

Jim physically participated in the cake tastings, but his mind was traveling between the past and present. He thought about Amanda, and how in love they used to be. Or at least, how in love he had been. He thought about the unbelievable sting of her betrayal, and the years it took him to get over, if he ever did. He wondered what the hell she was doing in Alabama, of all places.

"German chocolate?" Emily asked him.

"What?" he said, realizing he had lost track of the conversation.

"German chocolate is your favorite cake, right?" she asked.

"Oh, yeah," he said, "but it doesn't really matter to me. I'll be happy with anything you chose."

"He was telling us we can have different types of cake for each tier," she said. "Are you not paying attention?"

"No, I am," he said apologetically. "I'm sorry. I love German Chocolate cake."

"German chocolate can be a challenge for this type of cake," the baker said. "We can do it, but is there another type of cake you like?"

Jim felt betrayed by the baker. He didn't really care about the German Chocolate thing, but now he had to think of a whole other cake? Why was this guy fucking with him? How many damn cakes can there be?

"I like ice cream cake," he said lamely.

The baker stared back blankly, and Jim realized he wasn't alone. Thankfully, Emily's mother broke the silence.

"You're a huge help, Jim," she said. "We'll just skip this whole thing and head to Baskin & Robin's for a cake. Would you like baseballs on it, or would you prefer a Star Wars cake?"

"Mother!" Emily snapped.

"I'm sorry, but he's being a bigger dumbass than usual," her mother complained. "He's not coming with us to the fitting, right?"

Jim looked at the silver cake cutter and wondered if it was capable of killing banshees.

"I'm sorry," he said to Emily. "I'm a bit distracted from the call."

He turned to the baker. "I'm not totally hooked on German Chocolate. I like Devil's Food, and Red Velvet as well. But honestly, as long as it tastes great, I'm happy. I'm sure you're an excellent baker, but there is nothing you can do that will steal the show from my perfect bride."

Emily smiled and repaid his courtesy with a kiss on his cheek. She was easy to please when he was being romantic.

"Always the lawyer," Katherine sneered, looking as if she had caught him in a lie. Jim wondered how much it would cost to have the baker lace her cake samples with rat poison.

They finished up their session, and Jim hoped they had settled on a final cake, but wasn't quite sure with all the back and forth. The distraction of Amanda was temporarily replaced with the sticker shock of thirty-five hundred dollars for a cake. Which was three times more than the most expensive cake he had previously bought, and it had contained a live, mostly nude, woman.

"Get in the car, mom," Emily said when they got to the parking lot. "I've gotta talk to Jim for a moment."

"Fine, but don't let him make us late, too." Katherine delicately took her place in the passenger seat, and then unceremoniously jerked the door shut.

Emily noticed Jim glaring at her mother, and turned his face so she was looking directly in his eyes. "Ignore her," she instructed. "She's happiest when pushing buttons."

"Like to push her buttons," he said, suddenly realizing it sounded slightly sexual. "I mean I would like to shove her down an elevator shaft."

"She's being extra challenging today," Emily said with a consoling smile. "But I want to talk about you."

"What about me?" he asked.

"What's going on with you?" she asked.

"Nothing, I'm fine," he said.

Emily gave him a probing look. "The call threw you off, you've been somewhere else ever since. What's going on?"

Jim wanted to lie and tell her it was nothing, but he was starting to see the inevitable unfolding in his mind.

"I have to go take care of something," he said. "I need to go bail someone out of jail. And I may have to find them a good local lawyer."

"What's wrong with me?" she said. "I'm a local lawyer. Who's in jail?"

"It's complicated," he said.

"I'm a complicated girl," she replied. "What's up? What's the charge?"

"I don't know the charge yet," he said. "She's in Alabama."

He could tell he the pronoun caught Emily off guard. "I'm sorry, who is she, and why is she in Alabama?"

"Amanda, my ex," he admitted. "And I don't know why she's there, only that she's in trouble."

"Your ex, Amanda? The one who cheated on you, right in front of you?"

"Yes," he said, flinching at a memory refreshed too many times today.

"I wasn't aware you were talking to her again," Emily said with blatant jealousy. "When did this start?"

"About forty minutes ago," he said.

Emily put her hand on his chest and took a breath. "So, to be clear, after a heart-wrenching breakup which included cheating on you in your own bed and walking out the door, she calls you up a decade later and tells you she's in jail in Arkansas?"

"It's been closer to nine years," he corrected, "and it's Alabama."

"So glad you're counting the days," she snipped.

"It's not like that," Jim said.

A honk startled them both.

"Let's go!" her mother shouted from inside the car.

"I'm going to fucking kill that woman!" Emily growled.

Jim knew she was pissed, and rightfully so.

"Okay," she said. "Does this mean you're flying off to Alabama?"

"I'm going to try to take care of it from the office," he said, "but, yes. I might be flying to Alabama."

"To rescue the girl who scarred you for life?" she said.

"I guess so," he said shrugging.

"Why?" she asked.

Jim thought about it for a second.

"Because no matter what you did to me, I'd be there for you, too," he said.

"Fine," she said, patting him on the chest. "But never compare me to that tramp again."

Jim tried to kiss Emily goodbye, but she stopped him and began walking away.

"We'll talk when I get back?" he called across the parking lot.

"Oh, count on it!" Emily yelled back as she got into her car.

Chapter 6

Emily kept conversation in the car to a minimum to avoid giving her mother further ammunition on an already trying day. As they pulled into the dress shop parking lot, her mother could tell something was wrong.

"Is he leaving you?" her mother asked.

"What?" Emily yelled.

"Jim," her mother said. "Is he getting cold feet?"

"No!" Emily said. "And I don't want to talk about it with you. Now let's get this thing over with. Don't start your shit with me in there, understand?"

"Don't talk to me like that," her mother said. "It's not my fault you're having problems."

"We're not having problems!" Emily yelled. "You always do this, you make things much worse than they are."

"How am I suddenly the cause of all this?" her mother asked. "I was waiting patiently in the car!"

Emily got out of the car and began walking to the dress shop. Her mother stayed a pace behind until Emily spun around to face her.

"He's going to Alabama to help his ex-girlfriend, who's in some sort of legal trouble," she yelled. "That's it!"

"Okay, okay," Katherine said. "That's quite nice of him."

Emily looked her mother in the eye, waiting for the follow up comment.

"What?" her mother asked, looking back into Emily's eyes with pointed sweetness and submission.

Emily turned and walked into the shop, declaring to the woman at the desk she was there for her fitting.

Soon, Emily stood in captive motionlessness between a pair of seamstresses who stuck pins and grabbed fabric with the efficiency of long practice.

"I'm thinking we can go from a size five to a four with the notice we have, don't you think?" her mother asked one of the seamstresses.

"Mom!" Emily snapped.

"Okay," Katherine conceded. "Just trying to get this right. They're pulling in a lot of fabric, which is a good thing. You should be pleased."

"Just let them do their job," Emily snapped.

"What's she doing in Alabama?" Katherine asked.

Emily looked at her in the mirror. "Why?"

"I'm just wondering," Katherine said.

"He doesn't know yet," Emily said.

"Oh, they don't stay in touch?" Katherine asked.

"No," Emily said, "he hasn't talked to her in years."

"Oh." Katherine paused. "They must have been close for her to call him for help after all these years."

Emily scowled at her mother in the mirror. "Where is this going?" she demanded.

"Nowhere," Katherine said. "I'm just saying, years after a break up, and you can pick up the phone and call someone to your side from across the country. That's real love."

Emily didn't know who she wanted to hit most. Her mother was closest in proximity and current annoyance. But she was becoming increasingly angry with Jim. Was he really going to drop everything for some slut who'd treated him like crap eight years ago?

"I bet they'll be happy to see each other," her mother continued. "Where will he be staying while in town?"

Emily turned around and glared at her mother. "Get your damn purse, we're leaving." She began to pull at the fabric surrounding her, struggling out of the wedding dress. "I'm sorry, I have an emergency. I'll have to reschedule for next week," she told the seamstress. She was out the door before her shirt was fully buttoned.

"Let's go with the size four," Katherine whispered to the seamstress as she left.

Emily sped towards her mother's house.

"Where are we going?" her mother asked.

"Shut up," Emily said, grinding her teeth.

"What's wrong with you?" Katherine asked.

Emily slammed on the brakes. "One more word, and you're walking home. So help me god, I'll kick your boney ass out right here," she yelled.

Katherine leaned back and waited to be dropped in front of her house. Emily left without saying another word.

The office was closing when Emily walked in, and Jamie came running up.

"I got the motion emailed to you thirty minutes ago, and I tried getting you on the book for tomorrow, but the best we can do is Monday," she said.

"That's fine," Emily replied, walking briskly to Jim's office.

"Going to see Mr. Morgan?" Jamie asked.

"Yes," Emily replied.

"I think he already left for the day," Jamie said.

"He left?" Emily asked, pulling up short.

"I think so," she said, "I never saw him come back from lunch."

Emily was ready to turn around when she saw Jane walking towards her.

"Jane!" Emily called. "Did Jim come back from lunch?"

"Can you not reach him on his mobile?" Jane asked.

"I'll try in a second," Emily said. "I'm just curious if he came back and worked on anything."

"You'll have to talk to Mr. Morgan about his schedule," Jane said.

"But you run his schedule," Emily said. "It's a simple question."

"It is, and I'm certain Mr. Morgan will be happy to fill you in on his day," Jane said, smiling.

"I see," Emily said as Jane walked away. She turned to Jamie. "I need you to stay late."

"Okay, no problem," Jamie said.

"I need you to dig into arrest records in Alabama," Emily said. "I'm looking for one on an Amanda Jeffries. Also, find out who heads the PD office in the area, and get me his number."

"Got it," Jamie promised.

"And when you find the city of the arrest, book me the next flight out," Emily said.

"I'm sorry," Jamie said, "I don't have access to expense cards."

Emily grabbed her personal Amex from her wallet. "Take a picture of it," Emily told Jamie.

Jamie complied and took a snapshot of the card with her phone.

"I want the first flight that gets me there by morning." Emily said. "I'll be at the airport in an hour."

Chapter 7

Jim sat in the first class lounge and tried to not be nervous. He needed to treat her like any other client, or at least a distant friend who asked him for some legal help, which was really all it was.

He knew Emily was pissed, and he was going to have some serious groveling to do on his return. He knew she had every right to be angry; if the roles were reversed, he would never let her go without him. But she was always more level-headed than him.

Was there any comparison between Emily and Amanda? He sometimes thought that was what drew him to Emily; she was in many ways the opposite of Amanda. Emily was cool under pressure. She could be the sweetest person you ever met, but when it came to protecting her clients, she was better than a well-trained pit bull.

Amanda was the life of the party. She always was the funniest one in the room and wasted no time proving it. She had a way of bringing a room to life, no matter how beaten or tired everyone was. Within minutes, all eyes were on her. She had a magical quality that seemed to make people believe everything was going to be okay. It had worked wonders on Jim, until she decided to rip his heart out, of course.

But now she was in trouble, so maybe some of her magic had dissipated. Jim had tried to get information about Amanda's situation, but the town was small and lacked the streamlined data processes of the rest of the country. He'd been able to pull up a basic arrest report, but it left out any written statements and details. All he knew was she'd been arrested in Ashford, Alabama. Knowing her history, it was probably a driving issue gone way too far, and maybe she'd been carrying some weed.

His flight to Birmingham had been scheduled for 6:30, but it was now 7:15 and the board was flashing 8:10 as the departure time. He felt the waitress walk up next to him, and decided to get a refill.

"Another Bacardi and Coke," he requested.

"That's a girl's drink," Emily scoffed as she took the seat next to him. "Order something manly, like a Manhattan or something."

"Manhattan's taste like paint thinner," he complained. "What are you doing here?"

"That's the point, they taste like alcohol, not a soft drink," she replied, "and I'm catching a plane to Birmingham to meet a new client."

"I don't need any help," he said, trying to walk the thin line between being thankful and blowing her off. "I got this."

"If the roles were reversed, wouldn't you be going with me?" she asked as the waitress approached. "A couple rum and cokes for my girlfriend and me," she quipped to the waitress.

She had made her point.

As they boarded the plane, Emily brought out her iPad to display her plan.

"We'll be landing in Birmingham around two," she said. "We'll rent a car and be in Ashford by six at the latest. The courthouse doesn't open until nine, but we should be able to visit her in the jail right away."

Jim nodded along.

"I already sent out emails to the lead public defender, a Reginald Bayloch — love that name — and let him know I would like to co-counsel on this to work out a quick resolution," she explained.

"Since I failed to consider the need to get an Alabama law license, the only way I can have any official input is to have Bayloch back me in getting a judge to sign off on it."

"Where am I in all this?" Jim asked.

"You'll be assisting me. I'm the criminal lawyer. Once I meet with Bayloch, we're going to walk over to the DA, and either get a plea deal in place, or get a date set and have them release her to go home. I imagine there'll be some bond needing to be set, but it won't be too much. I mean, what could she possibly have done?"

"So, I'll just be holding your briefcase through all this?" he asked.

"That, and looking pretty for your ex," she breezed.

"I'm not liking this," Jim objected.

"Jim," Emily said, her voice taking on a sharp, serious edge. "I don't like this at all, but I'm here with you. Let's deal with this thing, and go home, okay?"

"Okay," he said, taking her hand. He had to acknowledge she was right, and Amanda was lucky to have such a kick ass lawyer coming to help her. But he knew the two of them were not going to get along.

"Get some sleep," she said. "Along with carrying my briefcase, you're also my driver."

As Jim reclined in his seat, Emily twisted toward him. "Does she know you're coming?" Emily asked.

"I pretty much told her to fuck off and hung up on her," he admitted.

Emily had practiced law long enough to recognize a non-answer when she heard one, and held Jim's eyes, waiting for the answer.

"Yes," he sighed. "She knows I'm coming."

Chapter 8

"Is there anything other than country music on the radio here?" Amanda asked.

Sam flipped from station to station until he came across a Journey song.

"I'm bored," Amanda said.

"I got a deck of cards," Sam offered.

"Nah," she said, "but you got a computer?"

"At home," Sam said, "but we don't have any WiFi."

The front door opened and Sam sat up straight as his father walked in.

"Pete's not here yet?" Chief Morris asked.

"Nope," Sam replied, "but he called in to say he'd be thirty minutes late; I told him it wasn't an issue."

"Why did you tell him that?" the chief asked.

"I don't mind hanging out," Sam said.

"Not really the point," the chief replied as he walked back toward the cells and saw Amanda sitting on the bench.

"Why is the prisoner's door open?" the chief asked.

"Oh," Sam said, "so she can use the bathroom in the office. That one has no privacy."

The chief slammed the cell door shut, making Amanda jump.

"This isn't a vacation," the chief said. "We're not here for her comfort. We have her for up to forty-eight hours, and then she gets transferred to county. She's not our first female guest."

"I know, Dad," Sam said. "But she's a lady, and that thing has no privacy."

The chief motioned Sam into his office, but Amanda could still hear the argument. The chief was still pretty pissed Sam was disarmed by a girl, and that it lead to the most expensive non-natural destruction the town had ever seen. And, he was extra pissed about the police car that went up in smoke — one of only two the department owned. Or, had owned, as the case was.

A small man with a mustache pushed through the door, and Amanda figured he must be Pete. He'd been manning the desk when she was brought to the station, and was still sporting the same obnoxious smirk from when he'd booked her in.

Sam came out and grabbed his coat. He gave a slight waive to Amanda, and she smiled and waived back.

She heard the chief giving Pete a run down of the day's activities. "She's heading to county tomorrow for arraignment," the chief explained. "We'll have to transport her there ourselves, and since we're down to one car, I'll be using my personal vehicle."

Amanda laid back and eventually dozed off. She awoke an hour later to see Pete leering at her. She had to pee, but she wasn't interested in giving him a show.

"Would you mind if I use the restroom?" she asked.

"You have one in there," Pete said. "Help yourself."

Amanda got up and began to unfasten her shorts.

"Can you go do something else?" she asked. "Don't you have work to do?"

"I'm doing it," he said, displaying that trademark smirk. "I'm watching the prisoner."

Amanda buttoned herself back up.

"I'm here all night," Pete said, smiling.

"Officer Stevens," the chief's voice bellowed from out of Amanda's eyesight.

"Yes, sir," Pete said.

"A word," the chief said.

Amanda moved closer to the bars to listen in.

"The prisoner, your wife, your two children, me, and yourself," the chief listed. "I'm sure there are more."

"Sir?" Pete asked.

"I'm listing the people you're disrespecting with your current behavior," the chief said. "I guess we can also count your parents, as I don't think they would be proud to hear they raised a Peeping Tom pervert."

"I'm sorry, sir," Pete said quickly.

"That behavior is unprofessional, and unacceptable in this station," the chief said. "Am I understood?"

"Yes, sir," Pete said loudly.

"Now you're going to deliver an apology to the prisoner," the chief said, "and if she finds it adequate, I won't call in your wife and mother to make you apologize to them, too."

"Yes, sir," Pete said.

Amanda hurried back to the bench so she could savor the moment to come, and Pete soon appeared in front of the bars.

"Ma'am," Pete began, "I apologize for my behavior. It was unprofessional and disrespectful. I was out of line and I do apologize. Please know I was raised better, ma'am."

Amanda tried to think if she had ever heard a more sincere apology, and couldn't come up with anything close.

Chief Morris walked up next to Pete. "I too apologize for my officer's behavior. If you feel you have been mistreated, I'll provide you with a pencil and paper to write a statement and we'll file it with the Sheriff's Office first thing in the morning."

"No, it's fine," she said. "I just wanted some privacy."

"Officer Stevens," Chief Morris said, "when the prisoner requests to use the facilities, you will walk her to the restroom, wait outside, and return her to her cell when she is done."

"Yes, sir," Pete said obediently.

"Fair enough?" Chief Morris asked Amanda.

"Fair enough, Chief," Amanda agreed, adding a nod to simulate his.

The chief walked away without any expression.

She didn't know what to make of him, other than the feeling he might be the world's most disciplined person.

Pete did as he had been instructed, and she even cajoled him into bringing her a cup of coffee.

"Does he sleep here?" she asked, pointing to the chief's door.

"Occasionally," Pete said. "He's pretty committed to the job."

"What's going to happen to Sam?" she asked.

Pete lowered his voice. "He's upset because the chief asked the county to investigate him."

"For what?" Amanda said.

"For your little bonfire," Pete said. "You got his gun away from him."

"That wasn't his fault!" she exclaimed. "He didn't do anything wrong!"

"Well, that's for the county to decide," Pete explained. "The chief didn't think it was appropriate for him to investigate his own son."

As she talked to Pete, Amanda found herself kind of liking him, smarminess aside. She learned a lot about the town, although she wasn't sure why she cared.

"Why were you being such a jerk to me?" she asked.

"Well, you blew up Eastwood's," Pete said. "It's the only convenience store within twenty miles. Some folks don't have a car, so you really done them over good."

"Shit," Amanda said. "I'm sorry."

"Well, yeah," Pete said. "Plus, it's where I got my scratchers and my lotto numbers."

"Ever win?" she asked

"No," Pete confessed.

"So, I saved you money," she said with a small smile.

"Yeah, but you're killing the dream," he said in a manner Amanda found profound. "It's a rough time around here, and we kinda need dreams right now."

Pete went back to shuffling his paperwork. Amanda curled up on her bench with her prison-issued blanket and a cushion Pete loaned her from his chair. She knew she'd be seeing Jim tomorrow, and she was nervous. This was not how she planned to see him again.

Chapter 9

The sleepy rental car agent handed them a set of keys. "Do you need directions?" he asked.

Emily could tell Jim was about to ask for help, but she rolled her eyes and dragged him out to the waiting car.

"I'm sorry," he said opening the car door, "do you know how to get to Ashford?"

"No," she said, "but we have expensive phones that do, and I have no interest in hearing that guy ramble on. Let's get there and get this over with."

She wasn't actually dreading this as much as she made out. In fact, she was working hard to focus on the idea of Amanda as a client in need, a poor girl trapped in a steel cage far from home, and she was starting to look forward to the coming battle. Now, if she could just keep the image of Amanda the Ex out of her head, and stop wondering how deep Jim's feelings for her still were ...

"You're their sword and shield," her father used to say about being a defense attorney. Emily believed whole heartily in this ideal, and she was armored up, sword drawn, and ready to fight Amanda's dragons, even if she was a nasty skank who probably wanted to steal Emily's fiancé.

The drive went quickly. Her phone was providing accurate directions, and the roads were wide open and empty, except for the occasional semi.

"What hotel were you thinking?" Jim asked.

"What do you mean?" she replied.

"Hotel," he said, "a place to sleep."

"We're not staying," she said, incredulous. "I'm getting this put to bed today."

"I'm not sure that's going to happen," Jim cautioned. "And it's Friday, so we may be stuck for the weekend at least."

"I don't think we're on the same page here," Emily said. "I'm going to get this girl the best deal humanly possible for whatever mess she's gotten herself into, and then we're going home."

"But we don't even know what the charges are yet," Jim said.

"That's right," she said, "because someone couldn't bother to ask while he had her on the phone. But like you said, it's probably a drug thing, or drunk driving, or some other crap. These towns just want their fines. I'll figure out how much they want, and we'll pay the damn fine for the girl. Then, home we go."

"And if it's bigger than that?" he asked.

Emily started to wonder if Jim knew more than he was letting on. "We'll play it by ear, I guess," she said. Refocusing on her phone directions, she noticed an email from Bayloch.

"I received your email, and I know the case. We should talk right away. I'll be in my office at 9:30. Since the defendant reached out to you, feel free to meet with her before, but obviously keep her from talking to anyone else," Bayloch wrote.

"We're good to go with Bayloch," she shared with Jim. "We'll meet with Amanda before going to his office."

Emily wasn't crazy. She knew it might take more than a day, and had packed three days of clothing just in case. But she didn't want Jim getting it in his head they'd be staying any longer than absolutely necessary.

"Well, I need to clean up," he said, and directed the car towards a Day's Inn.

"Fine," she said. "Want to look nice for your friend, I guess."

"Are we really going to do this the entire trip?" he asked as he pulled into a parking space. "I love you, and I have no interest in Amanda. I'm here out of an excessively built up sense of chivalry, even if she doesn't deserve it."

Emily didn't respond, and she didn't like him thinking he owed that slut anything. Almost a decade later, Emily could still sense the damage Amanda had left behind her. As she looked around the hotel parking lot, she noticed a small sign in faded red and blue, reading "Elect Chad Mitchell for District Attorney," and made a note of the name. She was planning to do a little damage of her own, and knowing her competition's competition could come in handy.

Jim went inside and got their room. Emily checked her watch and saw they had beaten her estimated arrival time by forty minutes. She could catch another ninety minutes of sleep, and still have plenty of time to shower and change.

The room was filthy by most hotel standards and was furnished with an ugly hodgepodge of styles covering several decades. Years of cigarette smoke and morning breath had made friends with the motel's cheap industrial cleaner, combining into an acrid odor nothing could cover. There were two beds in the room, and she considered for a moment making Jim sleep in one on his own, but realized she was being a bit hard on him.

"Do me a favor — move that comforter as far away from us as possible," she asked Jim. "I don't want it trying to kill us in our sleep."

He complied and threw it in a closet. Emily stripped down and got into bed as Jim tried to figure out the light switch.

"Are you nervous?" she asked him as the lights finally went out.

"No, are you?" he said getting into bed.

It was too dark to see his face react to the question, which disappointed Emily.

"A little, I suppose," she said.

Emily realized she'd never even seen a picture of Amanda and wouldn't know her if she walked right into her. The image in her mind was always a faceless, hot blonde with big breasts and a tramp stamp.

"Is she pretty?" Emily asked.

Jim took a beat longer than she would have liked in answering the question.

"I only date hot girls," he said as he ran his hand up her thigh. "Or hadn't you noticed?"

They spent a good thirty minutes of their ninety minute nap having sex, which put them both to sleep instantly.

Chapter 10

Amanda woke up with a sore back and the pain in her stomach was increasing again. Sam had been nervous when he patted her down and did a crap job, missing the six pills in her pocket. She took one of the remaining four and washed it down with the stale tap water. The Alabama summer heat had invaded the jail as she slept, making her skin crawl with its stickiness.

Sam walked to the cell and offered Amanda a cup of coffee.

"You're back already?" Amanda asked.

"Yeah," he said, "there are only four of us, so we work ten hour shifts and volunteer one day a week."

"That sucks," she said, sipping the bitter coffee. It did nothing to help, only filling her insides with the heat that blazed on her skin.

"It's not that bad," he said. "Not like there's a lot to do around here anyway, other than hang out with each other."

"Can I go to the bathroom?" she asked.

Sam unlocked the cage, performing a gentlemanly bow and gesturing her toward the communal restroom. Passing him, Amanda's attention was drawn by a cooling breeze swirling the hair on her arms. The side door was propped open, offering escape to the heat. She thought about it for a few moments while in the bathroom, and when she came out was considering making a run for it.

She eyed the door, trying to see if there was anyone outside.

"It helps cool the place off to have a nice breeze come through," Sam said, following her gaze.

She looked at him, then back at the open door.

"I will stop you," Sam cautioned. "I rather not have to do that."

She smiled and turned to walk back to her cell, "I got you in enough trouble as it is," she said.

Amanda finished her coffee and was about to toss the cup when she heard a new voice at the desk.

"My name is Emily Perkins," the woman said. "I believe you have a prisoner, Ms. Amanda Jeffries. I'm her attorney and need to speak with her right away, please."

Amanda didn't know the voice, and didn't recognize the name.

"I'm sorry," Sam said, "but have you met with Mr. Bayloch?"

"I have a 9:30 meeting with Mr. Bayloch, but you can see his written approval here on my phone," she said.

Amanda squeezed her head against the bars to try to catch a glimpse of this Perkins lady, but to no avail.

"I'm not sure about this," Sam said. "Can you come back with Mr. Bayloch?"

"No, I cannot come back over an hour later," the woman insisted, her voice taking on a harsh tone. "You are now denying my client her basic right to counsel, officer. I would suggest you take care of whatever paperwork you need, and bring me to my client."

"I can't bring in visitors without approval," Sam explained. "I don't know you. And this is serious."

"Just how serious?" the woman demanded. "What is she even charged with?"

"A lot of stuff," Sam said. "She completely destroyed our gas station and store."

Amanda winced thinking about it.

"What does that even mean?" the woman scoffed. "Did she

knock over a stand of Lynyrd Skynyrd CD's or something?"

"Now, just hold on, hold on," Amanda heard Chief Morris say in his deadpan voice. "No need to drag Lynyrd Skynyrd into all of this."

"And who are you?" the woman asked.

"I'm Chief Morris, this is my station house," he said. "And if you can provide me with some identification, I'll call Reggie right now and get this taken care of."

"Fine," she agreed.

There was a silence for a moment.

"Okay then, Ms. Perkins. Nice to meet you," the chief said. "And, who are you?"

Amanda's heart leapt when she realized he seemed to be addressing someone else.

"I'm Jim Morgan," the familiar voice said. "I'm just carrying her briefcase."

Amanda leaned back against the wall, giving up her efforts to see the desk. She knew what Jim looked like, and she had known he would come for her. He'd even brought some iron maiden, dragon lady with him to help rescue her. She knew it was all going to be okay, and soon. She wasn't alone any longer.

Chapter 11

Emily watched Chief Morris take their business cards and walk back into his office. She glanced over at Jim, who was keeping to his orders and letting her do the talking. He had an odd look on his face; it was almost a smirk, but more introspective. He noticed her looking and gave her a smile.

The burly chief returned.

"Reggie said you guys are good to go," he said. "We can bring you back to the holding cell, or we have a small conference room that's a bit more private if you prefer."

"The conference room will be fine," Emily stated. "I also need a full copy of the police report."

"We're still working on the final report," the chief said. "As you can imagine, there is a lot to put together. She caused quite the disaster."

"Allegedly," Emily said. "And surely you at least have an arrest report."

"Sam," the chief said while opening a drawer, "go make sure the conference room is cleared out for their meeting, and make sure they have enough chairs. Then, please escort the prisoner to the room."

Sam walked off, pulling some keys from a chain in his pocket.

"Allegedly, indeed," the chief said, smiling at Emily. "Let me grab the arrest report and some of the photos for you, and you can see for yourself what she did."

"Allegedly," Emily repeated, wanting to make sure it was clear to the chief she intended to question every facet of his report.

He brought back a folder containing about thirty pages of reports and statements, along with some photos. "Here's everything we have so far," the chief said. "We have a toxicology report coming back from the county next week."

Emily opened the folder, dropping a few of the pictures to the floor. Jim reached down to grab them for her.

Sam walked by and announced "The room's all set, if you're ready."

Emily looked down to see what was taking Jim so long, and found him still on his knee, examining the photos.

Frustrated, Emily decided to bottom line the severity of the issue.

"Do you intend on charging my client with a felony?" she asked.

The chief raised his eyebrow and smiled, "That's up to the state attorney, but I would hope so," he said. "Have you seen what she did?"

"Allegedly did? Not yet," Emily confessed.

The chief was clearly holding back from laughing.

"She assaulted one of my officers, grabbed his gun, blew up a gas station, a store, three vehicles, and put four people into the emergency room," he chortled, not unkindly.

Emily's involuntary deer in headlights impersonation was impossible to break.

"Allegedly," a faint voice said, breaking the spell on Emily.

Emily looked over and saw Amanda for the first time. She was much smaller than Emily had imagined the monster skank to be. She had the faintest tan, and light brown hair straightened from lack of a shower. Emily noticed her eyes were puffy, as were her lips. She was wearing a black Led Zeppelin shirt, the arms and collar shorn off, matching the tiny denim cutoffs that struggled to hug the few curves they reached. Even in handcuffs, she seemed to be striking a pose.

Emily realized she was still in shock from the severity of the crime, and on top of it was now a bit spellbound by the presence of the woman she had always been curious about. Recognizing she was missing an opportunity, she quickly glanced over at Jim to gauge his reaction. This time, the look wasn't foreign to Emily. It was longing.

Sam guided Amanda passed them. Amanda broke eye contact with Jim long enough to smile at Emily, who was trying hard to regain her momentum.

"We're going to need the full report as soon as it's available," Emily told the chief. "Our mobile numbers are on the cards."

"It should be done today," the chief said. "She's set for arraignment at 1:30."

"Fine," Emily said, and strode towards the conference room.

Sam was handing Amanda a cup of coffee and a donut when they walked in.

"Can I get you two a cup of coffee?" he asked.

"No, thank you," Emily said as she waited for Sam to leave.

"Okay, then, just let me know when you're finished." He closed the door behind him.

The door hadn't clicked shut before Amanda sprung to her feet and jumped into Jim's arms, squeezing him.

Emily stood, shocked again, and then angry. She wanted to rip the hair out of the girl's head while pulling her away. She looked at Jim, who was using his posture to show he was barely part of the hug, looking straight at Emily with an apologetic look.

The hug persisted too long and Emily was ready to break the moment and tell her to sit down when she heard the sobbing. She looked at Jim, who was clearly starting to be affected by the emotion.

"I'm so sorry," Emily heard Amanda mumble into Jim's shoulder.

Jim finally hugged her back. Emily watched him brush the hair from her ear, a familiar movement she could almost feel herself. He whispered something into Amanda's ear, and she laughed a little. He pushed her back and faced her, smiling. Amanda lunged forward and kissed Jim.

Emily slammed her briefcase on the table and Jim pushed her off him.

"Amanda," he said, "Stop. Don't do that. We need to get to work."

Amanda looked disappointed, but took her seat.

"Sorry," she said to Emily as she sat down, clearly not knowing the relationship yet. "I haven't seen him in a long time."

"Ms. Jeffries," Emily started

"It's Amanda," she corrected.

"Fine... Amanda," Emily said while trying hard to hide her contempt. "You're in a shit load of trouble, Amanda."

Amanda lowered her head. "I'm so sorry," she said again.

"First, don't ever apologize, it's a form of confession. As a matter of fact, stop talking to everyone, besides your lawyers. That includes the cute guard out there who you're clearly flirting with."

"Oh, Sam? He's a sweetheart," Amanda said.

"No," Emily snapped, "he's a law enforcement official obligated to report anything he's heard from you. Count on the fact he's putting you at ease in hopes of getting a confession."

Amanda giggled.

"What's so funny?" Emily demanded, glaring at Amanda.

"Well, you've just gotta spend five minutes with him to see he's not exactly the master detective type."

"Well, let's pretend he is and remember to keep your mouth shut," Emily snapped, having a hard time controlling her hostility.

Amanda looked down. "Fine," she agreed.

Emily took out a pad of paper and a pen. "We're going to start from the beginning," she said. "When did you first pull into this town?"

Amanda looked confused. "Should I start with the first time I got pulled over, or when I blew up the gas station?"

Emily could now feel a migraine coming on. "Let's start with the first traffic stop," she said.

"Okay," Amanda said, "this is going to sound bad, because I kinda showed the chief my boobs, and may have offered to blow him to get out of the ticket. But he's not charging me with that, I think. And I only did it because the car's stolen, but they haven't figured that out yet. And since the car blew up, I'm not sure they'll ever know."

Emily, despite being prepared for an elaborate story about the explosion, was once again dumbstruck. She was starting to feel like she was in a boxing ring, repeatedly getting pummeled on the head.

"Can you give us a moment?" Emily asked, standing up and glancing at Jim. The two lawyers walked out the door.

Sam looked up and Emily held up her finger, indicating they we're going to need a minute. She grabbed Jim's arm and pulled him outside.

"What the fuck?" Emily yelled.

"I know," Jim said. "It's bad."

"Bad!" Emily laughed. "I just counted three felonies in one sentence, and we haven't even gotten to the actual charges yet!"

"She obviously had a really weird day."

"Weird?" Emily laughed again. "Oliver Stone should just follow her around with a camera."

"Come on," Jim said, touching her arm. "It's not like she killed anybody."

"No," Emily snapped, brushing off his hand. "Somehow, they lived after she tried to blow them up." Emily reached into her bag, grabbing her ibuprofen. "And by the way, the next time you kiss that girl, I'm going to shove my ring up your ass."

"That wasn't me," he said, "I pushed her right off, you saw me."

"Oh, it must have been horrible for you," Emily said, downing the pills with some water.

"You're the one who didn't want her to know about us," Jim said. "She just doesn't know."

"But you do, right?" Emily asked, looking in his eyes. "Do you know we're together, or are you not sure?"

"We're together, and I love you," he said.

"Funny way of showing it," she sighed.

"I'd apologize, but I'm not sure if it would be taken as a form of confession," he said back.

Emily walked passed him and into the room.

"Let's start again," she instructed Amanda, who now had a mouth full of donut. "After you tried to bribe the Chief of Police by offering to perform oral sex, in an attempt to hide the grand theft auto, what did you do?"

Chapter 12

Jim sat next to Emily as Amanda walked them through the series of events. After she had received a ticket from the police chief, she went to get gas, took some painkillers for a headache, washed them down with a beer, and the next thing she knew she was waking up in a hospital bed. She didn't remember shooting up the place, but did have a slight recollection of the ensuing explosion.

Jim was trying to focus on the matter at hand, but found it difficult to concentrate. Amanda still looked great. A bit thinner than before, but still beautiful. And her demeanor was the same, so funny and playful, even during something as serious as this.

But Emily was agitated to a point Jim had never seen. She was clearly pushing herself to get through this, and was not happy with it or him. He was impressed at how well Emily was handling things legally speaking, and yet he couldn't help but feel she would be happy to see Amanda go away for life.

"What type of pain killers did you take?" Emily asked as she made her notes.

"Oxycontin," Amanda replied.

Emily looked up at her in annoyance. "You took Oxycontin for a headache?" she asked.

Jim looked down. He could feel Emily's stress level rising.

"Yes," Amanda said, "the Vicodin wasn't working."

Emily rubbed her head. "And you washed it down with a beer?" she asked.

"Yeah, I was really hot," Amanda said.

"I don't suppose you have a prescription for these pills?" Emily asked.

"No," Amanda said, "I got them from a friend."

Jim watched Emily jot down more notes. He looked over at Amanda, who was again smiling at him. He felt her foot gently press his leg. He looked up and she started moving it against him.

Jim immediately stood and leaned against the wall. Amanda threw him a pout that instantly turned to a mischievous smile. He tried hard to maintain his professional demeanor.

Emily's phone chirped, and she glanced at the clock.

"We have to wrap this up for our meeting with Mr. Bayloch," Emily declared, stuffing her pen and paper into her bag.

"So, what happens now?" Amanda asked.

"We're going to meet with your lead counsel, Mr. Bayloch," Emily said. "Has he introduced himself?"

"Yeah," Amanda said. "He introduced himself when I first got booked, and told me to not talk to anyone."

"Well, that was good advice," Emily said. "Start following it. You're going to be taken to the county courthouse and arraigned this afternoon. At which point, we'll argue for you to be released on your own recognizance, which will be denied, but then they will hopefully set a bail amount."

"I don't really have any money," Amanda said. "I got like three hundred bucks, but I don't know if that will be enough."

"I'll cover the bail," Jim said, earning an unhappy look from Emily.

"We will then go from there and see what can be done to get the charges reduced and work out some sort of plea agreement," Emily finished.

"I can't go to jail," Amanda said

"You're already in jail," Emily said as she got up.

"I mean I can't stay in jail," Amanda said.

"We'll do our best," Emily said as she opened the door, letting Sam know they were finished. "Do you have anything to wear?" Emily asked Amanda cautiously.

"My clothes blew up in the car," Amanda said. "But really, I cannot go to jail. I just can't."

Sam walked in and placed handcuffs on Amanda, giving Jim an unexpected urge to push him away from her.

"Jim, let's go," Emily demanded as she headed toward the front door of the station.

"I can't go to jail," Amanda cried as her tears started to fall. "Please, Jim. Please."

"You're not going to jail," Jim blurted out. "I promise, I'll fix this."

Amanda smiled at Jim, brushing away her tears. "I know you will, thank you," she snuffled, tears already drying on her face.

Sam led Amanda away and Jim looked over at Emily, but she was gone. He rushed out of the station and raced to catch up with her fast, angry pace.

"We're in that much of a hurry?" he demanded. "Do you even know where we're going?"

Emily stopped and spun to face Jim. "You promise?" she screeched. "You fucking promise?"

"It just came out," he said. "I got emotional."

Emily went to walk away but turned on him again. "Forgetting the idea you've just had a ridiculous emotional outburst, practically promising to kill or die for an ex-girlfriend you haven't seen in eight years, and putting your big boy lawyer pants back on, tell me this: how do you see this issue being resolved?" she demanded. "She got high on illegal narcotics, grabbed a cop's gun, and blew up a gas station!"

"Allegedly?" Jim said, trying to get her to smile.

"Fuck you," she declared as she walked away.

"Emily?" Jim asked softly.

"What?" she asked, spinning around again.

"Where are we going?" he asked.

"I'm looking up directions to Bayloch's office." Emily snapped back.

"Em?" Jim said, nodding to a green Subaru Outback parked in front of the police station. The license plate read "Bayloch."

They walked back into the station and saw Chief Morris speaking to a middle-aged black man by the desk. The chief pointed at them, and the man walked over with his hand extended welcomingly.

"Ms. Perkins?" he asked Emily.

"Mr. Bayloch, I presume?" she asked with the smile she reserved for respected colleagues.

"That's me," he said, pumping her hand, "but call me Reggie."

"I'm Jim. Just here to carry the briefcase."

"Nice to meet you, Jim," Reggie's smile grew. "Looks like you're doing a fine job, too."

"I'm sorry, I thought we were meeting you at your office?" Emily said.

"Oh, my office is in Dothan," Reggie explained. "I figured it'd be easier to meet here. How about I take you guys to breakfast and we can go over the case?"

Amanda walked into her cell and Sam removed the handcuffs.

"What's with the bracelets?" Amanda asked Sam. "Not like I'm going to run off on you."

"Sorry," he said. "Had to make it all look proper in front of everyone. How'd that go?"

"I'm not supposed to tell you," she whispered, teasingly. "You could be a spy."

"Makes sense, I guess," Sam said as he put the cuffs back in his holster. "Want anything to drink or anything?"

"A beer?" she tried.

"No can do," he replied, smiling. "But I got Diet Coke, Sprite, or Root Beer."

"Bottled water?" she asked.

"Nope, sorry," he said. "Just the tap."

"Doesn't any place in this town sell bottled water?" she complained.

"Yeah," Sam said with a smile, "but you allegedly blew it up."

Amanda looked down, "I'm not supposed to say this, but I'm sorry."

"I know you are." Sam closed the cell door. "Don't worry, it will all get worked out," he said.

Amanda winced as she sat down and pulled out another pill.

Chapter 13

The green awning of the Broadway Cafe was welcoming, even though the stores on either side were vacant.

"Not much shopping here I guess," Jim said as he surveyed the nearly empty shopping center.

"Nah," Reggie explained, looking a little wistfully at the shuttered windows. "The town's going through a tough time right now."

They sat at a table in the back and the waitress brought over a pitcher of iced tea and some menus. Emily decided to skip breakfast. Jim followed suit, despite his hunger, determined to follow her lead.

"How well do you know the prosecutor on the case?" Emily asked, jumping right in.

"Charlie Franks and I know each other well," Reggie said. "He's a fair guy, reasonable."

Emily rolled her eyes. "I worked as a public defender for years," she said. "Now tell me what you really think of him."

Reggie smiled and nodded to Emily, "Okay," he said. "Charlie's most aggressive when going after out-of-towners, or maybe even out of his skin color. His conviction rate on blacks is about fifty percent higher than whites. He has bigger political aspirations, and treats his office as a platform for earning favors from some of the banks, and making a name for himself. He and Chief Morris have been having some issues lately, ever since the chief refused to serve up a bunch of foreclosures on the people in Ashford, leaving it up to the Sheriff's office."

"Sounds like a lovely man. If we can show she was not in her right state of mind, and submit to rehab, do you think we can get a plea suspending jail time?" she asked.

Reggie poured them each a glass of iced tea. "Probably not," he said.

"What about Chad Mitchell?" Emily asked, referring to the sign she saw outside the Day's Inn. "Is he going to be the DA in a couple weeks?"

"Well, don't you pay attention to your local politics!" Reggie laughed. "Chad's a good guy, but he's young and doesn't have the support of the people who matter. Don't get me wrong, no one likes Franks, but people just don't see enough reason to vote him out." Sipping at his glass, he considered the two in front of him. "Let me ask you a question: where'd you to school?"

"Stanford, why?" she asked.

Reggie turned to Jim. "And you?"

"Harvard. We have an excellent briefcase holding department," Jim quipped.

"Enough with that joke," Emily shot at him.

Reggie nodded. "So, I guess my follow up question is simple. Why am I sitting at a table in a little restaurant in Ashford, Alabama, with two lawyers from a scary L.A. firm, with about half a million dollars in education between them?" he asked. "Who is this Amanda Jeffries?"

"She's a friend," Emily said. "This is a favor."

"Okay, fair enough. But one thing you have to understand here is this isn't L.A., and she isn't Lindsay Lohan. Someone can't just drive into town, shoot up the place and blow up the only gas station. Shit, even I got a little weepy seeing the place half burned down. Rehab and an apology is not going to cut it. Not for Charlie, and not for this town."

Emily looked over at Jim who was anxiously picking at his cuticles.

"This whole thing is a big screw up," Jim insisted. "She's got a clean record."

"Well," Reggie said, pulling a file from his case. "She's got a somewhat clean record. There's a bust for weed at nineteen ..."

"That was dropped," Jim interrupted.

"... Yes," Reggie continued. "It was. But there's another bust for weed at twenty-two, where she paid a fine. Then we have a domestic violence charge. Seems she used a stun gun on her boyfriend's testicles."

"What?" Jim asked.

"Yep," Reggie said. "Not just once, either. Poor man got tricked into letting her tie him up, and then she started giving him a good juicing. I asked her about it, and she claims he tried making moves on the fourteen-year-old neighbor girl, so she decided to take action. The guy ended up in the emergency room. They counted at least twelve shock points, meaning she hit him at least six times, right on the guy's balls."

Jim was doing his best not to laugh, as her record was only going to add to the complexity of the situation. But, it was just so Amanda!

"We're looking for the best, fastest resolution to this thing," Emily cut in. "From your experience, what do you think the prosecutor will go for?"

Reggie considered for a moment. "We got a young girl, she's pretty, and that will help because our juries always end up being about three-fourths male around here, and Charlie will know they'll like her. Most of her priors are minor, nothing like her behavior here. If we can show she got a little too much party in her for a day, we might be able to pull this off with a year."

"No way." Jim blurted out. "No. She's not doing a year."

"Jim, we're working this through," Emily said, putting her hand on his arm. "Let me do this."

Jim reluctantly retreated back to his iced tea.

"What if restitution arrangement were made to cover at least part of the damages?" Emily asked.

"Oh, I'm already counting on that," Reggie said. "Let's get her arraigned and figure out what we can do. This is going to be a long process."

"We'll be heading back after the arraignment," Emily said. "But we'll follow up with you via phone and email, if that's okay."

Jim looked over at Emily, but kept his silence.

They finished their iced tea and Reggie walked with them to their car. "You can follow the chief to the courthouse," he suggested. "He'll make sure you get to where you need to go."

"What's the deal with him?" Emily asked. "And the young one working the desk?"

"The chief?" Reggie said. "He's about as by-the-book as a man gets. He follows the rules and doesn't tolerate those who don't. The young one is his youngest boy, Sam. Good kid, smarter than people give him credit, but not exactly supercop, if you know what I mean."

"Really? Emily asked.

"Yeah," Reggie said, "matter of fact, when you read the full report, you'll see it was his gun she grabbed to shoot up the place. He's being investigated now," Reggie added.

"Good," Emily said. "That might be useful."

Chapter 14

Emily thumbed through the rack of clothing. "What size do you think she is?" she asked.

"Four," Jim answered, a little too quickly, and Emily shot him another dirty look.

"Really?" Jim asked. "For remembering her dress size? She's a C cup, in case you want to get mad about that, too."

"I could tell she was a C-cup, but thanks for the confirmation," Emily snapped as she quickly pulled three modest dresses from the rack.

"She would never wear these," Jim said looking at the paisley dresses.

"Then she can wear her dirty shorts and t-shirt to court," Emily snapped

They returned to the Day's Inn and Emily grabbed her computer. "I'm going to need to do some work, so can you give me some privacy?" she requested.

"Fine," Jim said. "But this is exactly why I didn't want you to come."

"Don't act like that," she said. "I'm doing this for you, and us."

"You're really going to let them send her to jail for a year?" he asked.

"No, I'm not going to let anyone do anything," Emily replied. "I'm going to fight like hell to get her a great deal. One so good, they won't even know it until well after the ink's dry. But she's not walking away from this thing without doing some time, so get that through your head."

Jim left the room, marching to the car and slamming the door hard enough to rock the rental on its wheels. He realized he was hungry and cursed himself for turning down three different offers of food today. As he hit the drive-thru at McDonald's, he couldn't help but remember the first time Amanda and he had gone to his parents for Christmas. Amanda was supposed to bring desert, but as usual they were running late. They showed up with fifteen McDonald's Apple Pies. His mother never did like Amanda.

He added an apple pie to his order, and ate his Quarter Pounder in the car. His phone started ringing; it was Jane.

"Hey," he said. "Everything go okay?"

"Yes, Mr. Morgan." Jane said, "Mr. Combs is meeting with Mr. Strickland at one, and both hope your mother recovers soon."

"My mother?" Jim asked.

"Of course, Mr. Morgan," Jane said. "You would not cancel such an important meeting for anything less than an immediate family emergency."

He loved Jane.

"But right now, I have Mr. Kyle Hill on the phone," she said. "He wanted to follow up on yesterday's meeting."

"Sure, please put him through," Jim said, taking the last bite of his burger.

"Mr. Hill, I'm transferring you now," she said.

"Kyle?" Jim said. "How's it going?"

"Good," Kyle said, "really good. I found out my dad was going to buy a new Lexus, and god knows what else, so ... thanks for taking care of me."

72

"No problem," Jim said. "What was their reaction?"

"My mom understood, but my dad was pretty pissed when I told him there wasn't going to be enough for him to get his new car," he said. "But seriously, thanks man. You really struck a chord with me yesterday."

"Yeah?" Jim asked.

Kyle fell silent for a minute. "It just feels like everyone supposedly looking out for me is really just looking out for themselves." He paused again. "I mean, I'm not saying they don't care, but every idea they seem to support brings them money. I guess that's part of their job, but it is nice to have someone who says they have no interest in what I do."

Jim was a little taken aback by Kyle's confidence in him. While he liked to think he was a trusted advocate for his clients, it never occurred to him he might be the one and only person really being honest with them.

"I don't know what to say, Kyle." Jim said. "I guess it's a little sad the person you have to trust most is a lawyer, but such is the world we inhabit, I guess."

Kyle laughed. "Yeah, that was a lot to lay on you," he admitted. "It's a weird time for me, with the show ending and all, and trying to figure out what comes next."

"You've got no shortage of offers," Jim said. "You've got so much going for you."

"Yeah," he said, "I hear that a lot."

Jim wished he had something more profound to share with Kyle, but he was not prepared for what was quickly becoming a soul-searching conversation.

"Well, I'm here when you need help sorting shit out," Jim said. "I'll warn you, though — I don't know shit about being a star. But, I can at least help you get what you want."

"Thanks, man," Kyle said. "I actually do want to run something by you soon. Are you free for lunch tomorrow?"

Jim admittedly felt he was letting Kyle down; he would be his first big celeb client, and now he was missing a lunch and risking him going to someone else.

"I'd love to, but I'm actually out of town," he said. "Can we do it next week?"

"No problem," Kyle said. "Where you at?"

"Um …" Jim thought about saying New York, but then he risked Kyle wanting to hang out. The truth would be better, anyway.

"I'm in Alabama," Jim admitted.

"Alabama?" Kyle asked. "Like, the state?"

"Yeah," Jim said. "A little town called Ashford."

"Cool," Kyle said. "Have fun with that."

"Thanks, but not likely," Jim said. "If you have something you want me to take a look at, you can send it over, and I'll review it with you."

"No, that's cool," Kyle said. "You're obviously taking care of something down there."

"It's not a problem," Jim reassured him. "I'm mostly hanging around and waiting right now. Pretty boring, to be honest." He really wanted to get working with Kyle, and he could feel the opportunity sliding away from him.

"Oh," Kyle said, "it's cool. I'd rather go over it in person, so it can wait."

When Kyle disconnected, Jim felt like he was missing out on something big. But he had another issue to deal with. He pulled into the bank parking lot and asked to speak to the manager.

Chapter 15

Emily was trying hard to keep her mind on the case. She had a ton of research to review, and motions to write. She was worried Reggie was going to be pissed at her for springing them on him, but she had to get this done so Jim and her could get as far away from Amanda as possible.

She was proofreading the last motion when her phone rang. She saw it was her mother and debated answering it, but it could be important. She hit the speaker button.

"Hey Mom, what's up?" she asked.

"Did you meet her yet? Is she pretty?" her mom asked.

Emily hung up and went back to searching for typos. Finally, she hit send on the email and picked up her phone. "Reggie, I'm really sorry, but I just sent you four motions I need filed immediately," she said.

Reggie was silent for a moment. "I wasn't aware you wanted to file motions," he said.

"Aren't you planning to file any?" she asked.

"Of course," he said. "A motion to dismiss, which will be tossed, and a motion for change of venue, since everyone in this town would like to hang her for blowing up the place they get their scratchers."

"I have a change in venue motion, too," she said, "and a motion to dismiss based on striking the testimony of Sam Morris."

"What do you mean?" Reggie asked.

"He's an incompetent police officer, Reggie. You said it yourself."

"I didn't say incompetent," Reggie insisted. "I just said he's not … great at being a cop, I guess."

"Right, so we're going to use that," she explained. "If we kill his testimony, they have nothing, and the judge will have to dismiss."

"Listen," Reggie said, "I appreciate the aggression, but I have to work with these people. I'm not sure I feel comfortable calling the son of the Chief of Police incompetent. And to be frank, he's a good kid. He didn't do anything wrong here."

Emily had known this might be an issue. Many lawyers talk tough, but backed down when it came time to unsheathe their claws.

"I completely understand," she said. "You can file that one under me."

"You can't file motions," he said, "you're not licensed here."

"I'm licensed in four states and have five years of experience, Reggie. You can submit me as a reasonably qualified attorney to consult on this case. Under your own state laws, you have the power to do that."

She could tell Reggie was getting the picture. This was her show, and it would be for as long as she wanted it to run it.

"And if I say no?" he asked, defeated.

"You would let your personal relationship with the police chief inhibit your ability to provide the best defense possible to your client?" she asked, with just a hint of warning in her tone. Reggie fell quiet, and she gave him time to consider the consequences of challenging her. She didn't like threatening him, but she felt somewhat legitimate in doing so.

"I'm not looking for trouble here," Reggie said. "You want the ball, you got it."

"I'm so glad I can help," she said. "Can you get these motions in before for the arraignment?"

"I'll have them ready, Ms. Perkins," he said.

"Please, call me Emily," she said.

"Stanford must be a very good school, Ms. Perkins," he said before hanging up.

Emily checked the time, 12:15, and looked out the window to see Jim parking the car. She grabbed her case and the bags from the dress shop, and hurried out to meet him. "We need to get these to her before she heads out to court," Emily declared as she carefully laid the dresses on the back seat.

Jim turned the car around and headed back to the police station. They walked in and saw Sam at the desk.

"We're heading out in a minute," Sam said.

"I'm here to provide my client with clean and appropriate clothing for her court appearance," Emily stated. "Please retrieve her and provide us a private location to change."

"Do you talk like this all the time?" Sam asked, making the corners of Jim's mouth twitch in a barely swallowed smile.

"I believe you said we only had a short time before we leave?" Emily prompted, giving Sam a dirty look.

"Okay, I'll get her," he said.

He appeared with Amanda a moment later, no handcuffs this time. "You can go in the conference room," he offered, pointing to the room they used previously.

Amanda smiled at Jim as she walked with Emily to the room.

"I brought two choices," Emily said as she closed the door.

"They're both hideous," Amanda said.

"Well, you have a choice between hideous in black or hideous in blue," Emily said, "and keep in mind, this is how they dress here. It helps to not look like an outsider."

Amanda stripped out of her clothes and slipped the dress above her head. Emily pretended not to look.

"It's important you do not say anything in that room until I tell you," Emily instructed. "Do you understand?"

"Yeah," Amanda said.

"When he asks you how do you plead, you're going to say Not Guilty. Do you understand?"

"Yes," Amanda confirmed. "What if he asks me other stuff?"

"He won't," Emily said.

"But what if he does?" Amanda insisted.

"It's illegal. I'm your lawyer," Emily said. "I speak for you."

Amanda reached into her shorts and grabbed the three remaining pills.

"What the hell are those?" Emily yelped.

"My pills," Amanda said.

"They let you keep those?"

"No," Amanda said, "they just didn't find them."

Emily looked around. "Well, they will likely search you at county, so you may want to get rid of them."

"Can you hold them for me?" Amanda asked.

"No, I'm not holding your illegal narcotics." Emily said.

Amanda looked around and placed two of the pills on the windowsill.

"Well, pop that other one in," Emily said. "Get right before court, I don't need you jonesing out in front of the judge."

"It's not like that," Amanda said.

"I don't care," Emily said, "let's just get on with it."

"Why are you here?" Amanda asked. "You clearly don't want to help me."

"I'm doing Jim a favor," she said.

Amanda looked Emily over. "When's the wedding?"

Emily looked down at her ring, and then back at Amanda.

"Two months," she announced. "Now let's get this thing done.

Afterwards, you're never going to bother him, us, again."

Sam clapped his hands in applause as Amanda glided out in her new dress. She did a quick spin for his enjoyment, and Emily pinned Jim down with her stare, making sure he was not watching, or enjoying, the show.

Chapter 16

The courthouse wasn't much bigger than the police station, and Emily was wrong, they didn't bother searching Amanda again. It was a big change from the bustling courthouses in Los Angeles, and much cleaner.

Emily walked up next to Reggie, who was already waiting at the desk.

"Got my motions?" she asked.

"I do," he said, not looking at her. "But trust me when I say this is a mistake."

"This isn't personal, Reggie," she said. "I'm not here to make friends."

"Well, then maybe this is a good plan," Reggie smirked.

Emily nodded to Amanda, who was now handcuffed to the table.

The bailiff announced Judge Clemens, and a man in his sixties came out and sat at the bench.

"Sorry I'm running late," the judge said. "I had to go an extra twelve miles to get some gas and my lunch," he added, shooting a glare at Amanda. "Mr. Franks, please begin," he requested the prosecutor.

"Your honor, we are still reviewing the entire case and

investigating the incident, but at this time we're filing two charges, assault on a police officer and felony criminal vandalism," Franks declared.

"Okay," the judge said. "Defense, how do you plead?"

Emily nodded at Amanda. "Not guilty," Amanda said.

"Very well, we'll set the trial date for thirty days from now," the judge decided.

"Your honor, at this time we have motions," Emily chimed in.

"I'm sorry, who are you?" the judge asked.

"My name is Emily Perkins, and I'm consulting with Mr. Bayloch on this case."

"Oh, yes," the judge said, "I've heard about you. I already ruled on Mr. Bayloch's motions. I'm not dismissing, obviously, and I'm not moving her trial. She'll get a fair trial here."

"I have another motion," she said, handing the papers to the bailiff.

"What is this?" the judge asked, looking through the papers.

"A motion to strike Officer Sam Morris's testimony, your honor."

"On what grounds?" he asked, reading over the papers

"His history of shoddy police work is currently being investigated by the county sheriff's office," she said. "He is even being investigated for this very incident, and because he may face personal penalties, we do not believe the court can count on him to be an honest and reliable witness."

"I don't like this." The judge shuffled quickly through the papers in front of him. "Is he being investigated, Mr. Franks?" he asked.

"Your honor, Chief Morris has asked the sheriff's department to investigate Officer Morris in this matter, as to defend his department from any appearance of impropriety," Franks replied.

"Yes, that would be proper, sounds like Morris," the judge agreed, returning his attention to the motion. He held his hand up to stop anyone from talking while he finished reading.

"I don't like this, Ms. Perkins," the judge repeated. "This is the exact type of maneuver that keeps people from getting fair trials."

"Your honor." Sam stepped forward. "I wouldn't lie, even if I did screw up. Everything happened exactly the way I put it in the report."

"Your honor, we should allow Officer Morris his right to remain silent so as to protect himself," Emily suggested. "There's no reason to let him dig himself into a deeper hole here."

Amanda stared at Emily. She wanted her to stop, but didn't know what to say.

"Ms. Perkins, don't tell me who to silence in my courtroom," the judge said. "This is bullshit, pardon my language. But it's well written bullshit, and I'm not going to give you the luxury of having any grounds for an appeal. We'll hold a hearing after the sheriff's department concludes their investigation."

"We would also like to be heard on bail, your honor," Reggie said.

"Prosecution objects to bail your honor. She was just passing through and is likely to flee," Franks insisted.

"Your honor, being a guest doesn't mean being dishonest," Reggie challenged. "She's been cooperative, and has a relatively clean record."

"She kidnapped a man and jolted his testicles a dozen times with a stun gun, your honor," countered Franks.

"It was half a dozen, your honor, and she showed up to the court date," Reggie said.

"I'm not letting her go without something showing significant good faith," the judge said. "Bail to be set at a hundred thousand."

"Thank you, your honor," Emily said.

"Don't thank me for doing my job," the judge said. "And I heard about your little comment. I happen to like Lynyrd Skynyrd, Ms. Perkins."

Amanda looked over at Sam. "I'm sorry," she said, a blush

spread across her face. "I didn't know that was going to happen."

Sam walked away without saying a word.

Emily turned to Mr. Franks. "We didn't get a chance to be properly introduced. I'm Emily Perkins, nice to meet you."

"Ms. Perkins," Franks said.

"Please, call me Emily," she said with a Teflon smile. "We should talk about making the next few years of your life as stress-free as possible, because that's how long I'm going to have my people drag this on."

Franks closed his briefcase. "I'm not intimidated," he said.

"Well, I would hope not!" Emily exclaimed, stepping in front of him. "To intimidate you would be illegal."

"You're going about this the wrong way," Franks said in a paternal voice. "I see the girl's broke and was obviously on something. I'll allow eighteen months with rehab and five grand in restitution, and we can call it a day."

"Ha," Emily laughed flatly. "You must have confused her for an unattractive, black male between the ages of nineteen and forty, because that's all they convict in this state."

"I take offense to that, Ms. Perkins," Franks said.

"Think about how they feel," Emily said. "Face it, she's a pretty girl. Two-thirds of her jury's going to be men. All we need is for one to develop a little crush."

"Let me know when you have something non-offensive to say," he spat, trying to step around Emily.

"You're elected, right?" she asked.

"Yes. Are you going to try to bribe me now through my campaign fund?"

"Why would I do that?" Emily tisked. "I hear Chad Mitchell is an excellent prospect, I'll just support him. I bet he would make better use of his time. I hear he only needs a bit more help in the fundraising department."

"Wow!" Franks said, "I'm really considering having you arrested. I think Sam might enjoy that, actually."

"My father had a saying: 'deal with the monkey before you try to take on King Kong.'" Emily said.

"What does that even mean?" Franks asked.

"I'm not sure, he drank a lot," Emily said. "But what I mean by it is you can't win this case, so don't look to make it harder on yourself. Six months in rehab, two grand in restitution, and she walks with a misdemeanor."

"That's crazy! She blew up the gas station with a cop's gun in front of three other people! There's no way!"

Emily stepped to within an inch of his face. "And that, Mr. Franks, is exactly what the papers are going to say when they write about your loss," she whispered. "How's that going to look? Assuming, of course, I allow it to go to trial during your tenure. Take the offer, and move on with your life."

Franks was visibly shaken. "Draft it up," he snapped as he stormed out of the room.

Emily turned around to see Jim standing there.

"Done!" she said, smiling.

"Be careful, Em," he cautioned. "I think that was a closer call than you think."

"God forbid you thank me," she said. "I imagine the asshole will make her spend the weekend in jail, but I'll make sure Reggie gets it counted towards time served."

"She'll make bail," Jim said.

"Not unless she's got a hundred thousand bucks hidden in those tiny shorts of hers!" Emily laughed, catching herself a moment later and looking at Jim.

"She doesn't belong in a jail cell," Jim said.

"Your money," Emily said, grabbing her bag. "Hope she doesn't try to skip town over the weekend. She's just going back in on Monday for rehab."

Chapter 17

Sam was quiet on the drive back, but didn't handcuff Amanda. It would have been a comfortable and enjoyable ride, if not for the silence.

"I'm so sorry," she finally blurted out. "I had no idea that was going to happen."

"It's fine," Sam said, "my own fault."

"This whole thing is my fault," she said. "I'll tell her to stop using you like that."

Sam looked over at Amanda. "It's not all your fault," he said. "I wasn't paying attention when you grabbed my gun. I should have been paying closer attention and none of this would have happened."

Amanda didn't know what to say to make him feel better. "When I get out of here, we're going to go dancing," she said.

"I'm an all right dancer," he said smiling. "Want some lunch?"

They stopped at a small place called The Old Mill. With the flimsy chairs and crochet tablecloth, it was decorated more like someone's home than a restaurant. It was nice to get away from the jail and sit on something not made from metal, Amanda thought. And with her new dress, she could almost pretend she was on a date. It was hard to believe it was a little less than forty-eight hours since she had been arrested.

"Do you come here a lot?" Amanda asked.

"Every couple of weeks or so," he said. "But my family used to come here a lot when I was younger."

"That's nice," Amanda said. "I never had a family thing like that. It was just me and my grandma for a long time."

Sam's phone rang and he looked hesitant to answer.

"Yes," he said, putting the phone to his ear.

"I'm on my lunch break," he said.

Amanda started buttering some bread and looked over the short menu, which didn't seem to contain one salad.

"Okay, we'll be back in about an hour," he said.

Sam hung up and picked up his menu.

"You're not going to get in trouble for bringing me here, are you?" Amanda asked.

"Probably a little, but it's worth it," he said.

"You're too sweet to me," she said. "I don't want to get you in more trouble."

"What are they going to do, fire me?" he said. "Also, you're being bailed out when we get back, so it won't matter much to them."

"Really?" she gasped.

"Yep," Sam said with a smile. "It's going to take a couple hours to push the papers through, so eat slow and when we get back you should be free to go."

Amanda jumped up and kissed Sam on the cheek.

"I didn't bail you out!" he declared with a laugh. "It was like a hundred grand. Must have been your boyfriend."

"Yeah," she said, "but I don't think he likes me much right now."

"Well, he just paid more than twice my year salary to make sure you don't spend another night in jail, so that's something," he offered. "But I think him and Ms. Perkins are together."

"Yeah," she said, "engaged, actually."

"How long were you two apart?" he ventured.

"Eight years," she said. "I made a huge mistake."

"That's a long time," he reasoned, "but still, he came when you called, just like you thought."

Amanda sat back and considered Jim. She could tell Emily was unhappy about all this mess, and wondered if maybe she might still have a chance. She had started with a plan, although she had known he might be with someone. But she knew whatever the cost, she needed him more than Emily did, or ever would.

Sam and Amanda wrapped up their meal and drove back to the station where a man from the bail bonds service was waiting.

"We just need you to sign here, Ms. Jeffries," the man said. "It says you won't run before you trial, or we'll be coming to find you."

She signed the paper and waited for more instructions.

"We have some papers for the chief here," the bondsman said.

"I have to admit, I'm glad to see you go," the chief said to Amanda as he got up. "You've been a bit of a distraction for my guys."

"Sorry," she said.

"Chief Morris?" the bondsman said handing him a pen.

"I don't imagine you'll be skipping town," the chief said as he took out his own pen and signed the document, "since it sounds like you got your plea agreement all worked out."

Amanda looked at him confused. "I got a deal?" she asked.

The chief looked at her, surprised she didn't know. "I guess your L.A. lawyers work pretty fast. From what I understand, you'll be serving six months in rehabilitation. Congratulations on getting less time than our last inmate, who stole a set of tires."

"Wait," Amanda said, "six months?"

"That's all," the chief said, shaking his head. "Congratulations."

"Okay," the bondsman said, "you're all set."

"You're free to go," the chief agreed. "Do you need a ride anywhere?"

Amanda looked around and saw Jim walking in. She rushed over and grabbed him, and since Emily was absent, she took the opportunity to kiss him, but he softly pushed her back.

She looked behind her and saw the chief and bondsman watching them. She waived as she left with Jim.

"Thank you so much, but we have to talk," she started.

"I know," Jim said, opening the car door for her. "Emily is waiting for you at our motel to go over your plea deal." Getting in the driver's seat, he reversed the car and headed back to the motel.

"Can we stop?" Amanda asked.

"Where?" Jim asked, "Do you need something?"

Amanda slid her hand on his thigh. "I need something," she said, smiling at him.

"Hey, hey, hey," Jim said, pushing her hand off him. "I'm with Emily. We're engaged, and I love her."

"You're still mad," she pouted.

"Yes," Jim laughed, "and I always will be, but that has nothing to do with it."

"Then why did you come?" she asked.

"Because you were in trouble," he said, "but seriously, this isn't the time."

"Fine," she said.

They pulled into the Day's Inn, and Jim lead the way to the room. Emily was perched on the bed in her most comfortable sweat pants and a t-shirt, a pen in her mouth and pencils in her hair, going through a stack of papers in front of her laptop.

"I need you to review this and sign it," she said, pointing to a document on the edge of the bed.

Amanda walked over and picked up the paper Emily pointed to and started reading.

"I can't go away for six months," she said.

"Amanda," Jim barked. "Six months is a gift from the gods, or

Emily, I should say. Take the deal, thank us, and move on with your life."

"You don't understand," she said, tossing the papers back on the bed. "I can't do it."

"Did you really think you were just going to walk away from blowing up a gas station while drugged out of your mind? Sign the deal!" Emily insisted.

Amanda walked towards the door. "I appreciate everything you've done," she said, "But I'm not going to sign it." She closed the door behind her and walked to the street.

"Is she serious?" Emily asked Jim.

"I don't know," Jim said.

"Well, fuck it," Emily said, "let's pack up our shit and go. Let her go with Reggie if she thinks he can cut a better deal."

"If we just leave, they'll come after her harder," Jim said.

"Probably," Emily said. "But we did our part. I should be taking victory laps naked for that deal. I got her a slap on the wrist after her little terrorist attack."

Jim watched Emily begin to pack.

"I need to set her up with a room and shit," Jim said heading to the door.

"Jesus. Fine." Emily continued gathering her clothes. "The first plane back to L.A. tomorrow leaves at 5:40 AM, and I want us on it."

Chapter 18

Jim walked out to the street. It was nearly seven, and starting to get dark. He found Amanda sitting on the curb in front of the hotel. He sat down next to her and stared across the street.

"What's going on, Amanda?" he asked.

"I'm sorry," she said, wiping the tears from her face. "I can't go to jail for six months."

"It's rehab," Jim said. "Emily told me about the pills you're popping, and after this gas station incident, I think you might need this."

"It's more complicated than that," she said.

Jim took a breath and leaned back. "Things always do seem a lot more complicated with you than they should be," he said.

Amanda smiled. "Some girls are high maintenance, I'm high voltage."

"Well, you've shocked the shit out of me a couple times," Jim said. "Why did you do it?"

"I assume we're not talking about taking out the local gas station?" she asked.

"No," he said. "We're not."

"It's complicated," she said.

"So you keep saying. But try me, I'm a smart guy," he said.

"I was going to hold you back," she said. "I didn't belong where you were going."

"Boston?" he asked.

"Harvard," she said. "Ivy league, and fancy parties with senators and BMW's, and people who would look down on me."

"For the record, I don't know a single senator," he said.

"You drive a BMW, don't you?" she asked.

"Well," he said grinning, "you know I wanted one."

"See?" she asked.

"No," he argued. "Why could you not be part of that?"

Amanda shrugged, "I feel differently, now," she said. "Now, I would follow you anywhere."

"Why?" he asked

"Because you're all I've thought about for the past eight years," she said. "I fucked up, and then I didn't know how to fix it."

"Well, I'm not sure you could have," he said.

"I know. That's why I did it that way. Had to burn the bridge."

Jim looked up at the stars. "Yet, here I am," he sighed.

"Yeah," she said, "thanks." She slid her hand under his.

"Tell me what's going on," he pleaded, looking into her eyes.

She looked back into his. "Do you trust me?"

"I did, once," he said.

She nodded and looked back into his eyes. "I can't do the six months, baby. I can't."

Jim was now consciously holding himself back from kissing Amanda. The familiarity of her breath that he could now smell, and the lips that were mere inches away were driving him closer to her.

"I'll get you set up in a room for a few days," he said, "and here's fifteen hundred in cash."

She pushed the money away.

"It's not optional, you'll need it," he said.

She took a single hundred-dollar bill. "I just need some beer money," she said, smiling.

"Oh, please," Jim said, standing. "When's the last time you had to buy yourself a drink?"

Jim walked back into his room and saw Emily lying on the bed, TV remote in hand.

"Got her room all set up?" she asked.

"Yeah, she's good to go." He walked to the bed and saw his suitcase was already partially packed.

"I left your toothbrush and stuff in the bathroom so you can get ready to leave," she said. "I think we should try to leave around midnight, just to be sure. We can grab a couple hours sleep now."

Emily's phone went off, and she walked over to where it was charging. "Once again, my mother calling to screw with me. Say hello to voicemail, mother!"

Jim stood close behind Emily. "You were really amazing today," he said, wrapping his arms around her.

"Well, thank you," she said, pulling him closer around her. "I'm glad you noticed."

"The way you handled that prosecutor?" he said, "Wow."

"I know, I totally made him eat his own testicles while I watched," she snickered.

"A bit vivid, but okay," Jim laughed.

"Thank you, babe," she breathed, resting her head on his shoulder. "I did my best for you."

"I know," Jim said turning her around and kissing her. He started walking backwards to the bed. "I mean, we got to the station at eight, no idea how serious it was, and by two you had this thing down to almost nothing."

"Yep," Emily said, pushing Jim to the bed and slipping down on top of him. "Who's the man, baby? Say my name," she laughed.

"You are," he said.

She started kissing his neck and chest as he ran his hands along the sides of her body.

"I can't help but wonder," Jim said, "if you had a few more days, what you could do then."

Emily moved her hand up to Jim's hair, and started kissing him.

Jim kissed her back, and slid his hand under her shirt. "I bet you could really bring this whole thing down to nothing," he continued.

Emily slowly raised her head. "What do you mean?" she asked.

Jim sat up a bit and pulled her closer to him. "I mean, I bet you could make this whole thing go away, if we gave it another couple days."

Emily's face changed. "You've got to be kidding me," she snapped, sliding off Jim in disgust. "What is this? Payment?"

"No, not at all," Jim insisted. "Well, maybe just a little coaxing."

"Fuck you, coaxing!" she spat, pulling her shirt back down. "Just say what you want to say."

"Okay," Jim took a deep breath. "I think you're right; I don't know if I can do this without you."

"But you're going to try anyway?" Emily said. "You're going to fight this thing?"

"I'd rather you help me," Jim admitted, "but I'll try to fight it alone if I have to, yes."

"Unbelievable!" Emily said. "Fucking, un-fucking-believable!"

"Em, it took you all of five minutes to talk him down to six months," he said.

"Yes, but there is diminishing return on talking down," she said. "It doesn't keep going by the minute until they owe her time."

"I know," Jim said, "but I think you can do it."

"She's guilty, Jim!" Emily yelled. "Have you thought about that? She's popping pills, even in jail, and god knows where she was hiding them before she put them in her mouth. She has a problem."

"She's not a junkie," Jim said. "I know something's up with her, but that's not it."

"Oh," Emily said, "now you know her so well. Did you know her well enough to knock before walking in on her getting taken from behind by a total stranger?"

Jim got up and walked to the door. "You should save the low blows for the courtroom," he said as he walked out.

Emily dropped to the bed and balled her hands into fists. She wanted to scream. No, she wanted to rip Amanda's head off and show Jim the vile insides of his little damsel in distress. But all she could do was tear up over the idea he still wanted to save a girl who had ripped his heart out. She was too afraid to wonder if he would do the same for her.

Her phone rang again and she grabbed it. "What?" she yelled into the phone.

"It's me, what's wrong?" Katherine asked.

"I know it's you, mother, what do you want?" Emily asked.

"Well, are you coming home tomorrow?" her mother asked.

Emily sat quietly for a moment and didn't know how to answer.

"Hello?" her mother said. "Do they have bad cell service in Arkansas?"

"Yes," Emily said, hanging up.

Emily drew on her shoes and walked outside. She glanced around and saw Jim sitting on the curb in front of the hotel. She walked over and sat next to him, starring across the street.

"What's going on, Jim?" she asked.

He looked at her and laughed a small, sad laugh. "Good question," he said.

"Do you want to be with her?" she asked

Jim looked at Emily and ran his fingers through her hair. "You're the one I love, you're the one I want to be with."

Emily smiled and nodded. "Good," she said.

"You should go back," he said. "I'll take care of this, it's not your problem."

"So, you're determined to stay?" she asked. "There's nothing I can do?"

Jim leaned over and took Emily's hand. "If you make me choose, I'll choose you," he said. "I'll get on that plane and I'll never speak to her again. But I will always feel like I let down someone I care about, and I don't know if I'll end up blaming you for that."

Emily nodded and leaned her head against his. "The stars are so much brighter out here," she said. "You can actually make out constellations."

Jim looked up and nodded.

"Poor Mr. Franks," she said. "His horoscope must have warned him to stay in bed this week," she laughed.

"Does that mean you're staying?" he asked.

"Well, yeah," she said. "My man tells me to kick someone's ass, that ass gets kicked."

Jim reached over and kissed Emily, and pulled her closer. "I'm never forgetting this," he said.

"Oh, count on that!" she laughed as she pushed him to the ground.

Chapter 19

Amanda watched Jim and Emily from her window. They were rolling around the sidewalk laughing. It reminded her of a trip Jim and she had taken to Madison together, and how they'd sat on the grass under a big tree and ended up wrestling over a Snicker's bar she'd discovered in his jacket.

She walked over to the bed, which looked much more comfortable than the jail mattress she had been sleeping on for the past couple days. The pain was subsiding now she'd taken the Oxy, and she was finally able to lie flat without the shooting spasms.

There was only one pill left, and then she would be stuck with Tylenol, maybe Motrin at best, until she could get to a doctor.

She thought about the plea agreement and knew she couldn't afford to take it. She had a plan, and was going to stick to it, despite this little misadventure. She pulled off the dress she had thought was ugly earlier, but now it had grown on her. She hung it up and crawled into bed, feeling the mattress's light support against her back, which made her feel better.

She played with the clock radio until it brought in something recognizable to her as music, and went through the plan in her head for the hundredth time. Getting Jim back was the important part. After that, she didn't care about the rest. Traveling didn't matter much anymore; she just wanted to be with him.

She focused on the radio and fell asleep to something sweet and acoustic.

The next time she looked at the clock, the sun had filled the floor. 9:34 am. She had slept nearly twelve hours, and felt well rested. She got up and walked to the shower. She normally hated cheap motel shampoo, but was just happy to have clean hair. And the water was the perfect temperature.

There was a knock at the door. She was still in her towel, but decided since it was likely Jim, that wouldn't be such a bad thing. She was surprised to see Emily's knowing expression as she opened the door.

"Expecting Jim?" she asked. "He's getting gas, in the next town of course. May I come in?"

"Sure," Amanda said.

Emily walked in and looked around. "You have a window facing the street," she said. "That's nice. We face the parking lot."

"Maybe you can upgrade," Amanda suggested.

"Nah, my room has something yours doesn't," Emily said.

Amanda smiled and rolled her eyes.

"I don't know what your game is," Emily said. "I don't know if this unwillingness to do the six months for taking out a chunk of the town is a genuine, selfish lack of accountability, or a ploy to get Jim here alone with you, but it's not going to work."

"I just can't stay that long," Amanda said.

"Fine," Emily said. "But realize, I'm going to have to possibly go to court for you, and if we lose, you go to prison for much, much longer than six months."

"Is that going to happen?" Amanda asked.

"No," Emily said. "Know why?"

"Why?" Amanda asked.

Emily walked in close to Amanda, expecting her to move back, but she didn't.

"Because I've never lost," she growled. "And I'm not going to start now. I'm not losing anything, do you understand?"

Amanda moved in even closer to Emily. "Yes," she said, "and you have beautiful lips."

Emily stepped back from Amanda, making Amanda smile.

"I'm glad you're so clever, Amanda," Emily said. "It will help when you're on the stand."

Emily walked out of the room, leaving the door open behind her.

Amanda sat on the bed, not worrying about the door. Emily didn't scare her. She actually liked her, and felt bad she was working so hard on her behalf. She got up and slid on a clean dress.

Chapter 20

Jim pulled into the gas station and filled up the rental car. He walked inside and grabbed some water bottles and trail mix and was about to pay when he got a new text from Kyle.

Kyle: Still in Alabama?

Jim paid the clerk and replied as he walked to his car

Jim: Yeah, through Tuesday, the earliest.

Kyle: Ok

Jim: Just waiting for info, but totally free to talk if you need to. Actually a bit bored.

Jim didn't know why he added that last part, as it sounded overly desperate.

Kyle: It's cool, we'll talk soon.

Jim got in the car and headed back to Ashford, stressing about missing potential opportunities with a new client. He drove back to the Day's Inn and saw Emily waiting.

"Should we bring Amanda?" he asked as she hopped in the Taurus.

"No," Emily insisted, "she was drugged out during the whole thing anyway. And I don't want her saying anything to these people. Just us and Reggie."

They pulled into the lot of semi-destroyed gas station,

underneath a slightly charred sign declaring "Eastwood's Gas and Grocery." There were people loading trucks with debris and making piles of salvageable items.

They saw Reggie step out of his car and walk over.

"Thanks for coming," Emily said as she got out of the car, "I know it's the weekend."

"Yeah," he said. "To be honest, I'm more wondering why you're still here. Didn't we get this all settled?"

"Well, not really," Emily admitted. "I feel I need to really look at the evidence more before recommending the deal to my client."

"But it was your deal," Reggie argued.

"Yes," Emily nodded, "and that's what makes this extra important. Is the guy working inside the one who was working that day?"

"Yeah, name's Clint. He owns Eastwood's," Reggie informed her. The three walked in the front door and saw a small bald man moving boxes around.

"Oh, hey, Reggie," Clint said, turning around.

"Clint, how you holding up, my friend?" Reggie asked, shaking his hand.

"Well, you know," Clint sighed, gesturing to the damage with his arms. "But these nice people out here are all helping me out on their weekend off, trucking some of this stuff to the dump. I might be able to start getting the store back up in a week or so."

"It's good to be part of a community," Reggie agreed. "What'd the insurance say?"

"Well, Tom handles all that for me," Clint said, "and he said things will be good as new."

"That's outstanding news," Reggie said, "I'm looking forward to the grand reopening."

"Yeah," Clint said, "we'll see what happens."

"Clint, these are a couple people working with me on the case, Ms. Perkins and Mr. Morgan," Reggie said.

"Nice to meet you, sir." Emily said. "Please, call me Emily."

"Always nice to meet a beautiful young lady like yourself, Emily," Clint said.

Jim reached over. "I'm Jim," he said, "but I have to ask; this is Eastwood's, and your name is Clint. Is your name really Clint Eastwood?"

"Oh," Clint laughed, "that's a funny story. See my name is Clint Nelson, but in school people would call me Clint Eastwood, because of the actor in the cowboy movies. And sometimes they would just point and say, 'Hey, Eastwood!' So when I bought this place back in '82, I decided to call it Eastwood's, like the movie actor."

Jim smiled and looked over at Emily, who had a dulled expression on her face. "That is funny, Clint," he said, "or should I say Eastwood?"

"Oh, get out of here," Clint blushed, "I'm not a tough guy like him."

Emily turned around and gave Jim a nasty look clearly meant to shut him up.

"Mr. Nelson," Emily said, "we have some questions about the event, do you think you can help us?"

"Oh, sure," Clint agreed, "how can I help?"

"That's great," Emily said. "First, we're interested in the interaction between Officer Morris and Mr. Jeffries. How did Officer Morris lose control over his gun?"

"Well, she dropped her purse, and when Sam bent over to pick it up, she just took his gun," Clint explained.

"Didn't Officer Morris notice the gun being pulled from his holster?" she asked.

"Oh yeah," Clint said, "and he asked for it back."

"And there was as struggle for the gun?" Emily prompted.

"Yeah," Clint agreed, "and then the gun went off."

"Have you seen Officer Morris display this level of incompetence before?" she asked.

Client scoffed at the question. "He may not be the best policeman, but he's not incompetent," he stated. "He's as brave as his father and brother. He pulled her out of here, put out the fire on poor Todd's jacket, and was already putting out the blaze when the fire department finally got here. The whole place would've been lost if Sam hadn't been here."

"That's wonderful, Mr. Nelson," Emily said dismissively. "We were going through the crime scene photos, and some of them left a few questions. I was hoping you could clear those up for me," she asked.

"I'll try my best," he said.

"Well, this photo here," Emily said as she pulled out her iPad and brought up a picture of the blown tanks.

"That's fancy," Clint said, pointing to the tablet.

"Thank you," Emily replied. "But in this photo, do you see what confuses me?"

"Well, see, those are the fueling stations you pay at," Clint explained. "I get those through a special company that supplies stations with equipment. Mine are leased and serviced by a fella out of Birmingham. Or, at least, they were."

"Yes, that's good to know," Emily said, cutting him off, "but look at the way the pumps are facing ..."

Clint looked closer at the picture, and Emily zoomed in on the picture of the pumps.

"Well, they're facing forward," he said.

"Exactly," Emily said. "I sent these photos to a friend in Quantico, Virginia."

"Oh, where the FBI is?" Clint said.

"Yes, Mr. Nelson," Emily said. "Have you had past run ins with the FBI?"

Clint looked surprised, "No, of course not!" he said, laughing.

"That's good, things go much easier for first time offenders," she said, pointing back to the picture.

"What do you mean?" he asked.

"Oh, nothing," Emily said. "I was just talking about the pictures here. Wouldn't it make sense, Mr. Nelson, that if the truck explosion knocked over the pumps, then the pumps would be leaning away from the truck?"

"Right," Clint said, "they aren't?"

"No, Mr. Nelson," she said, "they're leaning south and they should be leaning west."

"Hmm," Clint said. "I guess so."

"So, this indicates the explosion that caused the damage did not come from the exploding truck, but in fact from the exploding tanks underground," she explained. "But that's not supposed to happen. Those tanks, if set up properly, don't explode."

"Okay," Clint said.

Reggie was rubbing his head, turning as if to avoid an oncoming headache.

"Do you have an attorney we should be speaking to, Mr. Nelson?" she asked.

"An attorney?" Clint asked. "Mike Hutchins handles my taxes and will and stuff like that."

"Well, maybe we should be dealing with him," Emily said. "You may be dealing with a few potential lawsuits that could jeopardize your business."

Clint started to get anxious. "What did I do?" he asked.

"Well, Mr. Nelson," Emily said as if she was speaking to a child, "if those tanks were not properly installed and maintained, you might be liable for the all this damage, including the personal injury to those involved."

Clint started rubbing his neck. "I got everything signed off on when it was installed, and the inspector comes by every couple of months to check things out."

"Well, that should help," Emily said, putting away her iPad. "In the meantime, just some personal advice, I would talk to a good lawyer right away, and I'm certain he's going to advise you to not say anything to anyone unless they have a court order."

"Yeah, probably good advice," Clint said. "Thank you. I sure hope this isn't my fault though, I hate to think anyone got hurt because of me."

Reggie glared at Emily, walking away. "See you around, Clint," he said.

"Take care, Reggie," Clint said. "Tell Denise I said hi."

Emily walked out with Jim and saw Reggie waiting by the car.

"Are you serious with this shit?" Reggie demanded.

Although Jim agreed with Reggie about the tactics, he really couldn't say much.

"I told him my concerns and advised him to get counsel," Emily said confidently. "What's wrong with that?"

"You're scaring him into not talking so he can't be a witness against Jeffries," he said.

"If he didn't do anything wrong, why should he be frightened to talk?" she said

"Because you and I both know if he goes to an attorney, which by the way, he can't afford, he'll be told not to talk to anyone." Reggie said.

"Sounds like sound legal advice," Emily smiled. "Now, do you have the truck driver's address?"

The truck driver's interview went much the same, with Emily convincing him his smoking cigarette may have been the true cause of the accident, and he should probably protect himself by not speaking to the authorities without a lawyer, which they would provide if they intended on charging him.

Jim could tell even though Reggie was disgusted by Emily's

tactics, he was still impressed. She had already removed Sam's testimony yesterday, and now she had taken out the two other people present. And, since Amanda couldn't be forced to testify against herself, the prosecution wouldn't have a single witness to the event.

And with no video surveillance, they would have near to nothing on which to build a case. Jim started to remember one of the bigger reasons he loved Emily: she was one of the best attorneys he had ever seen, especially for under thirty years old.

"How did you know he'd recognize the FBI's in Quantico?" Jim asked as he drove Emily back to the hotel.

"What?" Emily asked, looking up from her iPad.

"Clint Eastwood back there," he said. "How did you know he'd knew where the FBI headquarters were?"

"He likes those types of movies," she said. "It's the type of trivia these rednecks enjoy. He could also probably tell you the name of Chuck Norris's dog. Why?"

"Just made me think a bit, watching you in action," he said.

"Oh yeah?" she said, sliding her hand to his neck and playing with his ear. "What are you thinking?"

"That we're getting one hell of a prenup," he said, smiling. "I never want to face off against you in court."

"Just keep that in mind," she said, turning her attention back to her iPad.

Chapter 21

Amanda saw Emily and Jim pull away, and figured by Emily's unpleasantness they must still be working on her case. She took her last pill to stop the pain and walked downstairs to discover semi-fresh coffee and a couple donuts.

A cute girl was working the desk, or more accurately, reading a book while sitting behind the desk. She looked up and starred at Amanda for a moment. "Are you one who blew up the gas station?" she asked.

"Sorry," Amanda said with a small shrug.

"That's okay," the girl said with a similar shrug. "Maybe we'll get a newer one now, with an actual coffee machine, not that thing from the seventies they had."

"Shouldn't you be in school?" Amanda asked, trying to decide which donut looked less fattening.

"It's Saturday," the girl said, returning to her book.

"Oh," Amanda said. "What's there to do around here on a Saturday?"

The girl rolled her eyes towards Amanda. "That donut will be the most exciting part of your day," she said.

"Isn't there a bar, or something?" Amanda asked.

"Oh, yeah," the girl said, "the Milky Way is across the street."

"The Milky Way?" Amanda asked.

"Yeah, it's got stars on the ceiling, or some shit like that," the girl said. "There's also Patty's, but not many people seem to go there."

Amanda didn't like being alone, and since the girl at the desk was proving more interesting than most, she decided to introduce herself.

"I'm Amanda," she said, walking up to the desk.

"Claire," the girl shared, giving half a wave.

"How long you worked here?" Amanda asked.

"My whole life," the girl sighed with a deadpan expression. "My parents own the place."

"Wow, that's cool," Amanda said.

"Oh, the coolest," the girl drooled. "Later today, you might see me scrubbing your toilet and making your bed."

"Oh," Amanda agreed, "that would suck. But you have like a bunch of rooms where you can party with your friends."

"Yeah, that's not happening," Claire said. "The parents are not what you'd call progressive … or fun, or nice, for that matter."

"Yeah, well I didn't have parents, and look at me now!" Amanda joked, trying to make Claire feel better. "I'm sure there is some trouble to get into around here."

Claire smiled, "I assume you have met our police chief?" she asked, raising her eyebrow. "He seem like the kind of guy to let there be trouble to get into?"

"No," Amanda admitted, "he seems like the killer of all buzzes, but he is sweet in his own way."

"Congrats on being the first to use that word in describing him," Claire said.

"Is there a pharmacy around here?" Amanda asked.

"Yeah," Claire said, "there's a drug store about fifteen minutes up the 84."

"Oh," Amanda said. "No place within walking distance to get

some aspirin or something?"

Claire raised her eyebrow again at Amanda.

"I blew it up, didn't I?" she said, smiling. "I really need something."

"You made your bed, now lay in it," was Claire's reply.

"Well, you'll actually be making my bed," Amanda returned.

"Touché," Claire grinned. "Thanks for reminding me."

"Well, you don't have to, I'll take care of it," Amanda offered. "But I don't suppose you have any ibuprofen or Tylenol, or anything stronger?"

"Are you asking me for drugs?" Claire asked.

"No!" Amanda exclaimed. "God, no!"

"Too bad, I might have been able to hook you up," Claire said.

Amanda thought for a second. "What kind of hook up are we talking?"

"One of my friends has ADD, so I can score you some Ritalin," Claire said.

"I was thinking more like pain killers," Amanda said. "Vicodin, or Oxy."

"They got some Oxy up in Dothan, but no one would dare bring that stuff around here with Chief Hardass," Claire explained. "But my mom had her wisdom teeth pulled last month, and I think she's got a bottle of Vicodin in the cabinet."

"Won't she notice it's missing?" Amanda asked.

"Not if I replace it with something else," Claire said, smiling. "A hundred bucks for whatever's left in the bottle."

Amanda didn't have to think about it long, as she could already feel the dull pain increasing to its well-known sharpness. "Okay," she agreed.

Claire hopped off her stool, "Wait here," she said as she passed through an internal door.

Amanda felt guilty for turning a nice, bright teenager into a drug dealer, but she was desperate.

Claire reemerged with a handful of pills. "There were twelve left." She handed Amanda the pills, and Amanda gave her the hundred she had gotten from Jim.

"Thanks," Amanda said, depositing the pills into her bag and taking one right away. "How long are you working here?" Amanda asked.

"Until I die," Claire said.

"No, I meant today," Amanda said. "Maybe you can show me around?"

"No offense, weird drug lady who blows shit up," Claire said, "but if my parents saw us hanging out, they would ground me for a month. Not that there's a difference between that and my life, but still."

"Okay," Amanda said, trying to not let her feelings get hurt. She walked towards the door.

"Wait, are you hitting on me?" Claire asked.

"What?" Amanda gasped. "No! I'm not. I mean you're cute and all, but no!"

"Okay," Claire said, returning to her book. "I can just never tell."

Amanda walked out into the daylight, the brightness highlighting the dinginess of the hotel lobby. She felt bad for Claire having to work inside on such a nice day.

She walked down the street and looked at the shops, most of which were closed up. She stood in front of a shop window advertising sewing machine and vacuum repair, two things Amanda barely knew how to use, and couldn't remember a time anyone she knew had one fixed. But they also advertised key-making, which Amanda could see being useful to people.

"Hey there," a voice called from behind her.

Amanda turned to see a guy in a flannel shirt and a John Deere hat. He looked to be in his forties, with half a straggly beard growing on his dirty face.

"Hi," Amanda said cautiously.

"What are you up to?" he asked.

"Just going for a walk," she said.

"Want to go for a drive?" he asked.

Amanda looked over his shoulder and noticed he had parked his truck along the street right behind her.

"No, but thanks." She wanted to continue down the sidewalk, but couldn't find a way without having to brush passed him.

"Are you sure?" he asked. "I think we can have a really good time."

"Are you for real?" she asked, deciding this guy didn't deserve politeness.

He put his arm in front of Amanda, blocking her from walking away, and leaned in. "How about you come back to my place, and I'll show you just how real I am?" he offered, breath reeking of what she thought might be chew.

"Fuck off," she said, trying to push passed him.

The guy laughed as she tried in vain to move his arm.

"Hey," a man emerging from a store doorway said, "leave that girl be, Wayne."

"How about you mind your own?" Wayne shot back.

"Leave her be or I'll call the chief," the shop owner warned. "I'm guessing from your behavior you've been drinking."

Wayne moved away from Amanda and towards the shopkeeper. "If you got such a problem with me, why don't you do something?" he blustered.

The shopkeeper stood his ground. "Hon," he said to Amanda, who was now clear of Wayne. "Why don't you head on your way?"

Wayne grabbed the shopkeeper and shoved him back into his door, nearly knocking him over. Amanda looked around for something to hit Wayne with, when she saw something better.

"Wayne, what are you doing?" Sam demanded as he walked up passed Amanda, placing her behind him.

"I ain't doing shit, Sammy boy," Wayne said. "What are you doing?"

"I'm going to give you the opportunity to apologize to Stan, and get in your truck and leave," Sam said.

"Or what?" Wayne smiled. "She going to take our your gun and shoot me?" he laughed, nodding at Amanda.

Sam looked unaffected by the slight. "Or I'm going to slam you against that car and slap my cuffs on you," he said.

Wayne stepped closer to Sam. "Be careful, daddy and your big brother ain't here to do your fighting, Sammy."

Sam suddenly grabbed Wayne, using his grip on his belt and shirt to throw him against the truck, and then just as quickly tossed him back to the wall. Wayne tried to rush Sam, but instead ran his stomach straight into Sam's boot, dropping to the ground with a whoosh.

Wayne was about to get up and Amanda saw him reaching for a knife holster.

"I'll put you down, Wayne." Sam warned quietly, placing his hand on his shiny gun. "Don't think I won't."

Wayne moved his hand away from the knife slowly and got up. "All right, I'm going," he said, moving to his car.

"Wayne?" Sam called, motioning towards the shopkeeper.

Wayne laughed a little and rubbed his ribs. "I'm real fucking sorry, Stan," he said. "And I'm real sorry, crazy gun lady with the nice ass," he added as he pulled himself into his truck.

"You really have to work on your apologies, Wayne," Sam said.

Stan walked over to Sam. "Thanks," Stan said. "But you probably should have taken him in."

"Nah," Sam said, watching Wayne pull away, "He's about to get picked up for his third strike today by county. I don't want to mess that up."

"Well, that's a shame, I guess," Stan said. "It will break his poor momma's heart."

"Yeah," Sam agreed.

"Eat lunch yet?" he asked Amanda, who was feeling a bit dizzy.

"I had a donut," she said, "but it wasn't very good."

"Well, let's grab something," he said, motioning to his police car.

Amanda walked up and hugged the shopkeeper. "Thank you," she said.

"Oh, don't thank me," Stan said. "You blew up Clint's station, and I hope you think about that when you're sitting behind bars," he added as he stormed off.

Amanda looked up at Sam, and he shrugged as he held the car door open for her.

"Any preference?" he asked.

"Is the Milky Way open yet?" she asked.

"Wow," Sam said, "you're like a local already, knowing all our places to eat. I mean there's only like four, but still, impressive!"

Chapter 22

Jim and Emily pulled into the Day's Inn parking lot. "I have to see what Amanda remembers about the shooting," Emily said, getting out of the car. "The more details she can give me about her interaction with Sam Morris before the shooting, the more I can give the sheriff investigators to hang him with. Once his testimony is gone, we're golden."

"You sure we need to go after him so hard?" Jim asked. "I mean, let's not ruin the guy's career."

"His dad's the police chief," Emily argued, heading into the room. "I'm sure he'll be fine."

Jim walked in and set some papers on the nightstand.

"What's that?" Emily asked, nodding to the flyer on top.

"Reggie holds a legal clinic on Sunday afternoons," Jim said. "I thought I would check it out."

"Why?" Emily asked, changing into jeans and a t-shirt.

"I'm curious," he said. "I always thought about volunteering at one of these things."

"He probably just uses it drum up personal injury stuff on the side or something." Emily kicked off her flats and grabbed her jeans.

"You're very cynical," he chided.

"Well, go and tell me I'm wrong," she said, finishing her outfit change. "Now I'm off to deal with your ex." She grabbed her bag. "With a little luck, I won't kill her."

"Should I come with?" Jim asked.

"No," Emily said, "please don't."

"Fine," Jim said, "I'll stay out of it." He flopped onto the bed, pulling his laptop closer and trying to look as unworried as possible.

Emily closed the door and prepared herself to deal with Amanda. She was still furious about having to stay and deal with the case, and the reasonable side of her knew Amanda deserved to do some time. But Emily was getting caught up in the game of defending Amanda, and loved the familiar pump of adrenaline that came from kicking a prosecutor's ass.

She walked up to Amanda's room and knocked on the door, wondering if the girl ever bothered to get out of her bath towel. A minute passed, and she tried again. She glanced into the window, but didn't see anything.

She headed down to the lobby and saw a teenage girl sitting behind the front desk.

"Excuse me, have you seen the woman in 204?" she asked.

"Why?" the girl asked.

"I'm her lawyer, and I needed to talk to her," Emily said.

"Oh yeah, the crazy lady with a gun," Claire said.

"Right, the crazy gun lady, have you seen her?" Emily repeated.

"Yeah, she came down earlier," Claire said.

"Did she say anything while she was here?"

Claire considered her for a moment. "If I tell you, you can't tell anyone else, right?" she asked. "Client, attorney privilege, right?"

Emily smiled at the question. "That's right," she agreed, "a lawyer can't divulge anything a client tells her."

"Cool," Claire said, nodding knowingly.

"So," Emily said, "what did she say?"

"Oh, she paid me a hundred bucks for my mom's Vicodin, and

then asked where the nearest bar was." Claire reported. "Then she totally hit on me, which is cool, because I've thought about it. Being with girls, I mean."

Emily stood silent for a moment, wondering how she still could be caught off guard by Amanda's behavior.

"Where's that bar you mentioned?" Emily asked.

"Which one?" Claire asked.

"The nearest one," Emily clarified.

"The Milky Way's across the street," Claire pointed.

"Thank you," Emily said as she walked towards the door.

"There's also Patty's," Claire added, "but that place is usually pretty dead."

Emily stopped for a second. Amanda was the kind of girl to go where the party was. The Milky Way was where she'd look first.

Chapter 23

Jim hopped on his laptop and surfed around a bit. He looked up Reggie and friend requested him. He liked Reggie, and felt bad about how Emily had treated him. He started Googling the other people he had met while in town.

Emily was much better at research, but it didn't take long for Jim to catch up. He read the local paper's coverage about the explosion, which the reporter confirmed was 'not the work of Al Qaeda, as previously rumored.'

He searched for information about Chief Morris, finding a short bio from 2002 that sounded about right. His father had been sheriff once, he had a wife and two sons, and used to box a little. He'd received two medals for heroism from the town's mayor.

Jim closed his computer and thought about taking a nap, since Emily had insisted on getting up extra early to start destroying the case against Amanda. He was impressed at how quickly she moved. Contract negotiations were all about dragging things out as long as possible, and then moving fast to close the deal. Emily had only one gear when going against a prosecutor: hair on fire.

He had no doubt he loved Emily, and he knew he wanted to spend his life with her, but he had to admit to himself, he'd missed Amanda. The way everyone seemed to fall in love with her, and how she kinda floated through life. She'd had it much rougher than

Em, and yet she'd somehow turned out less jaded.

And when it came to sex, he had to admit, even though Emily was incredible, he sometimes missed the softness of Amanda. The way she always wanted to please him, and that look of vulnerability in her eyes when they made love. Emily had one gear during sex too, and it was even more demanding than the one she used to run over prosecutors. She didn't seem to worry about pleasing anyone. She just did what she liked, and it was coincidence it corresponded perfectly with what pleased him.

He wondered briefly what the pairing would be like, and feeling desire rush through his body, held onto the thought. He thought about Emily's aggression, combined with Amanda's giggling and playfulness. He started to undo his pants, deciding there was no harm in indulging this fantasy. Things were moving in a good direction when his phone rang. It was Emily.

"Yeah?" he sighed, grabbing the phone with his free hand.

"Does your ex-girlfriend have a thing for teenage girls?" she asked.

He wondered briefly if his fantasy had morphed into a dream. "What do you mean?" he asked.

"I mean the girl at the hotel desk," Emily said.

Jim remembered the girl being cute, and was curious to hear more. "She experimented a bit in college," he said cautiously.

"Fantastic," Emily said. "And where were you during this experimentation?"

"I don't know, probably school," he said. "Are you coming back to the room? I thought it would be nice to spend some time together."

"What does that mean?" Emily said. "We spent all morning in a car together."

"Yeah, I meant more personal time," he said.

"Oh my god, you must be joking," she said, clearly understanding his implication. "No way. I'm trying to find your ex, who is now armed with a bottle of Vicodin, illegally obtained from a minor. So why don't you just lay back and jerk off about your ex and some teenage girl." Emily hung up with a huff.

"Way ahead of you," Jim said as he laid back down, "and you're joining the party, too," he thought, as he started playing in his head a brief, pornographic film featuring the three young women.

Jim had never told Emily about Amanda and his sex life, which had incorporated several additional people in its short run, including a waitress from the bar they hung out at, and a girl from down the hall on his birthday.

He'd tried to move Emily in that direction once while on a trip to Las Vegas. Someone had handed him a business card for a local escort, and he'd asked Em what she thought. The depressing lecture on prostitution he'd received meant even a commercial for *Pretty Woman* could now send him into a slump.

He was again reaching the climax of his little fantasy, in which he was merely an observer, when the phone rang again.

"What?" he groaned.

"Jim, how's it hanging?" Kyle's voice said.

"Well," Jim said. "How are you hanging, Kyle?" he asked.

"Good, man," he said. "Look out your window."

Spooked, Jim rushed to put himself back in his pants, doing a poor job of it.

"Why?" he said.

"Just look out," Kyle insisted.

Jim went to his window, but couldn't see much with the stairway blocking his view. He opened the door and spied a limo stretched across the parking lot.

"Surprise!" Kyle shouted from the sunroof. "You said you were bored and wanted to go over stuff, so I decided to come hang out."

Jim walked to the car in disbelief. "What are you doing here?"

"I came to hang out," Kyle repeated, stepping out of the limo.

"Looks like you're happy to see me," he said, looking down with eyebrows arched.

"That's not for you," Jim explained, trying to give his brain a cold shower. "How did you know where I was?" he asked.

"You said Ashford, Alabama." Kyle grabbed his bag. "And there's only one hotel here. If it's a problem, I can head back, no worries."

"No," Jim insisted. "It's cool of you, it's just a surprise."

"I know," he admitted. "Maybe a bit too much?"

Jim was confused and didn't know what to say, "Seriously, I'm glad you're here," he said, giving him a quick bro-hug.

Kyle looked at him. "Dude, you just totally poked me with your hard on."

Chapter 24

The Milky Way was dark and quiet, with the sense of authenticity everything in Las Vegas lacked. Amanda liked it. She wasn't hungry, but still ordered a basket of fries to split with Sam.

"How do you like being a free woman?" Sam asked.

"As much as I loved your company, it's nice to have some privacy again. And that mattress in your jail leaves much to be desired," she admitted.

"Yeah, I've slept on it myself," he agreed. "Not very comfortable."

Amanda laughed, but then suddenly excused herself to go to the bathroom, as the pain suddenly cramped her insides. She felt dizzy as she headed to the door marked "Women," and quickly sat down in a stall. She tried to steady her breathing. She got up and splashed water on her face, making sure to wipe off as much sweat as she could. She had gotten used to needing these sink baths, but they were becoming more frequent, and the pills weren't cutting it like they used to. Taking a last look in the mirror, she practiced her smile, and headed back to Sam.

As she walked back to the table, Sam got up. "You okay?" he asked. "You look a little pale."

"Gee, thanks," Amanda drawled as she sat down.

"I just mean," Sam spluttered, trying to find a word. "You're still beautiful," he finally breathed.

Amanda took a sip of his iced tea and felt a little better.

"My lunch is up," Sam sighed as he put cash down for the check. "I was wondering if you were free for dinner?"

Amanda had known this was coming, and should have cut this off a while ago. She liked the attention and was being selfish, but there was no reason to drag poor Sam into this more than she already had.

"Sam, I know this is going to sound really bad," she began.

"I understand," he blurted out. "No problem."

"I just don't think it's a good idea while all this is going on," she continued.

"I get it," he agreed, "and you're absolutely right. My father's been on me about us socializing too."

"I'm sorry," Amanda said. "Maybe we can have dinner and stuff after everything's over."

"That sounds like a plan," Sam smiled as he got up. "Take care of yourself."

Amanda watched him leave, feeling horrible. She had ordered another iced tea when Emily walked in. She waived and smiled, but Emily, as usual, didn't smile back.

"Do you like the idea of spending the rest of your life in prison?" Emily asked.

Amanda looked up and tried to speak.

"Do you?" Emily insisted. "Because I'm working very hard to try and make sure that doesn't happen."

"What do you mean?" Amanda finally got out.

"You bought some woman's Vicodin from her teenage daughter," Emily spat in harsh whisper, "and then you hit on her?"

"That's not true," Amanda said. "We just talked. She asked if I was hitting on her, and I said no."

"Oh, so she's making it up?" Emily demanded, starting to feel like a parent.

"Well, I think she misunderstood," Amanda answered, shrugging.

"She misunderstood and sold you Vicodin?" Emily asked.

"Oh, no, I bought the Vicodin," Amanda admitted. "I haven't been feeling well. But I wasn't hitting on her."

"You know what? I don't even want to get into this with you," she barked. "If you get one more criminal charge against you, I — we — are out of here. Do you understand?"

"Yeah, but won't Jim lose the bail money?" she asked.

"What?" Emily snapped. "No, you're staying. Jim and I are out of here. Is this an act or something?"

"I just got confused, sorry," Amanda said.

"We need to go back to the hotel and go over what happened at the gas station," Emily commanded. "Let's go."

"I already told you, I don't remember anything," Amanda said. "I remember going in and then I remember waking up on the ground with the fire trucks and everything around me."

"Well, we'll go over the going in part, then," Emily insisted.

"Can't we do it here?" Amanda pleaded.

"Why?" Emily asked, irritation growing by the second.

"I just like being around people," Amanda begged. "I'm no good when I'm alone."

The fragrance of French fries had already triggered Emily's hunger, and she could use a beer, she decided. "One hour," she declared, "then we need to go back to the motel and go over this."

"Fine," Amanda said as she sipped her iced tea.

Emily ordered a basket of fries. "Can I get ranch dressing with that?" she requested.

"We're out," the waitress snapped. "I'd run to the store and grab some more, but I can't." She glared at Amanda.

"Fuck," Amanda sighed. "I'm sorry. I'm sorry, okay?"

The waitress walked away saying something obscene under her

breath.

"I told you about the apology thing," Emily said.

"Yeah, but everyone's so mad at me!" Amanda whined. "What town has only one goddamned gas station and grocery store?"

"Well, we agree on the stupidity of that," Emily responded.

"I mean, look at this place," Amanda continued. "They have two bars, like twenty churches, and no Starbucks. How do they live here?"

"You should try finding WiFi," Emily added. "I asked your girlfriend at the desk if they have WiFi, and she laughed at me. Literally laughed at me. I've been using my cell phone data like it's oxygen."

"I do like this place, though," Amanda said, looking around the Milky Way. "It reminds me of Shank Hall."

"What's that?" Emily asked as she reluctantly put ketchup on her fries.

"The club Jim worked at," Amanda said.

"Jim never told me he worked at a club," Emily declared. "When was this?"

"When we dated," Amanda said, confused. "He worked the door for over a year, that's how we met. He caught me using a fake ID and still let me in, since I showed him my boobs."

"First off, charming story about the man I'm supposed to marry," Emily said. "Second, Jim was a bouncer in college?"

"Yeah," Amanda said. "What did he tell you he did?"

Emily thought about it, and realized they never talked about his life at UWM, other than mentioning Amanda as an ex-girlfriend, and being turned down for a frat.

"I guess it just never came up," Emily said, feeling a bit left out.

"Well, it's not a big deal," Amanda said. "But I am happy he finally got his BMW. He wanted one so badly when he was younger."

"He told you about that?" Emily said. "Actually, of course he did. Who doesn't he show that thing off to? Do you know he has it detailed weekly?"

"Every week?" Amanda asked.

"Every damn week," Emily confirmed. "I bet he has it detailed while we're gone.

"Weird," Amanda said. "He was such a slob in college."

"Oh, he's still a slob," Emily said. "He just has everything dry cleaned now."

Amanda looked around and shifted conspiratorially towards Emily. "Does he still do that, that thing, in his sleep?" she whispered.

Emily's eyes widened. "Oh my god!" she laughed with a mouth full of fries. "Yes!"

"It's so gross," Amanda declared.

"The first time, I thought for sure he was awake," Emily said.

"Nope, totally asleep," Amanda said.

"But he ...." Emily made a hand gesture as if to demonstrate a volcanic explosion.

"I know!" Amanda shrieked. "I can't count how many times I woke up because I felt something wet land on me."

"So gross," Emily agreed.

"Why do you think it grosses us out when it happens then, but it's kinda hot when we're ...." Amanda gestured with her hand and her mouth.

"Because," Emily said, straightening her back. "If I'm electing to perform such an action, we have entered into an agreement that ... *that* may be a result. And it's my skill that made *that* possible. But when I'm sleeping and wake up to it splattered across my body and hair ..."

"Oh, I hate when it gets in my hair!" Amanda chimed in.

" ... then I have been violated." Emily finished. "It's damn near rape, really."

They both looked at each other and started laughing. "He's so gross," Amanda repeated.

"Yeah," Emily agreed, but suddenly remembered to whom she was talking.

"Why did you call him?" Emily asked.

Amanda looked down at the table. She felt like she owed Emily the truth, especially since she had done so much for her, but the best she could do was provide a half-answer.

"Because I was in trouble, and I knew he would come," she finally said. "I didn't know about you, I swear. I won't lie and say it would have made a difference in the final decision, but I didn't mean to cause problems for you. I like you, Emily."

Emily looked away a moment. She realized this wasn't a personal attack against her. "I get it," she said, accepting the apology.

Chapter 25

"Nice car." Jim looked over the limo. "You took this thing all the way from the airport?"

"Yeah," Kyle said, "they won't let me rent cars yet."

"Oh, duh," Jim said, remembering Kyle was still under eighteen.

"Anyway, I didn't have plans this weekend, and I wanted to get your advice on some stuff," Kyle said. "So I thought I would come out and see you, since you said you were bored, too."

"Totally reasonable," Jim said, thinking it was completely insane.

"I'm heading back Monday," Kyle said. "Guess I don't have many options for hotels, huh?"

"Let's go see if we can get you the presidential suite," Jim said.

"Oh, that would be great," Kyle said, missing the joke.

"So, what are you doing out here anyway?" Kyle asked.

"It's complicated," Jim said, not sure how to explain his current situation.

"It would have to be to bring you out to this place," Kyle said. "I can't find a single Starbucks within twenty miles, and the only gas station looks like a war zone."

Jim walked Kyle to the front desk, where Claire was still reading her book.

"I need to get another room, please," Jim requested.

Claire looked up at Jim and Kyle as she pulled a registration card.

"Can you just make it all the same info?" Jim asked.

"No." Claire handed him the card, staring at Kyle suspiciously.

Jim started filling out the card with his own name, but Claire stopped him. "If he's staying, we need his name," she explained.

Jim looked at her and looked at Kyle. "He's who you think he is," Jim said, going back to the card.

"You're Kyle Hill," Claire stated.

"I am," Kyle agreed. "What's your name?"

"I'm Claire," she said, "and I'm having a weird day today."

"Me too, Claire," Kyle said.

"I brokered a drug transaction, and a woman hit on me."

Kyle smiled. "Me too, Claire."

She grabbed her book, a copy of *Illusionary Hearts*. "You're doing the movie, right?"

Kyle smiled again, more modestly this time. "We'll have to see what they decide."

"Oh, you have to do it, you are so Gavin!" she squealed. "Will you sign my book?"

"What if I don't get the part?" he cautioned.

"Well, then I doubt you'll be singing any others, which will make it even more valuable," she said. "Please?"

"Shit, can't argue with that logic," he laughed as he pulled a pen from his shirt.

"Why are you here?" she asked. "It must be because of the crazy lady with a gun, right?"

"What crazy gun lady?" Kyle asked.

"Oh," Claire said, "then how do you know the asshole lawyers?" she asked.

"Who calls us that?" Jim asked.

134

"Everybody," Claire tisked, scolding him.

"I'm just here to visit my lawyer," Kyle said. "I need his advice."

"Wow, you represent a lot of people," Claire said, looking at Jim with something closer to respect.

"The card's all filled out," Jim declared. "Can you bill everything to my Amex?"

Kyle slapped Jim on the shoulder. "I can't let you do that, Jim," he said. "Especially for the presidential suite."

"I was joking," Jim said, "there is no presidential suite. You'll be staying in the same shitty forty dollar a night room I am."

"Sixty," Claire clarified. "My mom raised your rates for the weekend. And with all the guests, we may have to raise them again soon."

"I forgot my contact lens solution," Kyle said. "Is there a place around here to grab some?"

"There was," Claire said, glaring at Jim.

"I'll get you some, Kyle," Jim said as he started to walk him out.

"Hold on!" Claire said, rushing through the door behind the desk.

"Where does that door go?" Kyle wondered.

"I think she lives here," Jim said.

Claire remerged with a plastic bottle in her hands. "Trade you for a picture," she offered, displaying the bottle of contact lens solution.

"Sold!" Kyle declared.

Claire ran up, grabbed Kyle tight, thrust the bottle into his hands, and sung out cheese, all while snapping the picture. She then kissed Kyle and took another photo before releasing him.

"I'm making a run to the grocery store tomorrow, to get stuff for people in town who don't have cars," Claire said. "Let me know if you need anything else."

"Thanks," Kyle said.

"Shit, this picture is going up right now" she gushed. "Oh, and I have a boyfriend, but just to let you know, you're on my list."

"Cool," Kyle said as he headed to the door.

"Sorry about that, Kyle," Jim said as they walked to the room.

"I don't even notice it anymore," Kyle admitted. "It's like having weird relatives everywhere you don't remember."

They walked to the room Claire had assigned to Kyle. "Did you want to go somewhere and talk about what's on your mind?" Jim asked.

"Sure," Kyle said, "just let me shower up first."

"Want me to send the car back?" Jim asked.

Kyle looked out into the parking lot. "Nah, I have it for the weekend," he said.

"Where does the driver sleep?" Jim asked.

"I don't know," Kyle admitted. "I think they just send another one every twelve hours."

"I'll take care of it," Jim reassured him. "Just grab a shower and call me when you're ready."

Jim checked with the driver and confirmed the company would be sending drivers every twelve hours to wait on standby for Kyle. Jim loved the idea this was normal for some people.

Jim tried calling Emily, but was sent straight to voicemail. "Sweetheart, things just got a little weird. Kyle Hill just showed up at the motel and is hanging out for the weekend. Call me back when you get this, okay?"

Chapter 26

Emily checked her phone, saw it was Jim, and let it go to voice-mail. One beer had turned into three, and she was now having an important conversation with Amanda.

"He tried to get you to sleep with a hooker?" Amanda asked.

"Yep." Emily's tone turned mocking. "He whips out this card with some tattooed chick in a fucking G-string, and was all 'Want to try something different tonight?'"

Amanda cracked up. "That's so sounds like him!"

"I assume you guys did a three-way," Emily sighed, "it being college and all."

"Well, and I went to art school, don't forget!" Amanda added.

"Please tell me it wasn't a hooker," Emily begged.

"No, we were far too broke for that," Amanda reassured her. "The first one was a waitress at this dive bar we would go to. She was in her thirties, which back then seemed so old."

"Of course," Emily agreed as she downed a shot.

"And this woman had a serious thing for Jim, so I just went along with it."

"And how was it?" Emily wondered.

"Well, maybe Jim's gotten better, but back then he wasn't really the best at ..." Amanda mimed a gesture with her tongue and fingers.

"What is that?" Emily asked. "What are you doing?"

"You know!" Amanda said, repeating the gesture and then pointing at her crotch.

"Oh! Oh!" Emily busted out. "Yeah, he still sucks at that!" she laughed.

"Well, this woman sure didn't," Amanda said.

"Really?" Emily asked, raising her eyebrows.

"Then we did it again for his birthday with the neighbor girl from down the hall," Amanda added.

"That was nice," Emily snorted. "Did you put a bow on her?"

They both started giggling uncontrollably, more due to the alcohol than the joke.

"What's up with all these people?" Emily asked, noticing it was getting crowded.

"I don't know." Amanda looked around. "Oh shit!" She grabbed Emily's arm. "Karaoke!"

"Oh, shit," Emily agreed. "Let's get out of here before some drunk mistakes herself for Mariah Carey."

"No way!" Amanda objected. "That's the best part!"

"Fine," Emily relented. "Night's shot anyway."

Two shots and another thirty minutes later, and they had finally moved on to talking about Amanda's case. Emily explained her plan to encourage each witness to lawyer up and go silent, blocking her from deposing them, which would allow her to throw out their previous testimony.

"Wow," Amanda breathed. "That's really smart."

"Thank you," Emily said. "It's effective, at least."

"So, what happens if the witnesses can't talk?" Amanda asked.

"What usually happens in a case with no witnesses? Now I just bring the physical evidence into question, which should be pretty easy since there's no actual crime lab here, and that's it. Poof!"

"Shit," Amanda said, admiringly. "I'm like one of those rich guys who kill their wives. I just get to go home."

"Yep," Emily agreed.

"What would this cost me if I was paying for this?" Amanda wondered.

"Well, if you were paying for this, I'd charge hourly, and this would take a lot longer," Emily explained, "so maybe eighty to a hundred grand, give or take."

"Wow," Amanda gasped. "You make that much money?"

"No," Emily laughed, "that's what the firm bills me out for. I get about twenty percent."

"Fuck, it's like a pimp," Amanda declared.

"No," Emily said. "Pimps dress better."

The two launched into another alcohol-induced burst of laughter until they cried.

Twenty minutes and another beer later, the first Karaoke singers went up on stage for a duet rendition of "Don't Stop Believing."

"Oh my god, it's so bad!" Emily complained.

"It's not that bad," Amanda said. "They're trying."

"Trying to kill the memory of the Eighties," Emily quipped.

Two more acts and one shot passed before Amanda started talking about them going up on stage.

"Never going to happen," Emily declared. And she was certain of that. She was self-conscious singing in her own shower, and would only do so when Jim was gone and all the doors were locked.

"Come on," Amanda cajoled her. "It must be a duet night or something, they're all in pairs. And there's prize money!"

"Which just makes them suck twice as bad," Emily said.

One act later, Emily was struck by a genius epiphany. "If you want to win, you just sing the same song that won the last contest," she said. "I mean, half of it has to be the song, right?"

"Makes sense," Amanda agreed. "I wonder if someone knows?"

"I tell you what," Emily offered, "find out what song won the last duet night here, and I'll do it with you."

"Really?" Amanda squealed.

"Really," Emily agreed. "And we'll take their money."

Amanda ran over to the bartender and asked him if he knew. After the bartender confirmed with someone else, Amanda came back smiling. "Got it!" she announced.

"All right then," Emily said, "let's do this thing!"

Amanda and Emily waited for their names to be called, then walked confidently to the stage. The crowd grew oddly silent when they saw Amanda. She took up the microphone.

"I know most of you are really mad at me," she said, "and I'm really sorry for all the trouble I caused."

"Screw you!" a voice shouted from the audience.

The announcer stepped out and took the microphone. "Now, that's not how we treat guests, now is it?" she demanded. "Let's not lose our religion just because we have to drive an extra ten minutes for a six pack, okay?"

She handed the microphone back to Amanda. "Ready?"

"We're ready!" Amanda said, smiling.

The announcer hit play and the background music for "Islands in the Stream" filled the bar.

"Oh my god, I know this song!" Emily declared. "My mother listens to this shit. Wait, who's the man?"

"What?" Amanda asked.

"Stop the music, give us a second!" Emily ordered.

The music stopped and Emily asked Amanda again, "Who's going to be the man?"

"How about you be the man?" Amanda decided.

"Fine," Emily said. "Go ahead and start."

The speakers were right behind Emily, and she could feel the music flowing through her. She started reading the words on the screen and it took her back to her childhood, moments spent in the back of a minivan, waiting in traffic while her mother insisted on listening to her music. She knew the words by heart, and by the second verse no longer needed the prompter. She closed her eyes and let her voice carry the emotion across the room.

Chapter 27

"Are they going to give me shit here?" Kyle asked.

"Don't you have a fake ID?" Jim asked. "You're rich."

"Yeah, and famous," Kyle explained. "Fake ID's don't really work in my situation."

"We'll deal with it when we get in," Jim promised, "and if they give us shit, we'll have your driver take us to the other one and get drunk on the way."

Jim opened the door and noticed the crowd of people, the music blasting. Something awful was coming from the stage. They couldn't see passed the people, but it seemed like there was a lot of laughing at a couple of drunks singing karaoke.

Jim and Kyle looked at each other and backed out the door.

"God, what was that?" Kyle demanded with a shudder.

"Don't quote me on this, but I think it was supposed to be 'Islands in the Stream.'"

"I don't know what that is," Kyle said, "But it was the worse thing I ever heard. We should go to the other place."

"Yeah," Jim agreed. "Let's call the car over."

The limo got lost maneuvering through the small-but-unknown town at night, and the two ended up sitting on the edge of an old bridge while they drank.

"I like this place, Kyle said. "It's quiet. In L.A., you get lost in crowds. Here, you can get lost all alone."

Jim wasn't sure about the role he was supposed to play in the conversation. Kyle still hadn't explained why he needed him, but it must be important to bring him out to Alabama.

"So," Jim ventured, "what's going on?"

Kyle looked down and smiled. "What, a guy can't just drop everything and come see his lawyer?"

"Of course you can," Jim said, "but call it lawyer's intuition. I can't help feeling you need something you're nervous to talk about."

"Yeah," Kyle sighed. "I'm a bit of a mess. Flaky Kyle, right?"

"Who says that?" Jim asked.

"I don't know, some paper or blog printed it once." Kyle brushed it off. "Better than some of the other stuff."

"Do you read a lot of those things about you?" Jim said, worried he wasn't equipped to fill the role of psychiatrist at this point in the evening.

"Sometimes," Kyle said, pouring himself another drink. "Is Kyle dating this girl, or will he do this movie, or is Kyle gay?"

"What's the point of reading it?" Jim wondered. "It's just written by people who have nothing to really say, so they speculate bullshit."

"Yeah," Kyle said. "I'm sorry I came. This was weird, I'm sorry."

"Hey, I'm not." Jim soothed. "I was bored and you're giving me something to do. I was just sitting around the motel jerking off. I mean that, literally, I was jerking off when you called."

Kyle laughed. "And with that, I should probably go." He moved to stand up, but Jim stopped him.

"Talk to me, Kyle, what's going on?" he asked.

"Why do you care?" Kyle asked. "We only met two days ago, for about an hour."

"And we liked each other," Jim said. "You're here, so something's bothering you. Do you not want to do this movie you're being pushed into? Are you unhappy the show's ending after eight years? Tell me the problem, and I'll see what I can do."

Kyle shook his head. "Yeah, all that shit bothers me," he admitted. "You're right, I don't want to do the shitty tween flick, and yeah, my TV family is breaking up after eight years, seven years after my real family basically dissolved because of the show. But why should I get into it with you? You won't even tell me why you're here."

Kyle stood up and walked away.

"Crazy lady with a gun," Jim blurted out as he got to his feet.

"What? Where?" Kyle asked, looking around with wide eyes.

"No, that's why I'm here," Jim said. "The crazy lady with the gun the desk girl was talking about. She's my ex."

"Your ex shot someone in Alabama?" Kyle asked.

"Kinda sounds like a country song," Jim laughed, "but no, not technically. She's the one that blew up the gas station."

Kyle laughed. "And you're down here to be her lawyer?" he spluttered as he took a couple steps back towards Jim.

"Oh," Jim said as he sat back down, hoping Kyle would join him, "it gets better."

Kyle took the bait and reluctantly sat down next to Jim.

"My fiancée works at the firm with me, she's a defense attorney," Jim said. "She came down to defend her."

"That's fucked up," Kyle said. "Did they even know each other?"

"No," Jim said, pouring himself another drink

"Were you married to the ex?" Kyle asked.

"No," Jim said, "we dated for a couple years. I wanted to marry her. I loved her."

Kyle thought about the situation. "Your fiancée must be pretty cool to do this for you."

Jim realized he had been underestimating how this sounded to other people. "Yeah, she's awesome," he sighed.

They sat quietly for a few moments.

"I lost my virginity on the set of the show," Kyle said.

"Really?" Jim asked "Not to your TV sister, right? That would be weird, although she is pretty hot."

"No," Kyle said, "one of our wardrobe people."

"You're bummed it's ending?" Jim asked

"Yeah," Kyle said.

"Well, it's been eight years," Jim said. "You grew up with the people, it's only natural you feel frightened about losing them. But I'm sure they'll keep in touch, and you know how America loves reunion shows."

"I'm gay," Kyle blurted out.

Jim sat for a moment, wondering if that was the thing Kyle had been holding back.

"And is that a problem?" Jim asked.

Kyle was rocking back and forth, tightly gripping the edge of the bridge.

"Are you worried about it being an issue?" Jim asked.

"I'm gay," Kyle repeated. "I've never said those words to anyone before."

Jim realized Kyle was actually coming out, and not just to him. He put his arm around him.

"You know that's okay, right?" Jim said. "I mean, no one is going to judge you for being gay."

"Bullshit," Kyle said.

"We live in L.A.," Jim said, "no one gives a shit about that."

"No," Kyle clarified, "they give a shit about money. That's all they care about."

Jim knew what Kyle was saying: openly gay actors rarely get the big roles. The luggage of their personal lives carries over to their on-screen roles, kills the romance. And Kyle, being someone America watched grow up on TV, would be a big story.

"There are plenty of closeted gay actors," Jim said, "I hate that you would have to live like that, but it is an option."

"No, it's not," Kyle said, his voice shaking.

"Okay," Jim said, "then you walk into this thing head on and don't let people judge you."

"I'm being blackmailed," Kyle declared. "It's going to come out."

Jim's lawyer instincts kicked back in. "Who's blackmailing you?" he asked. "What do they have?"

Kyle smiled, "Video," he said, "what else?"

"The video is of you ... engaging in ..." Jim was trying to find the words.

"Engaging, being engaged ... all of it," Kyle finished.

Jim's mind raced. "You're a minor. They can't shop the tape around; they'll go to prison. Give me the name of the person doing this, and I'll take care of it," he promised.

Kyle nodded his head. "There's more to it than that, though."

"Okay," Jim breathed, "what else?"

"They don't want money. They just want me to admit it. Publicly."

"What do you mean, who are they?" Jim asked.

"Some gay advocacy group," Kyle explained. "The whole thing was a set up. I met this guy, and we went back to his place and got drunk. We ended up fucking, and the next day he called me and told me if I didn't come out, he'd release the video on the web."

"Did you see the video?" Jim asked.

"Yeah, he sent me a clip." Kyle wiped at his eyes.

"And you haven't told anyone else?" Jim asked.

"What, and make them think their next payday is in jeopardy?" Kyle took another shaky breath. "Tell my dad, who wants me to buy him a new Lexus, or my agent, who loves me now that I have a five million dollar price tag? Or better yet my mom, who still won't let me watch R rated films?"

"I'm sorry," Jim said. "This is a lot for you to carry, especially on your own."

"He said I should tell people because people like me are the problem," Kyle continued.

"Who, this guy who seduced and videotaped a minor? Fuck him!" Jim insisted.

"Yeah, too late." Kyle laughed weakly.

"How do you know he's part of a group?" Jim asked.

"He tried to get me to join," Kyle said. "He said once I'm out, I'll help other people with my courage."

"What an asshole!"

"I wasn't even sure myself until a year ago," Kyle added. "I'm still not sure, to be honest."

"It's no one else's business!" Jim declared.

They sat for a while and eventually got up and walked back to the limo, waking the driver. They drove back in silence, until Kyle got out of the car and started walking to his room.

"Kyle," Jim said, closing the distance between them. "You don't owe it to anyone to be something you're not, or not ready to be," he said. "You don't owe it to the gay community to come out, and you sure as hell don't owe it to your parents, or agent, or anyone else, to be straight."

Kyle nodded.

"We'll deal with this more tomorrow," Jim said. "I promise, this is going to turn out okay."

Kyle nodded again and went to his room, clearly too drunk to comprehend all of Jim's speech.

It was now nearly one in the morning, and Emily had never called him back. He slipped quietly into their room and saw her passed out on the bed, pants half off. He stripped and was about to get into the spare bed when he noticed a DVD sitting on the table.

Chapter 28

Emily ached all over. Her mouth felt chalky and dry. Her eyes were physically unable to open. Her head throbbed. But the worst part was the noise. There was a sound, a melody that seemed to be repeating over and over. She raised her arm toward the source and grasped at air, as if hopping to capture and crush the sound with her hand. She was startled by a familiar laugh.

"Oh my god!" Jim was laughing while shaking his head. Emily slowly lifted her head from the pillow, pushing the mountain of invisible bricks she were certain were holding it down.

"What are you doing?" she asked, clearly meaning 'stop what you're doing.'

"Oh, you're up," Jim smirked, an evil grin splitting his face from ear to ear.

"No, I'm not." She let her head fall back to the bed. "What is the awful noise?"

Jim lost control and started laughing, "Yes, I imagine that would be most people's reaction!"

Concern started to overcome Emily's aching. "What are you laughing at?" she demanded.

Jim turned up the volume on his laptop, and an awful screeching erupted from the speakers. The familiar melody made Emily pause, recollection setting in. The events of the proceeding night bloomed bruise-like in her brain and she leapt, at least the best she could, at the laptop. The screen revealed a nightmare: a cartoonish version of herself and Amanda on a stage, microphones in hand, eyes closed and belting out something reminiscent to Yoko Ono being tortured to the melody of "Islands in the Stream."

"Where did you get this?" she demanded.

"It was on the table," Jim said, unable to control his laughter.

"Give me the DVD," she commanded.

Jim, paying more attention to the video than her, hit eject on the computer and handed her the disc.

"You're not even singing the real words after the first part," he said. "There's a part where you ask her to 'flail with you in the underworld.' That's a dark Freudian slip, if you ask me."

"Wait, why is it still playing?" Emily asked, staring down at the DVD in her trembling hands.

"Oh, I'm playing the video from YouTube." Jim said, nonchalantly. "It was easier to post it to my Facebook from there."

Emily froze, staring at Jim, waiting, praying for a sign he was kidding.

Sensing her stare, he turned around to face her. "Are you mad? Was that not okay?"

Jim used Facebook with the frequency of a thirteen year old girl, friending everyone he met, and posting the most mundane, stupid things imaginable, which has garnered him, last time she checked, over two thousand friends.

"Tell me you're kidding," she warned, tensing up.

"It's not so bad, it's funny!" he said.

Emily's head was exploding and melting at the same time. "Jim, the senior partners are on your Facebook!" she screamed, her head immediately punishing her like a dog with an anti-bark collar.

"Yeah, Ellis actually clicked 'Like,'" Jim gushed. "He never does that!"

"They can't have see it yet, it's only 7:30 there!"

"They're old," Jim explained. "They only sleep like three and half hours a night now."

The words "They're old" made Emily pause again. Regardless of mutual disdain, there was another 'friend' on Jim's Facebook she feared even more than the senior partners.

"No, no, no!" she gasped as she stumbled off the bed trying to find her phone.

"You okay?" Jim asked.

"No!" she yelled, immediately having to grab her head. "And take that shit off your Facebook, you imbecile!"

"Wow, imbecile!" Jim whistled. "That's a word I don't hear often anymore."

"That is a mystery," Emily agreed, looking around for her phone, "I'm serious, take it down, now!"

She finally found her phone amongst the pile of clothes she'd shed last night. One message from Jim, and two from her mother. She skipped Jim's and played her mother's, praying she hadn't seen it.

"Sweetheart, it's me," her mother cooed. "I am so sorry. If I had known how much talent you had, we never would have wasted all that money on law school. You're such an artist. I really love the way you made the song your own by using all new words. Hold on, your sister has something to say ..."

Emily hung up, glaring at Jim.

"I'm sorry, it's down," he said. "I guess I should have asked first."

"Why the hell would I want this on the Internet?" she said, waiving the DVD.

"I don't know, why did you bring the DVD back to the room?" he asked. "I figured you thought it was funny and cute."

Emily sunk on to the bed, dropping her head into her hands as tears coursed down her cheeks.

Jim walked over and knelt in front of her. "I'm sorry, I didn't think it was so bad," he said.

"How many people saw it?" she asked.

"Probably almost no one," he said. "It was only up for about fifteen minutes."

Emily slowly started to get up. Jim held out his hand to help her, but she slapped it away. "I'll get you back for this," she warned as she walked into the bathroom. She went to the sink, rinsed out her mouth and washed her face. When she returned, Jim was sitting on the bed.

"Told you she's fun," he said.

"What?" Emily said.

"Amanda. I saw you up there. You were having a blast with her."

"I was drunk," she explained.

"Yeah," Jim agreed, "but you were also having fun."

Jim got up and walked into the bathroom. Emily found a pair of shorts and looked in the mirror. Her hair looked like a Japanese cartoon and her makeup made it look like she'd been beaten. This was already possibly the worst day of her life, she thought.

A knock came at the door, and she was certain it would be Amanda. She walked over and answered it, only to find herself breathing into the face of one of the cute boys from the show her sister loved.

Kyle recoiled in shock from Emily's appearance. "Is Jim here?" he asked, certain he had the wrong room.

Emily, who couldn't fail to notice Kyle's reaction to her appearance, stood there as a new bucket of humiliation poured over her. "I'll get him," she said as she closed the door.

Emily walked to the bathroom door and knocked. "There's an adorable TV star at the door," she called, then got back into bed and pulled the covers over her head, seeking sleep.

Chapter 29

Before she was fully awake, Amanda was rushing to the bathroom, crushed by intense abdominal pain. She threw up what little food she had eaten last night and laid against the bathroom wall, drained.

She thought back over the evening and laughed to herself. She'd had fun with Emily. It was sort of nice to talk to someone about Jim who really knew him, she thought.

She picked herself up and carefully walked back to the bed, quickly learning the movements that triggered the pain. She lowered herself slowly to the mattress and checked her phone. Another message from Bobby about his car. She deleted it, much like the car.

She popped a pill and waited until she could rise, and then walked back to the bathroom to shower. Stepping out and grabbing the towel, she heard a knock at the door. Emily was standing there looking like hell, wearing big sunglasses.

"The towel again?" she asked.

"Sorry, showering," Amanda said.

"Well, we have to go over the shooting," Emily said. "I need to get this done before tomorrow so I can catch Franks with his pants down."

"Okay," Amanda agreed. "I need some coffee, though. Let me get dressed."

She opened the door for Emily to step in, closing it behind her.

"Did you know they made a DVD of us last night?" Emily asked as Amanda grabbed her last clean dress from the closet.

"Yeah, you bought one for each of us," Amanda said. "Don't you remember?"

"Not that part," Emily sighed.

Amanda let her towel drop to the floor as she slid on a pair of panties. Emily looked away, but caught herself stealing a long glance. She envied Amanda's breasts. They were a full cup bigger than hers, and she knew Jim must have preferred them. She knew she would.

Amanda flipped her hair over the back of the dress and grabbed her bag. "Okay, ready," she announced.

They headed downstairs to the lobby for coffee, where Claire sat with several girls her age, clearly hanging out in the hopes of spying a certain TV star. They were giggling, but stopped momentarily as Amanda and Emily walked in.

They headed for the coffee, but Emily could see the girls looking over and pointing, whispering to each other.

"Is there a problem?" Emily finally demanded, thinking they were making fun of how she looked. "I had a rough night."

"I know, we totally heard," one of the girls said, breaking the others into peals of laughter.

Amanda filled her cup and grabbed Emily's arm. "Let's go sit outside, it's a beautiful day." They walked towards the door.

"Nice singing," one of the girls called, sending Emily into a near rage.

"Fuck you, you little bitch!" Emily snarled, turning back sharply to the group of girls.

Amanda grabbed her arm. "Let's just go," she begged Emily. "Don't you have someplace else to hang out?" she snapped at the girls.

"Why, going to blow that up, too?" one of the girls said.

They walked outside and Amanda felt better in the sunlight. "We should go for a drive or something," Amanda suggested.

"No, we have to go over this stuff," Emily insisted.

"We will," Amanda agreed as she spotted Sam driving by. She waived and he pulled over next to them.

"Hey, pretty girl," he said. "Staying out of trouble?"

"Trying," Amanda said with a flirty smile. "Where can we picnic?" she asked.

Sam laughed. "That's one thing we don't have a shortage of," he said. "Want me to drop you at a nearby place?"

Amanda looked at Emily and smiled her sweetest smile. "It's a great day, and it's Sunday," she pleaded.

"Fine," Emily sighed, feeling better in the fresh air. "But we're going over this stuff, and without him," she nodded at Sam.

"I have to work anyway," Sam said. "Hop in."

Sam took them to a beautiful park with a stream and a couple small benches. "This place should be quiet while everyone's in church. And I have a couple bottles of water back there if you want," he offered.

Emily noticed he had a dozen bottles of water and six bags of chips.

"You always keep this much stuff back here?" she asked, trying to see how he would transport a prisoner.

"No, but I'm grabbing everything I need for the day when I go out to get gas because ..." he stopped suddenly.

Amanda rolled her eyes, "I'm sorry!" she said, again.

Sam smiled and handed Amanda a pair of sunglasses as she got out of the car. "It's a bright day," he said.

She smiled back. "Thanks," she said.

Emily and Amanda found a bench and sat quietly for a few minutes before Emily took out her pad of paper and pen. "Tell me about the first time you saw Sam Morris," she began.

Chapter 30

Jim pulled into the library parking lot and noticed Reggie's green Outback, confirming he was in the right place.

"What exactly is a legal clinic?" Kyle asked.

"It's a place for people to get legal advice," Jim said, "usually from law students. A friend of mine is running it."

"Like in *The Rainmaker*," Kyle said.

Jim was happy Kyle and he had a book in common. "Yeah, did you like *The Rainmaker*?" he asked.

"Hell, yeah," Kyle said, getting out of the car. "Helped make Damon's acting career."

Inside, Jim saw Reggie prepping a small group of four law students. Reggie waived him over.

"This is my friend, Jim," Reggie stated. "He practices law on another planet called Los Angeles, where everyone has a lawyer."

"It's a beautiful place," Jim added.

Two of the law students, both women, started looking at each other and at Kyle. They had already recognized him, despite the clever disguise of his designer sunglasses.

"This is my friend, and client, Kyle," Jim offered, hoping to defuse the weirdness.

"I'm a big fan," one of the students said, "I'm Summer."

Kyle smiled and shook Summer's hand, "Thank you," he said.

The other young woman moved in passed Summer. "I'm Bree, I'm a big fan, too."

"Nice to meet you, Bree," Kyle said, shaking her hand.

"Can I get a picture?" she asked.

"Sure," Kyle said, noticing Reggie getting a little impatient about losing his class to Kyle's celebrity. "How about I take one with everybody after the clinic?"

Kyle followed the students into the clinic, leaving Jim with Reggie. Reggie looked at Jim with a questioning expression.

"Sorry," Jim said. "You should have seen the car he wanted to come in."

"All right," Reggie said, laughing. "You can make it up to me by letting me get his autograph for my daughter, she loves that show."

"I like your team," Jim said, motioning to the law students.

"They're second year," Reggie said. "I usually have Chad Mitchell here helping me out, but his son's recovering from a tonsil-lectomy, so it's just me today."

People started to arrive at the clinic, and Kyle volunteered to hand out the numbers to those who were waiting. Most were over fifty years old, and therefore didn't recognize him.

The students impressed Jim. They were professional and courte-ous, a trait lost on many Los Angeles lawyers. But they were green. Although they had no formal method of bringing Reggie to the ta-ble, he was an expert at spotting their blank expressions and rushed to help each as needed.

Jim floated from table to table, listening in on some of the is-sues this small community faced. A few were farm related, which he found oddly interesting; a couple involved personal disputes the attendee wanted to turn into a legal issue, which of course the stu-dents advised against; one was a sad story of an older woman who feared her family would put her in a home now that her husband has passed. But by far the largest number of cases, at least a dozen by Jim's count, revolved around home foreclosures.

Time and time again, Jim heard stories of people being coaxed into taking loans on their homes by offers of extremely low interest rates, and then finding themselves upside down due to property deflation. Now their payments were going up, making it difficult, if not impossible, for them to pay.

The students' advice was unsophisticated to say the least: call and try to work it out with the bank. Pay what you can, and realize they don't want to take your home, they suggested. Fair enough advice, especially for the price of free, but not really a solution to the problem.

As the clinic started to wind down, the students got together with Reggie to discuss the cases and go over their notes, which was a big part of the learning experience for them.

Jim and Kyle went outside to wait for Reggie and get some fresh air.

"This was interesting," Kyle said as he opened a Coke.

"I'm glad you thought so," Jim said.

"You went to Harvard, right?" Kyle asked.

"Yeah," Jim said, surprised Kyle remembered.

"Was it hard?" Kyle asked.

Jim laughed, "Well … yeah!" he said.

"Duh!" Kyle said, laughing. "When did you know you wanted to be a lawyer?"

Jim thought about it. He had been asked this question a million times, but always felt like the answer was bullshit. "I think when I first saw a lawyer on TV," he said, surprising himself. "I remember watching L.A. Law when I was a young kid, and they all seemed so important. Every week they took on life and death cases, or sometimes just funny ones. But they seemed to be so respected."

"One of the producers from my show worked on L.A. Law," Kyle said. "I'll have to tell him it inspired you."

"No," Jim said. "I always tell people I was inspired by Atticus Fitch. Let's just stick with that."

"That a TV show?" Kyle asked.

Reggie and the students emerged from the library, and true to his word, Kyle headed over to sign autographs and take pictures.

"I have to say," Reggie said, "you and your friends bring a bit of excitement to this old town."

"We'll be gone soon," Jim said.

"Yeah, I don't think I've ever seen a case get dismantled as fast as your fiancée has taken apart the Jeffries case," Reggie said.

"Hey, about that," Jim said, "I'm sorry if things have gotten bad. We're just trying to make sure we give her the best defense we can."

"I get it," Reggie said. "Just remember it's easier to piss in a sandbox when you don't have to play in it the next day."

"Understood," Jim said.

"Now, about my daughter's autograph," Reggie said, smiling.

"How about we do you one better than that?" Jim suggested. "What's the family doing for lunch?"

Chapter 31

Amanda recounted the few details she could recall from her visit to Eastwood's. She remembered going inside.

"I think I may have grabbed a beer," she said.

"Did you open it?" Emily asked. "In the store?"

Amanda thought about it, trying to see through the fog. "Yeah," she said. "In the bathroom, I took the pills with the beer."

"So no one saw you drink it?" Emily asked.

"No," Amanda said.

"And you took how many pills?" Emily asked.

"I don't remember, two or three." Amanda said.

"Oxy? Do you remember the dosage?" Emily asked while she started a new sheet of paper.

"I don't remember the dosage," she said.

Emily went back and reviewed some of her notes.

"When Chief Morris stopped you, did he do a sobriety check?" Emily asked.

"No," Amanda said, remembering that encounter pretty well. "He wasn't checking me out at all."

"Did he look through your car?" Emily asked.

"No, but the top was down, so he could see everything," Amanda said.

"And no drugs or alcohol were visible?" Emily asked.

"No," Amanda confirmed.

"Interesting," Emily said, underlining some previous notes.

"So," Emily continued. "You came out of the bathroom and what happened next?"

Amanda strained to remember. "I think I fell down, or tripped?" she said, having a slight recollection of hitting her knee on the floor.

"Could you have been pushed?" Emily asked.

"I guess so, but I don't see why," Amanda said.

"Did you talk to anyone before grabbing the gun?" Emily asked.

"I don't think so," she said.

"And when you grabbed the gun, do you remember at all what you were thinking?" Emily asked.

"No," Amanda said, "that whole part is a blank."

Emily lost herself in her notes for a few minutes, and Amanda watched some squirrels rush around the park. It was nice, she thought, to just sit quietly with someone. You could try to forget they didn't like you very much.

"Okay," Emily said, "I think I have what I need to throw out some of the physical evidence."

Amanda smiled. "That's good," she said. "Do you think they will still move forward?"

"The plan is to make this case a nightmare for the prosecutor, to the point he'll take about any offer he can legitimize to the public," Emily explained. "We're going to fight him on all fronts, and do it so quickly he wants us gone right away. Monday, he's going to get a taste of what this case will be like, and hopefully by the end of the week, he'll be dying to get you out of his life."

"Rejected again," Amanda said, laughing.

"I'm guessing rejection isn't a problem for you," Emily said, standing up and stretching her legs.

"So, if the prosecutor caves, what am I looking at?" Amanda

asked, deciding to ignore Emily's last comment.

"Well, I originally offered six months, which evidently you feel is too long for taking out the town's only source of milk and bread, so my new offer will have to be three years probation, a big fine, maybe ten grand, and time served," Emily said.

"I don't have that kind of money," Amanda said. "Are they going to make me pay that before I leave?"

"I imagine whatever the fine is, Jim will cover it," Emily said. "Small price to pay considering how far we've already come on this thing."

Amanda felt bad, but it was what she wanted, and what she had known would end up happening when she called Jim. She decided to change the subject.

"Where are you going for your honeymoon?" Amanda asked.

Emily looked at Amanda, trying to determine if she was being sincere in her interest, or just trying to hit a nerve.

"We haven't decided yet," Emily admitted cautiously.

"Oh," Amanda said, disappointed. "If it were me, I would want to go Paris. I know it's a bit of a cliché, but it looks so beautiful."

Emily, deciding Amanda's interest seemed sincere, sat back down, excited to talk to someone about her idea for the honeymoon.

"Jim and I have both already been to Paris, and I want to go somewhere new for us both," she said. "I was thinking someplace like Fiji."

"Wow," Amanda said, "that would be cool. The water looks so blue there."

"Yeah," Emily said, "it would be nice to be alone with him, and Europe is so crowded."

"I don't do well alone," Amanda said, "I get lonely easily. I'd probably love Europe."

"Well, he and I will have each other, and that's all we need," Emily said before remembering who she was talking to.

Amanda smiled and nodded.

"You're going to take him if you can, aren't you?" Emily asked.

Amanda looked up, surprised at the directness of the question.

"It's okay," Emily said. "You can be honest."

Amanda thought about it for a couple seconds. "Yes," she said, finally having the courage to look Emily in the eye.

Emily was certain when she asked the question she had the upper hand, but suddenly with Amanda's big, sad, blue eyes looking into hers, she wasn't so sure.

"Why did you cheat on him?" Emily asked. "Was it just a sex thing?"

Amanda felt the little courage she was able to muster dissolving into shame at the question.

"He told me all about how you were fucking some guy in your bed, and admitted cheating throughout the relationship," Emily blurted out. "If you were so unhappy with him then, why do you want him back now? Money?"

Amanda laughed. "I don't want his money," she said.

"Sure you do," Emily countered. "You need it, in fact, to get out of going to prison."

Amanda felt a sharp twinge and knew the pain was going to come on strong this time. She reached in her bag and grabbed a pill.

"Those the pills you bought from the front desk girl?" Amanda asked

"Yeah." Amanda popped it in her mouth. "I'm not feeling well."

"Right," Emily said, nodding.

They sat silently for some time. Amanda wanted to go back to having a nice conversation; she hated the cold silence.

"Are you heading back to Vegas when this is over?" Emily finally asked.

Amanda nodded.

"What were you doing in Florida?" Emily asked, surprised she hadn't thought of asking before.

"Visiting a friend," Amanda said.

"Boyfriend?" Emily asked.

"Kind of," Amanda said, "more just a guy I met in Vegas who asked me to come out to see him."

"That's romantic," Emily offered.

"Not really," Amanda admitted.

The weight of the silence carried through the mundane conversation, and when Sam finally returned, they were both happy to go.

Chapter 32

Reggie's family pulled up to the BBQ Shack, a little place that looked promisingly authentic for some good southern barbecue. Reggie walked over to greet his family, consisting of Reggie's sixteen year old daughter Lisa, ten year old son Todd, and wife Denise.

"Hon, this is Jim and Kyle," Reggie said. Denise seemed eager to meet them both, but the daughter was definitely more interested in Kyle.

The meal was a little less authentic than Jim had hoped, feeling there were better barbecue places in Los Angeles, albeit at five times the price. Kyle didn't seem to mind the food, or playing twenty questions from Reggie's family about his show. They were disappointed it was ending, too.

Denise switched their conversation to Amanda, with whom she seemed fascinated.

"Why did she do it?" Denise wondered. "Was she on something, or is she bipolar?"

Reggie laughed. "You know we can't really talk about this," he said.

"But you're her ex boyfriend?" Denise asked. "Right?"

"Yeah," Jim said, feeling a bit of a celebrity himself now.

"And your current girlfriend is the one representing her?" Denise asked with a big smile.

"Fiancée," Jim corrected, knowing it added greatly to the story.

Denise shook her head. "No way, no way would I put up with your shit, no offense," Denise declared. "You got some ... well you know, asking her to do that for you."

"Well, technically speaking, your husband is representing Amanda," Jim said, "and doing an excellent job."

Denise looked over at Reggie and smiled proudly, "He's all right I guess, for a local boy."

Reggie laughed.

"He's much better than I expected, to be honest," Jim said. "No offense."

"Oh, no offense," Reggie said, "I'm guessing you're just surprised to see black folks at all," he laughed.

"Well," Jim admitted, "when imagining the public defender in a small town in Alabama, I admit I was going more Matthew McConaughey than Bill Dee Williams."

Denise laughed loudly. "Billy Dee?" she spluttered. "More Bill Cosby with James Early Jones on the horizon!"

Reggie sat up his seat, "Bill Cosby?" he asked, affronted. "Mr. Huxtable? Really?"

Kyle told Jim he had made plans with the law students, which surprised Jim.

"We still have to go over that issue," Jim said, "I need to get more info from you to help."

"I know," Kyle said. "Let me just have a day to think."

Jim agreed, in part because he wasn't exactly sure yet how to fix the problem.

Lunch was over, and the limo pulled up in front of the BBQ Shack.

"I'm so sorry, Mr. Hill," the driver said as he walked inside. "I needed gas and had to drive all the way to the next town. Evidently, some crazy lady blew up the only one here."

"I gotta meet this chick," Kyle said to Jim as he got up.

Kyle signed autographs and took pictures with Reggie's family, as well as a couple of other diners, and the restaurant's owners, who wanted to put his picture on the wall.

"He's as nice as I thought he would be," Denise sighed as the limo pulled off. "So many young stars today end up looking so jaded, but he still smiles and acts like a young boy."

Reggie kissed his family goodbye and told them he'd be home soon. Denise thanked Jim for giving her daughter something to brag about, which the girl was already in the process of doing via cell phone.

"Thanks for lunch," Reggie said. "Now, how about I buy you a beer?"

They sat on the patio of the BBQ shack, which reminded Jim of a typical southern home porch, overlooking a quiet street.

"What'd you think of the clinic?" Reggie asked.

"I liked it," Jim said. "I never got to do those, I clerked for a judge in school."

"Yeah, me too," Reggie said. "That has its perks, but it's not really the same as working with the people. I could have used a bit more of that in school."

"I rarely deal with people," Jim said. "I mean, I deal with them, but more through their contracts. I guess I deal in people."

"That what you're doing with Kyle?" Reggie asked. "Putting together a contract for his white person version of slavery?"

Jim laughed, "He's a different situation all together," he admitted. "Something bothered me about the clinic, to be honest."

"What's that?" Reggie asked.

"The people there about their foreclosures," Jim said, "they didn't really get much advice."

"Not much to say, unfortunately." Reggie sighed. "A lot of people in this town, all over I imagine, made some bad decisions, and now they're screwed. The bank keeps raising the rates, and the house is worth less than they owe. All we can do is tell them to pay what they can and try to work it out."

Jim nodded. "But what if there was something we could do?" he asked.

"I'm open to any ideas," Reggie said. "Chad Mitchell, our wannabe DA, keeps ranting about how the banks should be charged with predatory lending. But realize, these are not people with a lot of means."

"There's a strategy that works pretty well for buying time," Jim said. "The banks are in such chaos, and these mortgages are sold between the banks to other investors, and then back to other banks."

"Right," Reggie said. "That's what helped cause this big mess."

"Right," Jim said, "but in all this mess, the home owner still has the right to request a copy of the original mortgage note. I've read about people using this tactic, and I've never heard of anyone getting one in less than three months. All the foreclosures would be halted until the bank can produce the note."

Reggie thought about what Jim had said, and took a sip of his beer. "It would slow things down a bit, maybe give the people a chance to at least save up for other arrangements," he said.

"Time is a good thing in this situation." Jim said, "And there's always hope things change, or we come up with a fix."

"We could template out a note request and just fill in the blanks with information from their last statement," Reggie said, becoming more accustomed to the idea.

"Exactly!" Jim said.

"You got a good request template?" Reggie asked.

"I work at a firm with over a hundred lawyers," Jim said. "Someone does."

"I do envy the resources," Reggie said.

Jim threw out his beer bottle and grabbed his keys. "I'll get to work on this tonight."

"Oh, when you get home, tell Emily I got her emails. Everything is all set for the morning," Reggie said. "She's very specific on timing. It feels less like law than a strategic air strike on poor Charlie Franks."

"Yeah, she can be pretty menacing," Jim said.

"For what it's worth, and I know she's kicking his ass and all, but I think she's going about this all wrong," Reggie warned. "I don't know how things go in L.A., but people down here only take so much crap, especially publicly, before they have to hit back."

"I hear what you're saying," Jim said, pausing on the steps. "I'll try to keep her from going too far."

Chapter 33

Emily sat in front of her computer, sending out the last batch of instructions for Reggie. As a former public defender, she felt bad for the work she was piling on him, but she had to hit the prosecutor hard and fast if she wanted to force this good of a deal.

Her phone buzzed, displaying the fourth voicemail of the day from her mother, who was obviously interested in continuing her mocking session over Emily's drunken rendition of Kenny Rogers.

She heard Jim unlock the door and pulled back her hair, hoping it wouldn't look as straggly as she knew it must.

"Hey," Jim said, walking into the room, "how goes the war?"

"Fine," she said. "How was the clinic?"

"Good," Jim said, clearly excited about something, "I think I really might be able to help some people."

Emily smiled, but had little interest in hearing about it. She was still angry with him over posting the video, and she was mad he'd decided to take a fun day to go and explore his inner humanitarian, while she was stuck defending his ex-girlfriend.

"Do you want to tell me why Kyle Hill is here?" she asked.

Jim stretched out on the free bed and rolled to face her. "I do want to tell you," he said, "but I have to get his approval first. I think I need some help on his situation."

"Oh, good," Emily said. "Just put it on top of the rest of the work I'm doing for you."

"It's not like that," Jim said. "It's firm work, and billable."

"Speaking of firm work," she said, "have you let them know you're not coming in tomorrow?"

"Jane took care of it," he said. "Dying mother."

"Lucky you," she said with a glance at her phone.

"Just say that you're with me, helping me through my grief," he suggested.

"Thank you, but I'll take care of my own lies," she said. "God knows I can't tell them the truth without looking like the world's biggest idiot. And I'm sure my singing debut is going to make me look really grief stricken. Thank you for that, again."

She knew she was unloading on Jim, but she needed to unload on someone. Amanda had unnerved her, and she was angry. She wanted to fight. That's when Jim used the worst words one can use when their significant other wants a fight.

"Sorry," he said. "I'm going to take a nap, let me know when Kyle shows up. Love you."

Emily regretted buying such a light laptop, as she would like to have beaten Jim with it.

Jim increased his annoyance of Emily by snoring, and Emily thought several times about smothering him with a pillow. Not like the town had a good prosecutor.

A couple hours later, a knock came at the door. She knew it might be Kyle, so she stressed about her appearance and tried to fix up her hair. Looking in a mirror at the wreck she was, she gave up and opened the door to see Amanda standing there.

"Hi," Amanda said.

"What's up?" Emily asked.

Amanda looked in and saw Jim sleeping. "I was wondering if you wanted to grab some coffee or something," she whispered.

"I'm working," Emily said.

"I know," Amanda said. "Want me to bring you some coffee?"

"No, I'm fine," Emily said, even though she now wanted coffee.

Amanda gave a slight nod and was about to walk away.

"Hold on," Emily said, "let me do something with my hair, it's driving me nuts."

She motioned Amanda in and headed to the bathroom.

Amanda noticed the mountain of notes on Emily's bed, and was amazed at how many hours she must have worked on her case. She then looked over at Jim sleeping. She knew his face impossibly well. She used to watch him sleep all the time, and would play with his hair and close her eyes while she traced the outlines of his face. She walked over to the bed and touched his hair. She watched his chest breath in and out and noted how much more muscle he had now that he was older.

She hadn't heard the bathroom door open and the look on Emily's face was somewhere between an angry dog and a frightened child.

Amanda froze and slowly moved her hand away from Jim. "I'm sorry," she said as she slowly backed away from the bed, Emily's eyes following her every inch.

"Let's go," Emily said, surprising and frightening Amanda with the realization they were still going out together.

They walked out the door and turned towards the lobby. Emily stepped in front of Amanda, blocking her. Amanda stood still and had a quick flashback of being beaten up by an older girl in the third grade.

"If you ever touch him again, I'll hand that dick prosecutor enough to send you away for twenty years," she growled, giving Amanda a stern look. "Do you understand?"

Amanda nodded.

"Say you understand," Emily emphasized.

Amanda's voice failed the first attempt. "I understand," she finally got out. "I'm sorry."

"Good," Emily said, "now let's get some coffee."

Amanda's stomach was already in pain and now it had an additional knot. "We can go to the Milky Way," she said.

"That's never happening again," Emily said. "Rule number one of not making a fool of one's self is to never get drunk in a Karaoke bar. Especially one with cameras. I should sue those assholes."

They walked into the lobby and saw Claire sitting at the desk.

"Are you ever not working?" Emily said while Amanda waived to Claire.

"You're not here to serenade me, are you?" Claire asked, looking up from her book.

"That's very funny," Emily said as she lifted the coffee pot. "There's no coffee."

"Sure there is," Claire replied. She pointed at the coffee can. "Use your imagination."

"I'll make it," Amanda offered.

"When is Kyle coming back?" Claire asked.

"I don't know," Emily said as she examined the coffee cups.

"Who's Kyle?" Amanda asked.

"One of Jim's clients from L.A.," Emily said, "he just showed up."

"Weird," Amanda said.

Amanda and Emily sat on the lobby couch, waiting for the coffee. There was an awkwardness between them they both wanted to break.

"Are you nervous about court tomorrow?" Amanda asked.

Emily smiled at the question. "I don't get nervous before court," she lied.

"I would be," Amanda said, "I mean, I am nervous."

"The only one who should be nervous is Franks, and he's probably not even aware he's going to court tomorrow." Emily smirked.

"I can't wait to see the look on his face."

"You're a really good lawyer," Amanda said. "I mean, you're like the best I've ever seen."

"Seen many lawyers?" Emily asked.

"Well, the ones who represented me," Amanda said. "Most of them were kind of crappy."

"So, you really took a stun gun to your boyfriend's balls?" Emily asked, trying to picture what Amanda's sweet face must look like when angry.

"He was trying to fuck our fourteen year old neighbor!" Amanda said. "He was totally hitting on her and tried to get her to come over when I wasn't home."

"Wait!" Claire yelped. "You did what?"

"It's a long story," Amanda said.

Claire hopped over the desk and ran to the couch to sit across from Amanda. "I'm stuck here my whole life, I got time," she said.

Amanda recounted the story about how she began to suspect her boyfriend, Nick, was talking up the neighbors' teenage daughter, despite a fifteen year age difference.

The girl liked Amanda, so when Nick texted the girl an invitation to stop by at a time he knew Amanda would be at work, the girl forwarded the message to Amanda. Amanda came home early and told Nick she and a "friend" had a special surprise for him.

Being the pig he was, he somehow thought Amanda and the girl were going to show him a good time, and let Amanda tie him to the bed. Amanda pulled out her stun gun, and with his eyes closed, she pushed the metal contacts hard against his testicles, pushing the trigger.

The screams were substantially louder than Amanda had planned, so she tried to muffle them with a pillow, while she continued his punishment.

"I just kept thinking about what he wanted to do to that poor girl," Amanda said. "I mean it's bad enough I let him do it to me, but to expose a child to that was sickening."

The neighbors, alarmed by the constant blood curdling screams, called the police. When they arrived, Amanda was unable to convince them it was only fun and games, especially with Nick crying and begging for help. She was charged with a dozen crimes, and locked up.

Because it was her first real criminal offense, and since she'd been lucky enough to pull a female judge who found it challenging not to laugh while the whole story was told, Amanda was given probation and ordered to undergo anger management therapy, where she met a nice guy named Tony. He ended up throwing a beer bottle at her when she asked how long he'd been living with his parents.

"You're awesome," Claire said. "I'm so buying a stun gun."

Emily, who was still trying to be angry with Amanda, couldn't help but be taken in again. The angelic face with that sweet voice relaying a tale of such brutality, all with the tone of a babysitter telling a bedtime story.

They had lost track of time, and noticed the coffee had probably been done for a while.

Claire's phone rang.

"Hey, can't talk, hanging out with the crazy lady with a gun and the cat strangler," she announced before hanging up.

"Cat strangler?" Emily asked.

"Yeah, you know, because of your singing? And also, you're really mean," Claire explained.

"I'm not mean," Emily said. "Who the fuck said I was mean?"

Claire retreated back. "Sorry."

"She's not mean," Amanda agreed. "She's been helping me and she has every reason not to."

"Yeah," Emily said, pointing to Amanda. "See?"

"Sorry," Claire said. "Still doesn't make that singing okay."

Chapter 34

It took two rounds of knocking to wake Jim, who fumbled to the door in the dark.

"Oh, you already in bed?" Kyle asked.

"No, I was just taking a nap," Jim said, scanning the room for Emily. "How was your evening with the law students?"

"They're cool," Kyle said. "They just had mucho questions about the show and other celebrities. Standard stuff."

"Come on in," Jim said, knocking a trash can out of the way. "We should talk about your situation a little."

"Do we have to?" Kyle pleaded.

"I just want to get a few pieces of info from you," Jim said. "Ten minutes."

"Fine," Kyle said.

"By the way, do your parents know where you are?" Jim asked.

"They think I'm in New York," Kyle said, as if New York was a friend's house.

"Okay," Jim said. "First, I want to get your permission to bring Emily into this, she's a great criminal attorney, and I think we could use her help."

"That's your fiancée?" Kyle asked.

"Yes," Jim said.

"Isn't she busy defending your girlfriend?" Kyle asked. "Does she handle all your cases?"

"No, she does not," Jim snapped at hearing this suggested a second time, "but I'd like to get her help with this."

"Will she tell anyone?" Kyle asked.

"Absolutely not," Jim assured him.

Kyle thought about it, but finally nodded. "Fine," he said.

"Okay," Jim said, "I also need the name of the guy who took the video."

"Steve Lange," Kyle said. "At least that's what he said his name was."

"Can you forward me the text messages he sent?" Jim asked.

Kyle squirmed in his seat.

"What's wrong?" Jim asked.

"Are you going to watch the video?" he asked.

Jim leaned back, knowing how Kyle must feel. "I may have to, Kyle," Jim admitted. "But I won't before asking you."

Kyle's mood changed. "It's not a big deal," he bluffed. "I mean it's not like I'm embarrassed." In fact Kyle looked very uncomfortable, and embarrassed.

"I understand," Jim said, "and like I said, I won't watch it right now. If I feel I need to see it, I'll come to you and ask your permission."

Kyle looked down and nodded.

"What's the name of this organization?" Jim continued.

"I don't remember," Kyle said. "It's something like Rainbow Party or some stupid shit like that."

"Is it in the messages?" Jim asked.

"Yeah," Kyle said.

"Okay, send it over tonight if you can," Jim said.

They looked up when they heard the women's voices laughing as they opened the door. Emily and Amanda walked in, stopping when they noticed Kyle.

"Oh, hi again," Emily said.

"Hey," Kyle said standing up.

"Hi," Amanda said from behind Emily.

"Oh, hey!" Kyle said, pointing. "Crazy lady with the gun!"

"That's me!" Amanda declared with a smile.

"Very cool," Kyle said. "Oh, and I saw your video tonight," he added, looking at Emily.

"What?" she asked.

"'Islands in the Stream,'" Kyle laughed, "I didn't know the song, but now I'm hooked!"

Emily shot a look at Jim, who shrugged. "It wasn't me," he said.

"Oh, no," Kyle said. "Some people had a copy of the DVD at the party. They love it."

"Fantastic," Emily said. "I'm glad I can entertain everyone."

"Is that your limo?" Amanda asked

"Yeah," Kyle said. "Well, it's a rental."

"Can we go for a ride?" Amanda asked. "It's such a beautiful night."

"Sure," Kyle said. "Want to come?" he asked Emily and Jim.

"No," Emily said, "you two should go and have fun. I've got work to do, and a busy day tomorrow."

Emily liked the idea of Amanda spending time with Kyle. Maybe it would distract her from Jim. And, more importantly, maybe Jim would lose interest if he saw her with another man again.

Kyle walked out with Amanda.

"Don't forget to send me that stuff, Kyle!" Jim called as he closed the door.

"What stuff?" Emily asked as the limo pulled away.

"I need to talk to you about that actually," Jim said.

He sat Emily down and went through Kyle's dilemma. He told

her about Kyle coming out to him, his issues with his family, and then the blackmail.

"Shit," Emily said. "He's just a kid!"

"I know," Jim said, "and the worst part is, I don't know what to do to stop them."

"Why would a gay advocacy group want to do this to a young gay guy?" she asked.

"Well, I don't think they speak on behalf of the entire community," Jim said. "It's just a couple assholes who think they have the right to do whatever they want in the name of a cause."

"Want me to call the DA?" Emily offered. "I have his mobile number, we can try to keep this discrete."

"No," Jim said. "These guys are like terrorists. If they think they're going down, they'll blow up Kyle first."

"Well, we have to get to them somehow," Emily mused. "Maybe find some dirt on them?"

"Like what? They sound like they're okay being considered total assholes," Jim said.

"I don't know," Emily said, "but we have to find something to kick their asses with."

"You know, Em, not every problem requires a sledgehammer," Jim said.

"If you don't want my help, then why did you ask me?" she said

"I guess I was hoping for some advice other than a full attack," he said.

"Fine," Emily said. She turned to her laptop. "I got other shit to do, anyway."

Jim went back to sleep, but would occasionally wake to find Emily still typing away on her laptop. She was tireless, and he did admire that.

Chapter 35

Emily woke and noticed Jim was already gone. She rolled over and checked her phone: 8:32 AM. She had overslept. She checked her email and saw Reggie was already on top of things.

She got out of bed and stretched. The benefit to oversleeping was she'd gotten a full seven hours, and she felt good, rested. She threw on some sweats and t-shirt and went for her run.

She always liked to run before court; it gave her time to think things through. By the time she returned to the hotel thirty minutes later, she felt confident, and had a new idea. She grabbed a copy of the local paper and a cup of coffee from the lobby, waiving at the older woman working the counter, whom she assumed was Claire's mother, and headed back to her room.

An hour later she was dressed, waiting by the phone. It rang.

"Okay," Reggie said. "You were right. Both witnesses have retained counsel and are unwilling to talk," he said. "I got us on the docket at noon for an emergency hearing in the judge's chambers."

"On the record, right?" she asked.

"Of course," Reggie said.

"Excellent," Emily said. "Great work, Reggie."

"Gee, thanks," he said as he hung up the phone.

She knew he didn't like her tactics, but they would work.

She called Amanda's phone.

"Hi," Amanda said.

"We're good for noon," she said. "We'll be leaving at eleven, so be ready."

"Okay," she said, "I'll put on the blue dress, I think it's the prettiest."

Emily had grown to appreciate Amanda's lose grasp on the important details, and usually found it cute, but she wasn't in the mood for it. She was in warrior mode, which was probably why Jim had made himself scarce this morning.

Emily did some additional research and made some final notes before heading out. Reggie wasn't kidding about Franks being buddied up with the banks. She'd easily found photos of him golfing with bankers, as well as confirmed Franks' extra aggression in prosecuting black men. Those facts, accompanied by Franks' deep interest in Civil War reenactments, made Emily dislike him even more. It was then she noticed the car was gone. Jim must have taken it.

She panicked and grabbed her phone. She was about to dial Jim and rip into him when she saw Kyle's limo pull up and Amanda's head popped out the sunroof.

"We went all the way to Starbucks," Amanda said. "I wanted to do something nice for you, so Kyle called Jim and asked what you like. One Cinnamon Dolce Latte for the best lawyer in the world!"

Emily took the coffee and thanked Amanda. Maybe she could get used to her lack of priorities thing, just a little.

They pulled up to the court house where Reggie was waiting by the door.

"I should have rode with you guys," he said as they walked up the steps. "Looks like you're getting married," he laughed, pointing at the limo.

"Franks here?" Emily asked, eager to see his face.

"Not yet," Reggie said. "I don't imagine he'll be happy."

They sat outside the judge's chambers and waited to be called in. Franks showed up with only five minutes to spare.

"What the hell do you think you're pulling?" he demanded of Reggie.

Emily got up and walked over. "I'm sorry, is there a problem?" she asked.

Franks gave Reggie a dirty look before turning his scowl on Emily. "Do you know the meaning of witness tampering?" he asked.

"Of course I do," Emily said. "Obviously you don't, or you wouldn't have brought it up."

"You're intimidating the witnesses, and I'm going to have you disbarred!" he threatened.

"I did nothing of the sort," Emily said. "Repeat that allegation in public again, and I'll file an action against your office, and you personally. Maybe go after your ridiculous Civil War memorabilia collection, too."

"What, now you're digging into my private life?" he yelled.

"What private life? Tramping around the woods, pretending to fight for the right to own black people?" she said, referring to the civil war reenactment photos she found of him online.

"The judge is going to see right through this, the same way I have," Franks said.

"We'll see what the judge says," Emily assured him with a confident smile. "I think you're about to experience a whole new level of humiliation. But I'll give you one chance: drop the charges and we'll just go home. You'll only look a little foolish."

"Not on your life," Franks spat. "You're going to learn a little humility in that room."

Emily was afraid, but hid it well. For her, this was a planned maneuver, but for him, it was nothing more than an emotional outburst. She had known he wouldn't go for the first offer; that's why she hadn't offered him one.

The judge opened the door, "What the hell is the screaming about?" he said. "I feel like I'm back in divorce court!"

"Your honor, we have a serious breech of conduct we need to address," Franks began.

"Well, come on in, let's get this over with," the judge sighed, leading them back into his chambers.

Franks, Emily and Reggie walked to the front of the desk. Amanda, not knowing what to do, held back by the couch.

"And who are you?" the judge asked Kyle.

"I'm Kyle, your honor," Kyle replied.

Reggie looked back over his shoulder to Kyle. "Sorry, you're going to have to wait outside for this, man."

"You look familiar," the judge interrupted. "What's your name again?"

Reggie smiled as he knew the judge was about to recognize Kyle.

"Oh, you probably know me from my show," Kyle said.

The judge clapped his hands together. "That's it!" the judge agreed, coming out from behind his desk. "My granddaughter loves that show," he gushed. "It's one of the few good family shows left on TV."

"Well, thank you, your honor," Kyle said. "That means a lot coming from an actual judge in the real world. We don't get much positive feedback in California."

"Well, I just love the show, just love it!" the judge insisted. "Can I trouble you for an autograph?"

"It would be an honor, your honor," Kyle said, trying to be witty. The judge handed him a piece of stationary as the attorneys stood by.

"How are you connected to this case?" the judge asked.

"Amanda is part of my church group, your honor," Kyle said. "We're all worried about her, so I came down to offer my support."

Reggie rubbed his neck, hoping Kyle didn't get caught lying to a judge.

"Well, that is very decent of you," the judge said.

"Who should I make this out to?" Kyle asked.

"My granddaughter's name is Amanda," the judge said.

"Another angel named Amanda," Kyle said, smiling at the judge.

"Yeah." The judge glanced skeptically at Amanda. "She hasn't blown anything up yet, so we're mighty proud of her for that."

Kyle handed the paper back to the judge.

"Thank you so much," the judge said. "But I'm afraid you do have to wait outside."

"No problem," Kyle said. He stopped in front of Amanda before leaving. "I'm going to be out there praying for you. God will get you through this," Kyle said. He looked back to the judge and smiled. "I know that now," he added, before hugging her and leaving.

The judge admired his autograph and walked back behind his desk. "That's a fine, Christian boy," he said. "That show is about the only damn thing on TV we feel safe letting our little granddaughter watch."

"It's a fine show," agreed Reggie. "My family loves it, too."

"Okay," the judge said. "It's been less than five business hours since I last laid eyes on you people, and I've got twelve motions on my desk already. What the hell is going on?"

"Your honor, the defense has gone to two of the state's witnesses and intimidated them into not speaking," Franks said.

"That's B.S., your honor," Emily said, remembering the judge's usage of the phrase. "We did nothing of the sort."

"Your honor, she told them both they may be held criminally and civilly liable for the explosion her client caused!" Franks yelled.

"Allegedly caused. And all I did was ask them some basic questions, your honor," Emily said.

"You asked them if they had lawyers and mentioned the FBI is involved! Now they both have lawyers who are advising them to not say anything!" Franks snarled in disgust.

The judge put his hand up for the lawyers to stop.

"Did you intimidate the witnesses?" the judge asked Emily,

"No, your honor," Emily said. "I asked them the same type of questions I would have asked in an official deposition. Of course I asked them about other potential causes for the explosion, but that's my job, to look at what else might have happened."

"She's splitting hairs, your honor," Franks insisted. "It was her intent ..."

The judge cut him off. "Hold on," he demanded.

"Reggie," the judge said, "I've known you a long time. I don't know Ms. Perkins, and to be honest, I'm not too inclined to take her at her word. Did she intimidate the witness?"

Reggie thought about it for a moment. "Your honor, I can't speak to her intent, but the questions she asked were fair questions in establishing alternative possibilities for the event."

"Good enough for me," the judge decided.

"Your honor, this is his case," Franks complained. "Of course he is going to side with her!"

Reggie went to speak, but stopped himself. The judge held up his hand again.

"Reggie is too much a gentlemen to respond to that, but I will not let it pass. He is an officer of this court, and a good man. I take him at his word. You were not there, Mr. Franks, thus you are in no position to challenge it."

Franks threw his arms in the air.

"Your honor, since the witnesses are unwilling to cooperate with our requests, we respectfully request their statements be excluded from the evidence," Emily said.

"Mr. Franks?" the judge asked.

"So, I'll have one witness, and his word is no good until he's cleared by the Sheriff's investigation," Franks huffed.

"That doesn't sound like an argument, Mr. Franks," the judge said.

"Fine," Franks said. "But we reserve the right to resubmit their statements if they agree to talk later."

"Fair enough," the judge said. "Next."

"Your honor, the defense did not get a chance to inspect Officers Morris' weapon before it was handed back to him," Emily said. "We therefore would like the ballistics report thrown out."

"It hasn't even come in yet!" Franks argued.

"Well, there's no point if it's not relevant," Emily said.

"Are you arguing it wasn't the gun that shot the bullet?" Franks asked.

"No, we're arguing that we can't say when, or how the bullet was shot." Emily said. "We had no opportunity to examine the weapon for potential malfunctions, it was simply put right back out on the street, with a police officer under investigation for incompetence."

"Christ!" Franks swore, "Are you for real?"

"Language, Mr. Franks," the judge reprimanded.

"I'm sorry, your honor, but she's tearing apart evidence that hasn't even come in yet, and picking at every corner of this case before it's started!" Franks whined. "What would you have me do?"

"Oh, man up, Franks!" the judge said. "Just file your responses and get back to me. The witnesses are tossed until such time as they are willing to be deposed by the defense. The gun's out too if you don't respond with something compelling."

"Thank you, your honor," Emily said, packing up her bag

"Grace, I forgot you were there, dear," the judge called. "You watch that show, right? Did you want that young man's mark before he leaves?"

"Oh, if he's not busy, that would be wonderful!" the elderly court reporter declared, getting up. "Maybe one for Mary Lou's little girl in the hospital, I know she likes that story, too."

"That's a terrific idea," the judge said, holding out his arm for her. "I'm a judge, so let's see if I can throw some weight around and get a couple more autographs for folks. Lord knows we could all do with a little cheering up."

They all walked outside and Emily watched as the judge introduced Grace to Kyle, who gallantly kissed her hand.

Emily approached the judge's secretary. "Excuse me," Emily said. "Can I get a copy of today's transcripts sent to these two email addresses?"

"Certainly," the woman said, taking the paper from Emily. Raising an eyebrow, she smiled conspiratorially at Emily. "Oh, you're good. Just between you and me, I don't like Mr. Franks much. Not done anything for anyone in this town, unless you count the bank. I'll make sure those transcripts go out immediately, Ms. Perkins, don't you worry."

"Thank you so much," Emily said before striding after Franks, who was making a hasty retreat down the back stairs.

"How'd that go?" she said, cutting him off.

"That's a real annoying habit," he said, pointing to the fact she was blocking him from leaving again.

"Oh, believe me, I can be much, much more annoying," she promised. "This would be an excellent time to discuss what you're willing to do to save yourself from continued humiliation."

"What do you want?" Franks demanded. "I already agreed to the best possible deal you could hope for."

"No jail time," Emily said. "The rest I'm flexible on."

"She does time," Franks insisted, staring Emily in the eye.

"We'll promise to get her into a treatment program in Las Vegas," Emily offered.

"Oh, so she can just walk in and leave?" Franks said. "Here's where she did the crime; here's where she'll serve the time."

"Okay," Emily cautioned. "But tomorrow's going to make today look like Christmas, and all the Dr. Seuss rhymes you can muster are not going to save you from that nightmare."

"Look for my responses to your motions, Ms. Perkins," he said as he pushed around her. "I'm not done yet."

"Oh, you're done. You just don't know it yet," Emily called softly.

Chapter 36

Jim was scouring the county records when the call he was waiting for finally came.

"Mr. Strickland, thanks for calling me back," Jim said.

"Jim, how's your mother?" he asked.

"Oh, she's a fighter. Still holding strong," he said.

"That's good," Strickland said. "I see Emily's doing her best to cheer you up. We loved the video."

Jim had to think a moment. "Oh, the video," he said. "Yes, it was pretty funny."

"The whole office loved it, we're considered putting it on the website to show how fun we can be," Strickland said.

"Oh, that's very thoughtful, but you shouldn't go to the trouble," Jim said. "To be honest, she's a bit embarrassed about the whole thing, so maybe we could just let it die?"

"No problem," Strickland said. "But Ellis did buy a Karaoke machine for her office, I'm sure she'll think it's funny."

"Yes," Jim said, "I'm sure she will. The reason I called was to see if I can get a direct number from you for a client?"

"What for?" Strickland asked.

"It's a delicate issue, and to be honest, I can't disclose the details," Jim said. "But I give you my word it's of high importance, it's for a client, and the person I'm trying to get a hold of will appreciate the call."

"I don't like being kept in the dark," Strickland said. "They pay me not to be. But who are you looking to contact?"

"Jason Mackenzie," Jim said. "I need his direct phone number, if possible."

The line went quiet and Jim prepared himself to come up with a more valid explanation.

"Got a pen?" Strickland asked, coming back on the line "It's 213-423-4982. Please make sure it's important, Jim. He's a big client."

"I promise," Jim said. "Thank you very much."

Jim snapped a couple final pictures from the books he was studying and packed up his things. He walked out to his car, pulled out his computer and brought up his notes on the Rainbow Action Committee, the organization the man blackmailing Kyle claimed he was with.

Jason Mackenzie was an A-list actor, and he was openly gay. He had also just spoken at an event for the RAC, and sat on its board. Jim hoped Mr. Mackenzie knew nothing about the blackmail. If he did, Jim was not sure how this call would go. He pulled out his phone and dialed the number Strickland gave him.

"Yeah?" a voice said.

"Mr. Mackenzie?" Jim asked,

"Who is this?" the voice asked.

"My name is Jim Morgan, I work with Mr. Strickland, your attorney," he said.

"Okay," the voice said.

"This is Mr. Mackenzie, right?" Jim asked.

"Yeah, what can I do for you?" Mackenzie asked.

"Mr. Mackenzie, I'm calling about the Rainbow Action Committee," Jim began. "I have a situation involving them, and I was hoping you might be able to help."

"What's that?" Mackenzie asked.

"I have a client, a young man, not yet eighteen, and he is gay," Jim continued. "A couple weeks back, he was approached by a man who took him back to his place where they engaged in sexual activity. Unbeknownst to my client, it was recorded."

"I'm sorry to hear that," Mackenzie said.

"Well, sir, the worst part is that now he is being blackmailed," Jim explained. "This young man is an actor and a public figure. And to make it even stranger, the blackmailer doesn't want money. He wants him to come out of the closet, or he will release the tape and out him to the whole world."

There was silence on the end of the phone. "Mr. Mackenzie?"

"Yeah," Mackenzie said. "Are you going to tell me it's someone at the RAC?"

"I'm afraid it is," Jim said. "Would you like the name of the person?"

"Yes, please," Mackenzie said.

"Steve Lange," Jim said. "I believe he works for the RAC, according to their records."

"Yes, he does," Mackenzie said.

"Mr. Mackenzie, I would like to think you had nothing to do with this, as you yourself must know how hard it is in this town and this business to be gay," Jim said. He took a deep breath. "And I hope you can help. Because if this tape becomes public, I'll be sure to let the press know exactly who released it, and how the group sent a man out to seduce a teenage boy for the purpose of blackmailing him."

"What did you say your name was?" Mackenzie asked.

"Jim Morgan," Jim said. "M-O-R-G-A-N. My name is Jim Morgan, and if that tape leaks, you'll be seeing me on every station, and the conservatives will be picketing your movies for years."

"I heard you the first time, Mr. Morgan," Mackenzie said. "I'm going to take care of this. Tell whoever it is this happened to I'm sorry. He can call me anytime to talk."

Jim was relieved. "That's it, then?" he asked.

"I'm going to take care of this right now," Mackenzie promised.

"Thank you," Jim said.

"Thank you, Mr. Morgan," Mackenzie said, and the line went dead.

Jim sat for a moment, not sure how the interaction had gone. It was a precarious call, but Jason Mackenzie had never struck him as an extremist, or an asshole. He had always come off as a pretty normal guy, which was probably why he was popular. Jim cautiously hoped the issue had been put to rest. But he knew there was one way to know for certain.

He started the car and went back to the motel. He didn't see Kyle's limo in the parking lot, and figured they must still be at the courthouse. He decided to grab a beer, and figured the Milky Way would be free of Karaoke singers at this hour, and was thankfully correct.

As he sat with his beer, admiring the stars projected on the ceiling, he thought about Amanda. He had faith in Emily's ability to resolve the criminal issue, but then what? He, of course, would go back to Los Angeles with Emily, but would this whole endeavor mark the beginning of some sort of new relationship with Amanda? Was he now obliged to have the occasional call, or have the rare, awkward dinner when they were in each other's city?

He ordered a second beer, and it contained a small dose of animosity. Who was Amanda to initiate this whole thing, he thought? What gave her the right to tumble back into his life, and allow him to reach out his hand, when it was her who had pushed him away? Now, he had to face her and remember the pain all over again. He had to see the way Emily looked at him, with constant suspicion and pain of her own. Emily didn't know him anywhere near as well as Amanda, and that was painfully clear to all three of them.

Amanda hadn't come between them; she'd simply shined a light on the chasm that already existed.

As he finished his third beer he could hear her voice, laughing, saying "I love you" with her girlish giggle that had always melted his heart.

Chapter 37

Kyle had the driver drop them off in front of The Milky Way. He and Amanda had convinced Emily there was no Karaoke at this hour, and they promised not to let her get drunk.

"I can't believe how bad it went for that guy," Amanda said. "I almost feel sad for him."

"Well, I think our 'fine Christian boy' helped a bit," Emily said, tousling Kyle's hair.

"What can I say? America loves me," Kyle sighed as he opened the door to the bar for the ladies.

"I love you," Amanda giggled as they piled through the door.

"Jim!" Emily said, walking up behind him, sliding her hand across his shoulder. "Hey, babe, you're here!"

"I am," Jim said, spinning on his seat to kiss Emily.

"Guess what?" Emily said with the giddy voice she got after demolishing someone in court.

"You knocked the poor man to the ground and stomped on him repeatedly?" Jim said.

Emily gave a mischievous smile and nodded. "I was so bad!" she said, failing to contain her laughter.

Jim glanced over at Amanda by the door. He then grabbed Emily around her waist and pulled her close, "Come here, bad girl," he ordered as he kissed her hard and deep. He opened his eyes long enough to see Amanda look away.

"Hmmm," Emily gasped as he finally released her. "I'm coming straight to you after all my wins," she said.

"Please do," Jim said sliding his hand down to grab her ass, making Emily jump and yelp.

"Bartender, whatever you're giving him, keep it coming!" she yelled to the burly guy behind the bar.

"So, is it over?" Jim asked.

"Just about," Emily said. "Some people refuse to tap out, but that's when you start breaking bones."

"Brutal." Jim agreed.

Kyle and Amanda sat at a table and ordered a pitcher of beer. The waitress looked at Kyle and smiled.

"I heard you were in town, but I didn't believe it," she said, smiling and moving closer.

"Well, I am," Kyle said, "and I love this place."

"Let me know if you want a guided tour," the waitress flirted, despite being over twice Kyle's age. "I have somethings I would love to show you."

"Thanks," Kyle said. "I just might do that."

"Hey, you did stuff today, too," Emily said to Jim as she pulled him to the table with Kyle and Amanda. "How did that go?"

"I think it went okay," Jim said. "I'll find out soon on that one thing; the other's going to take a lot more work."

The waitress returned with a pitcher of beer, a coke, and five glasses.

"This is how this is going to work," she announced, "I'm setting this pitcher of beer here for all you grown ups, and a coke here for this cutie," she said, rubbing Kyle's shoulder. "As far as I know, that's what he's drinking."

"Well played!" Emily said to the waitress.

The waitress moved behind Kyle and ran her hand down from his shoulder to his thigh, moving her hand into his pocket.

"This is my number," she whispered in his ear, "or just flag me down whenever you like and I'll show you our storage room. I think you would really like it."

The waitress walked away, leaving the table staring at Kyle. "Believe it or not, she was more subtle than most." He poured himself a beer.

"I really can't stay long," Jim said, filling his glass. "I promised Reggie I'd get some info to him today."

"Oh, come on," Emily complained. "Let Reggie do his own work for once."

"It's not just for him," Jim replied.

Someone turned on the music and Amanda got excited. "Let's dance," she said, "I feel like dancing!"

Emily finished her second beer. "Jim doesn't dance, he's too embarrassed," she said.

Amanda looked up at Jim, but he ignored her.

"How about you?" Amanda asked Kyle. "There's no such thing as a non-dancing gay guy, right?"

Jim and Emily looked over at Kyle, shocked at Amanda's comment.

"I told her last night," Kyle said, seeing their expressions. "Relax. It feels good to tell people. But no, no dancing yet for me, I need at least one more drink."

Amanda moved her eyes to Emily.

"Oh, I'm not going to be the last to be asked," she said. "I'm not someone to be settled for!"

Amanda smiled and held out her hand and Emily grabbed it. "Okay, but don't think this leads to singing again."

The two walked off to the dance floor, leaving Jim alone with Kyle.

"We need to talk," Jim said, raising his voice above the music.

"Are you breaking up with me?" Kyle asked.

"It's good news, I think," Jim said. "I looked into that guy's organization, the one he said he was with. It ends up one of their most prominent members and spokespeople is Jason Mackenzie."

Kyle smiled. "I always wanted to meet him," he said.

"Well, good," Jim said, "because I think you should call him."

"For what?" Kyle said, "He wouldn't do something like this."

"No," Jim said, "but I called him because I thought he might be able to end it."

"You told him?" Kyle asked in a panic.

"I didn't mention your name," Jim said, "I just told him it was a client and asked if he could help. He said he would take care of it, but I can't say for certain if I believe him."

"But if I call him, he's going to know it's me," Kyle said.

"I know," Jim said. "But I think that's a good thing. People like you, Kyle. If he knows it's you, and you open up to him, I think he's more likely to fix this. It has to come from within that organization. Anything else just increases the risk of the video being leaked."

"I don't know if I can tell him," Kyle said, shaking his head.

"You told Amanda!" Jim said.

"Yeah, but she's really sweet and understanding," Kyle said, "and there's something about being away from everything that makes it easier for me to be honest with myself."

"I can't make you call him," Jim said, handing Kyle the phone number. "But it's what I recommend."

Jim walked over to the dance floor and kissed Emily. "I have to get that stuff over to Reggie," he said. "I'll see you back at the room."

"You bet you will," she said, slapping his ass as he turned to go.

Chapter 38

Emily returned to the table with Kyle while Amanda went to the bathroom. "That girl has to pee every five minutes," she said.

Kyle looked up from his phone and smiled.

"Everything okay?" Emily asked.

"Yeah, just adding a number to my phone," Kyle said.

"Did Jim make any headway on your problem?" Emily asked.

Kyle nodded, "Yeah, we think it might be taken care of."

"Really?" Emily said, grabbing Kyle's hand. "How did he do it?"

"He called someone who said they can take care of it," Kyle said. "I'm going to follow up tomorrow, when I'm not quite as drunk."

"That's great news," Emily said. "I'm really sorry you had to go through that."

"Thanks," Kyle said. "I know you know what it's like to have an embarrassing video on the Internet."

"Right," Emily said, promising herself to get Jim back for that.

Emily looked up and saw Sam walk in. She instinctively waived him over, forgetting her constant lectures to Amanda about consorting with the enemy. But Emily was in a good mood and drunk, more on adrenaline than beer.

Sam walked over and she hugged him. She saw him glance

around the bar.

"She's in the bathroom," Emily said smiling.

Sam blushed.

"You're in a good mood," he said.

"Yep!" she said.

"You're not going to be singing tonight, are you?" Sam asked.

Emily rolled her eyes and poured another beer.

"I'm Kyle, by the way," Kyle said.

"Oh, shit!" Emily said, "I forgot you two haven't met. Kyle, Sam, Sam, Kyle. Sam's a police officer."

"I kept hearing you were in town," Sam said. "It's nice to meet you, I really like your show."

"Thanks," Kyle said

"What's brings you to town?" Sam asked.

"I'm just here to see Jim, he's my lawyer," Kyle said.

"Oh," Sam said, glancing at the beer in Kyle's hand.

"Oops," Kyle said, grabbing the cup of coke.

"I'm off duty," Sam said, smiling, "and I don't recall how old you are."

"Oh, thank god!" Kyle said, grabbing his beer again.

"Your dad's not coming in here, is he?" Emily asked. "No offense."

"You mean you don't think he's fun?" Sam asked with a laugh. "No, this place isn't really his thing."

"Hi," Amanda said, walking up behind Sam.

"Hi," Sam said. "You look beautiful tonight."

"Thank you," Amanda blushed.

"Do me a favor, Sam," Emily requested, "dance with her, I'm exhausted."

"She did say she owed me a dance," Sam reminded her, holding out his hand.

Emily watched Amanda walk to the dance floor with Sam. She liked the two of them together. Plus, it might take her eyes of Jim.

"They look right together," Kyle said.

"They do," Emily agreed.

"She doesn't like being alone," Kyle said. "She's very sad about something."

"Yeah, she was looking at a long prison sentence," Emily said.

"I guess," Kyle said. "But I think she's lonely. Maybe she'll end up with the cute policeman."

"Here's hoping," Emily said, raising her cup.

Chapter 39

"I'm not sure I get what it all means," Reggie said.

Jim switched to his headset and pulled up more copies of the book to forward to Reggie. "The first form I sent over is a quick template to request a copy of the mortgage note. I checked with four different attorneys who have worked with these, and all of them agreed the tactic will buy at least another sixty days, more often over three months."

"Okay, I get that," Reggie said. "It's after that you lose me."

Jim went through the plan with him again, this time focusing on the need for the whole town to participate.

"Has anyone done this before?" Reggie asked.

"Not that I'm aware of," Jim admitted.

"It feels like there could be a criminal issue, but damned if I can think of one," Reggie said.

"I thought the same thing, but there really is nothing," Jim said. "It's basically using the same system the banks use to screw people."

"I have to say, I'm surprised at the response from people so far," Reggie admitted. "I went through the last few months of the clinic records and found over a hundred residents facing potential foreclosure."

"There's probably over twice that many still out there," Jim said.

"Give me tomorrow to look this over and absorb everything," Reggie said, "but then I think we should talk to the mayor."

"Sounds great," Jim said.

"Jim," Reggie said before Jim could hang up, "either way I want you to know that I'm grateful you care enough to have spent so much time on this."

"Not a big deal," Jim said.

"It is," Reggie said. "Thank you."

"You're welcome," Jim said, feeling unusually like Atticus Finch.

He put all the papers away and stretched out on the bed. He awoke an hour later to a woman kissing him, running her hand down his chest and into his pants.

"I'm still a bad girl," Emily breathed.

Jim could taste the beer on her breath. "You're drunk," he said, smiling.

"And horny," she said, tugging his pants off. "Lucky you."

Chapter 40

The shifting mattress woke Emily, and she saw Jim getting up. "Where you off to?" she asked.

"The bathroom," Jim said, "but I was thinking about getting some coffee."

"Umm," Emily said, "grab me one too. Oh, and grab me a copy of today's paper, the Herald or Sun, or whatever they call it."

She watched Jim throw his pants on and close the door behind him. She laid in bed smiling. She felt good this morning, no hang over. Jim returned and tossed the paper on the bed.

"I assume this is what you wanted to see?" he said.

Emily sat up and grabbed the paper, excited to see her handiwork herself.

"Man Up, Franks!" read the headline. She wiggled in glee; it was even better than she had hoped. She read the subheading, "District Attorney Franks chastised by judge for whining about loss in gas station explosion."

"Did you read it?" Emily asked Jim. "I wonder if Amanda saw it yet?"

"Em,'" Jim said, grabbing the paper, "What are you doing?"

"Kicking ass," she said, grabbing the paper back. "What's your problem?"

"My problem is that you're leaving this guy no choice but to go after her harder," he said. "You have to stop."

"You're the one who insisted I push for no jail time," she said. "You think that'll happen by playing nice? I have to show him this case is going to cost him his career if he keeps going."

"If I were you, I would back off," Jim said.

"Well, you're not me, Jim," Emily said, getting out of bed. "I'm trying to keep Amanda out of prison, not get her a bigger dressing room. This is what law's like when it matters."

"What the hell does that mean, 'matters'?" Jim asked. "You're saying my work doesn't matter?"

"Let's face it Jim, what happens when you lose a case?" Emily said. "Some actor has to do a film he'd committed to, or maybe he doesn't get a cheese plate delivered to his dressing room daily."

"We'll deal with your utter lack of respect for my career later," Jim said. "Right now, I need you to listen to me."

"What?" Emily asked.

Jim paced back and forth, genuinely concerned about Amanda and knowing getting into a bigger argument with Emily wasn't going to help.

"I once saw a man's arm ripped off by an alligator," Jim said.

"What?" Emily asked.

"Ripped off, visible bone, screaming, all that shit," Jim said.

"Where would you have possibly seen this?" Emily asked skeptically.

"My family drove down to Disney World one year, and I saw a sign for one of those roadside shows where the guy sticks his head in an alligator's mouth," Jim said. "I begged my parents to stop so I could see it."

"Why?" Emily asked.

"Because I was ten!" Jim snapped, annoyed. "Anyway, we get there with about three other families and I watched this guy stick his head in the mouth of a huge alligator. I thought it was so cool; the guy had no fear. And then, as he was doing this part of the show where he has the 'gators roll over each other for scraps of food, one suddenly lunged out and grabbed his arm. A few thrashes, and the guy's arm ripped clean off."

"Shit," Emily said.

"It was awful," Jim agreed. "The families freaked out and started running, but I wouldn't go, I just watched as two other men came rushing in to grab him. The other alligators, I guess smelling the blood, were trying to get to him then, too. And off to the side, I saw this woman crying and screaming to get him out. I think it was the guy's mother, the place looked family run. My parents did their best to cheer me up, but the thing I kept thinking about was all the times he did that routine and nothing happened. At some point, he probably forgot the thing he was messing with had teeth."

"You saw this at ten?" Emily said. "Why have you never mentioned this?"

"Because it was disturbing and still freaks me out," Jim said. "But do you get what I'm trying to say?"

"Well, first off, your parents have a surprisingly white trash sense of children's entertainment," Emily said, "but yes, I get it. You're afraid Franks, who is as dumb as an alligator, is going to get the upper hand somehow, and that it's Amanda who's going to take the hit. But that's not going to happen. I won't let it happen. I know I'm pushing hard, but he has to feel like this case can't be won."

"Em, I'm asking you to be careful," Jim said.

"I am," Emily said. "You worry too much. Once he sees this, he's going to realize this case could cost him the election. He'll take the deal, and we can go home."

"I hope you're right," Jim said.

"I'm going to get dressed and go there now," Emily said. "I'll be back in a bit, and then you should go shopping with us."

"With who?" Jim asked.

"Me, Kyle, Amanda, and Sam," she said.

"I'll see, I got work to do," he said.

"Cheer up," Emily said, kissing him, "we're almost done."

She walked into the bathroom to shower.

"We're still going to have a conversation about what you think of my work," Jim said as she closed the door.

Emily got dressed and drove to meet Reggie and ambush Franks in his office. She pulled up and could already see Reggie was pissed.

"You're not happy," Emily said, squinting at Reggie's face.

"Does it matter?" Reggie said.

"I know it's harsh, but I'm sorry, I have to get this put to bed," she said.

"Well then, let's go slap the bear in the face again," Reggie said walking towards the office.

"Ms. Perkins and Mr. Bayloch to see Mr. Franks, please," Emily said to the secretary.

"He's expecting you," the woman replied, glaring at Emily.

Emily and Reggie walked into the office and saw Franks sitting at his desk with his back to them, the paper unfolded on his desk.

"My mother reads this paper," Franks said, back still turned to them both.

"I gave you your chance," Emily said. "It doesn't start getting better until this case is gone."

"I'm supposed to just roll over, right?" Franks said. "Like a trained dog."

The image of an alligator crossed Emily's mind, but she continued. "Why keep playing this game?" she said. "We'll get her treatment, but it can't be here. We'll up restitution to twenty-thousand, and promise she'll never step foot in this state again."

Franks turned to face them. "And if I don't?" Franks asked. "If I defy your bullying and push forward, what will you do then? More cheap tricks, or theatrics? Maybe bring more television celebrities to impress the judge? Have you ever actually practiced law?"

Emily, now having had enough of his crap, decided he hadn't quite gotten the point yet. "Fine, Franks, let's keep doing this. Want to go back into a court room? Let's go. I gave you my final offer. Quite frankly, going against you in court makes me feel guilty, like parking in a handicap space, but if that's what you want, let's do it!"

Franks stood up and resisted the urge to knock everything off his desk. Emily walked closer and looked him in the eye. "Take the deal and move on with your life," she said.

Franks looked over at Reggie, who was standing behind Emily but clearly feeling his pain.

"Charlie, can you do something without jail time?" Reggie asked. "They just want to get the girl home to her people."

Franks looked down. "Five years probation," he said. "Twenty-five in restitution, a letter from a drug treatment center somewhere in this country saying she's enrolled, and a personal promise to never return to the sate of Alabama."

"Done," Emily said. "Let's write it up and get it to the judge."

"I'll go do it right now," Reggie said. "Thanks, Charlie."

"Yes, thank you," Emily said, reaching her hand across his desk. He looked at it and then looked her in the eye. She got that image of the alligator again and quickly withdrew her exposed limb.

"I don't think anyone has ever looked at me with such contempt before," Emily said as she took the stairs with Reggie.

"I doubt he's ever been treated with such contempt before," Reggie said, grabbing his phone.

"It's not personal," Emily said.

Reggie held his hand up. "Hey, it's me," he said into the phone. "I need a plea agreement drawn up right now for the Jeffries case. Five years probation, twenty-five thousand restitution, a letter within thirty days from a drug treatment center, and time served. This is to cover all counts stemming from the arrest. And get me on the judge's docket, today if possible. I want it sent over to Franks within an hour."

"Thanks, Reggie. I appreciate it," Emily said.

"Well, then you can buy me lunch while we wait," he said.

Chapter 41

Amanda looked at the last two Vicodin, and opted to take a couple over the counter pain killers she picked up while out with Kyle and conserve the bigger stuff. She headed to Emily's room and knocked. Jim opened the door, his phone glued to his ear. He motioned for Amanda to come in and finished his call.

"So, as long as the trust wasn't in place at the time of the original note, then we're not looking at any sort of issue?" he said into the phone. "And, if the properties are already in foreclosure, is there a fraudulent conveyance issue?"

Amanda looked around and saw lots of crumpled, yellow paper. She assumed Emily must have gone back to the courthouse, as she'd said she was hoping to get the deal with Franks done today. Amanda sat on the edge of the bed and waited patiently. Jim looked over and wrapped his call.

"Thanks for much, I think I've got everything I need. I'll call if there's anything else," he said, and hung up the phone.

"Hey," he said, looking at Amanda, "What's up?"

"I was hoping Emily would have some news," she said. "She said she was going to show me something in the morning I would like."

Jim handed Amanda the newspaper with the Franks-inspired headlines.

"Oh my god!" Amanda gasped. "He's going to be so mad!"

"Yeah, I would imagine," Jim said. "But that's part of her strategy, I guess."

"Wow," Amanda said, "I feel bad, like I caused all this."

"Well ..." Jim said, shrugging.

"I know," she said. "I'm sorry I caused all this trouble, but you know me, it seems to find it's way into everything I do."

"Yeah, I remember," he said.

"Do you?" she asked, looking up at him.

"Yeah," he said smiling.

"Ever think about me?" she asked. "I mean, before all this?"

"Oh yeah," Jim said, "you gave me lots to think about."

"I'm sorry," she said. "You'll never know how sorry I am."

"Sorry, as in sorry I blew up the gas station, sorry?" he asked.

"A hundred gas stations, a thousand gas stations," she said, standing up. "I'm sorry."

"It's in the past," he said, "I'm over it."

"Yeah, I can tell," she said.

"I'm sorry, what did you expect after eight years?" Jim asked. "For me to be curled up into a ball, crying out your name? I got passed that after only two years, thank you very much."

"I'm sorry," Amanda said again.

The old anger gripped Jim. "What do you expect from me?" he demanded. "I dropped everything and came out here for you. Did you know I would do that?"

"Yes," she admitted.

"Well, I didn't," he said, "and it makes me sick I did, to be honest. I thought I was over all this shit, Amanda. But now you're here, and everything is weird and strange."

"So, you're not over me?" she asked, trying to look him in the eye.

Jim avoided eye contact but finally gave in. She stepped in closer. "I'm here," she whispered. "Please don't be over me."

Jim grabbed Amanda and kissed her. She wrapped her arms around him and he pushed her against the door, running his hands all over her body. She felt so familiar to him that eight years turned into a week and suddenly they were back in Milwaukee making up from a fight. He grabbed at her ass and lifted her dress. She started unfastening his pants and he pushed her back onto the bed.

She slid up the mattress while he pulled at her dress. She lifted her arms and he pulled the dress off. He grabbed at her breasts as she reached down between his legs.

The phone startled them both, and they looked first to the door instead of the buzzing device on the nightstand.

He looked at the phone. Amanda knew what he was thinking before he did, and she reached out as he rose from the bed, reaching for but not touching him.

He picked up the phone. "Hey, hon," he said.

Amanda lay on the bed, her hands covering her breasts. She felt cold.

"That's great, I'm glad it worked," he said. "I'll let her know."

Jim hung up the phone. "It's over," he said as he fastened his pants.

Amanda nodded and tried to sit up, failing on her first attempt because of the pain.

"You okay?" Jim asked, looking at her suspiciously.

"Fine," Amanda said, "you're just a little heavier now." She pushed through the pain to grab her dress.

"Sorry," Jim said as he watched her dress. "I still love you," Jim said. "I don't think I'll ever not."

Amanda tried to smile although the pain fogged her vision as she fixed her hair and got off the bed. "I understand," she said.

"I love Emily, and I want to have a life with her," he said. "I'm sorry for what almost happened here, being around you again is difficult, and I have missed you."

Amanda nodded.

"I can't be around you, Amanda," he finally said. "I'll fuck up what I have, and she means too much to me. I'm sorry."

"Well, like you said, it's over now," she said as she walked out the door.

She started slowly back to her room, balancing herself on the walls until she reached her door. She walked in and tried to sit on the bed, but fell short and ended up on the floor, doubled over in pain. She reached for the bottle of Advil where she had stashed her Vicodin and was struggling with the lid when she saw Claire above her.

"You okay?" she asked.

"No," Amanda admitted.

"I'll get help," Claire said, trying to step passed Amanda.

"No, stop," Amanda said. "I just need to take a pill and that will help."

Claire looked at the door, "I think I should get some help," she said. "You look like shit."

"Please, don't," Amanda said. "I don't want to be alone."

Claire grabbed a bottle of water and knelt down to Amanda. "Give me the pills," she ordered. Claire opened the pills and gave both to Amanda, along with the water. She sat on the floor. Fifteen minutes passed before Amanda felt like she could sit up. Claire carefully helped her to the bed.

"What were you doing here?" Amanda asked.

"Cleaning your bathroom," Claire said. "Thus is my life. What's wrong with you?"

"Nothing," Amanda said. "Just feeling ill."

"Yeah," she heard Kyle's voice, "I noticed you weren't feeling good."

Amanda looked at the door and saw Kyle standing on the threshold.

"Oh, hey," Claire said, obviously relieved.

"Hi," Kyle said, walking in. "I'll take over."

"Okay, cool," Claire said, looking at Amanda. "Let me know if you need anything."

Kyle closed the door behind Claire and turned to Amanda. "I told you my secret," he said, "now let's hear yours."

Chapter 42

Reggie set down the slice of pizza and grabbed his phone. "Okay, thanks," he said. "We're not able to get into see the judge until tomorrow at one," he reported.

"That's okay," Emily said. "We'll stick around another day."

"Well, that's good," Reggie said. "Jim's helping us out with something and he and I are meeting with the mayor."

"Really?" Emily asked. "I thought he was just helping some people drag out their foreclosures a bit longer."

"Well, that's part of it," Reggie said, "but it's bigger now. If all goes well, we'll be addressing an open public forum this week in the town hall. Just might be that little girl blowing up our gas station is the best thing that could have happened to this town."

"Let me guess, you're declaring her a natural disaster and getting a FEMA grant?" Emily said.

"Not a bad idea," Reggie laughed. "You know, you're a fun person when not in court."

"I get that a lot," Emily said. "I'm a bit gladiatorial when it comes to my cases." She wiped her mouth, folding the greasy napkin closed and dropping it on her plate. "Well, I'm off to my motel. I'll meet you at the judge's chambers at one tomorrow?" she said.

"Sounds good," Reggie agreed.

Emily pulled into the parking lot and stopped by her room first. Jim was going through some papers, but set them aside when she walked in.

"Well, you return triumphant," he said.

"Told you, you worry too much," she said, jumping on top of him. "Now tell me I was right and you were wrong," she demanded as she started punching him in the arm.

"Fine, fine!" he exclaimed. "You win. Congrats!"

Emily kissed Jim and straddled his hips. "I like when you admit I'm the better lawyer."

"I didn't say you were a better lawyer," he corrected, "I said you were right in this one, limited instance."

Emily stopped kissing him and looked him in the eye. "Do you want sex, or not?" she asked.

"You're a better lawyer," he relented, believing any good lawyer will lie through his teeth to get what he wants.

Twenty minutes later, Emily rolled off the bed and grabbed her clothes. "I should go tell Amanda," she said. "She's going to be thrilled she gets to go home tomorrow."

"I'm sure she will be," Jim said, getting out of bed.

"Speaking of which, Reggie said you're meeting with the mayor of Mayberry. You're not dragging us into anything that's going to keep us here, are you?" she asked.

Jim sighed and leaned against the wall. "One extra day at most," he said.

Emily turned around and gave him an exasperated look. "Are you kidding me?"

"I'm doing something to help these people," he said. "It feels good."

"Oh, baby, is this because I said your work wasn't important?" she asked.

"No, but that's an issue we'll deal with when we get home," he said.

"One day, promise no longer," Emily said.

"One day. We'll leave the day after tomorrow," he affirmed.

"Fine," she said. "We taking the TV star with us, or is he staying here?"

"I think he wanted to see this thing through, for some reason," Jim said. "He needed a break from L.A. He's seventeen and already dealing with an ulcer, you know."

"That sucks," she said. "We'll have to do more for him when we get home. Now I'm off to tell Amanda."

Emily kissed Jim while heading out the door. Jim felt relieved they were going home. Amanda was going to be okay, and he and Emily could move forward with their lives. He called Kyle to see if he had called Jason Mackenzie yet, but it went to voicemail.

Emily knocked on Amanda's door and was called in by Amanda and Kyle in stereo.

"Hey, guess who's going on five year probation tomorrow?" Emily asked.

"Are you kidding?" Amanda said, getting up from bed. "You did it?"

"I did it," Emily agreed.

"That's it, just probation?" Amanda asked.

"Well, twenty-five in restitution, but let's not worry about that now," Emily said.

"Shit!" Amanda said, "When do I have to pay that?"

"I imagine you won't," Emily said. "Just promise to stay out of trouble."

Amanda wanted to reject the gift, but she didn't have much to argue with. "Thank you so much," she said, hugging Emily. "I can't believe you did this."

Amanda felt weird hugging Emily. Not more than two hours ago, she had been ready to have sex with her fiancé, and now she felt horrible about it. She started to cry.

"Hey, don't cry!" Emily said. "It's good news!"

"Yeah," Amanda sniffled. "You're amazing, and I don't know what to say."

"Just say thank you and stay out of trouble," Emily said.

"Okay," Amanda said. "Thank you."

Amanda still wanted Jim, but knew even if she had a chance before, she couldn't possibly do anything to hurt Emily. Not now. Not after Emily had given her back her freedom.

Kyle, who had been sitting back, finally spoke. "I know we have plans, but I have to make a call," he said. "I'll be around later."

He waived to Amanda on the way out and she smiled back.

"Let's go do that shopping," Emily said. "You need something clean for court tomorrow."

Chapter 43

Kyle finally appeared at Jim's door, holding up a six pack of Coors Light.

"Hey, I've been trying to reach you. Did you call Mackenzie?" Jim asked.

"I did," Kyle said, handing Jim a beer.

"And?" Jim asked, waiting to hear if the problem was resolved.

"He says he took care of it," Kyle said. "We had a good talk."

"That's good," Jim said. "You know, his box office records have been good, and no one's shorting him on salary for being gay."

"I know," Kyle said. "He gave me some good advice, but I'm not sure yet."

"I know I'm not your agent, but maybe you can run it by me?" Jim said.

"He said I should do what makes me happy," Kyle said.

Jim took a moment and pretended to think about it. "That's the stupidest thing I ever heard. We live in L.A., where we do what makes other people happy, so they will make us rich," he said, laughing.

"Yeah, yeah," Kyle said, "but I do think I have to give some thought to that."

"For what it's worth, Kyle, I agree," Jim said, growing serious.

"You're in the public light, and frankly, you belong there. You're smart, talented, good-looking, and despite years of Hollywood training, not a total douche."

"Thank you!" Kyle said, raising his beer to Jim.

"But that also means the more you try to hide who you are, the bigger deal it's going to be when it comes out," Jim finished.

Kyle nodded and thought for a moment. "The producers of my show wanted me to have more lines the third season," Kyle said. "I was terrified about the idea. So they got me this insanely expensive comedy coach who insisted 'one has to build a house before they can move in their furniture.'"

"Please tell me there's context to that?" Jim said, finally opening his beer.

"He told me I have to build a character before I can worry about the jokes," Kyle explained. "Everyone's a character actor whether they know it or not. The style of comedy, and acting for that matter, has to be consistent. I don't know how to blend this into being consistent with my character."

Jim followed the problem and realized Kyle was dealing with something profound for a celebrity. Kyle was known for being the cute, wholesome teenage boy on a dramedy, and it carried through to his personal life. Everyone saw him as that character, and he didn't act much differently in person. What would happen when his sexuality was thrown into the mix?

"You don't have to be that character," Jim said.

"But I do," Kyle said, standing up. "And that's what Jason Mackenzie helped me see."

Kyle walked to the door and left. Jim didn't know what to say. He wasn't the arguing kind of lawyer, and he understood what Kyle was saying. If he came out, he risked losing the fan base that currently supported him. It wouldn't be easy, giving up that kind of love, even if it meant being true to who he was.

A few hours later, while enjoying a beer outside, Jim noticed the limo pull up. He watched Emily and Amanda spill out of the car, laughing and babbling on over some inside joke.

He wasn't surprised Emily had a good time with Amanda. That was Amanda's gift, to lighten the room and make everyone love her. It was a gift that cost Jim his heart every time he saw her.

He went inside and waited for Emily to come back to the room.

"I got you something," she announced, storming into the room.

"What's that?" Jim asked.

Emily was holding half a dozen bags filled with various junk she'd purchased, and after a minute found Jim's gift: a very authentic, very big cowboy hat.

"Oh, how did you know I didn't already have one?" Jim said, trying it on at a rakish angle.

"You look sexy," she decided. "I should have known you'd look hot in a cowboy hat."

Jim looked in the mirror and thought he looked ridicules. "I don't think I'm a hat guy," he said.

"Nonsense," Emily said. "The saleslady said all people think they look bad in hats, but they look great."

"Really?" Jim said. "A woman who sells hats told you everyone looks great in hats? What fortunate insight!"

Emily pulled out her own hat and slid it on her head. Jim got her point, as she did look kinda sexy.

"Take off your clothes, partner," she drawled.

Jim, happy to oblige, took off his hat and began to remove his shirt.

"No, no," she said. "Leave the hat on."

Jim smiled. "Are you leaving your hat on?" he asked as he returned the hat to his head.

"Yep, I'm going cowgirl," she said. "Or a reverse cowgirl, if you prefer," she added with a mischievous smile.

Jim kissed Emily, and went for the reverse cowgirl option.

Chapter 44

The phone was never this loud, what was it? Emily thought, then jolted up thinking a fire alarm was going off. It went silent, and then hit again. She looked over at the phone on the night stand, it rang hard and the little red light kept blinking.

"Oh my god, what?" she said, answering it.

"They're arresting her! They're trying to take her!" Claire shouted, "Do something!"

"What?" Emily said, trying to shake the fog in her head.

"Crazy lady … Amanda," Claire screamed. "Hurry!"

Emily hopped out of bed, pulled on pants and Jim's jacket and ran outside, leaving the door open and Jim still coming to.

She saw a police car in the parking lot, along with the chief in his truck, and Franks standing by. She looked towards Amanda's room and saw her being lead out in handcuffs, crying.

Emily ran up to Franks, hands clenched into fists. "What the fuck?" she demanded.

"Oh, did we wake you?" Franks said, looking over Emily's outfit.

"We have a deal," Emily said. "What the hell is this?"

"We *had* a deal," Franks corrected smoothly, "like we had a deal the day of arraignment, but I guess they're not really binding until the judge signs off, right?"

"I'm going to destroy you," Emily said. "I will bring down everything in your life. That gas station is going to look good next to the wreck I will make of you. Count on it."

"Threaten all you want, Ms. Perkins," Franks said smugly, "but you and her are not going be my problem for much longer."

"What does that mean?" Emily asked

"It means I'm dropping all charges, for the time being," he said. "Be happy, you won."

Emily glared at Franks, waiting for the rest.

"But the grand theft auto charge ..." he clucked his tongue. "I'll just let Broward County handle that."

"Florida?" Amanda asked, incredulous.

"That's where she boosted the car," Franks explained. "Normally, we prosecute here on those, but I figure this time, I'll make an exception."

Emily was about to be sick.

"I had the chief rerun those plates, and wouldn't you know, stolen! Oh, and I checked for you," he said. "They're not quite as keen on the idea of consulting counsel there, so unless you have a Florida license, she'll have to make due with what they give her."

Amanda was being walked passed Emily, her eyes pleading for help. Emily's guard was down, and for once her look of certainty was absent. Amanda sought deeper for it.

"Ms. Jeffries, you're going away for three to five years for grand theft auto," Franks said as she walked by. "Maybe after that, I'll refile the charges here and you can spend some more time in our jail, as well."

Amanda looked back at Emily, pleading for reassurance, but Emily was lost in her own head, searching for a solution she knew wasn't there. She looked up and saw Amanda's eyes, hopelessly welling up with tears.

"I'm sorry," Emily said, softly starting to cry herself. "I'm so sorry."

Amanda broke down, and Pete had to carry her gently towards the waiting police car.

Emily surveyed the parking lot, dazed. She saw Kyle standing by Claire, not sure what to do. She looked over at Jim, who was watching helplessly as Amanda was lead to the police car. He'd been right, Emily thought. This was her fault.

She felt something strike her chest, and looked down at the newspaper Franks had pushed at her. "That man enough for you?" he snickered, turning his back to walk away.

She glanced at his teeth and thought about the alligator. Emily threw the paper to the ground and screamed, running forward and shoving Franks to the ground with all her weight and furious momentum.

Kyle leaped forward and ran to the limo, reversing it to block the police car's exit.

Franks tried to push Emily off him, but she started slapping at his head and face, forcing him to use his hands for cover.

Claire ran up to Pete and tried pulling Amanda away.

Emily felt herself being lifted into the sky and heard Jim's voice from far away. "Stop! Stop!" he commanded. "Kyle, move the damn car!"

Emily was kicking out at Franks as he pushed himself to his feet, and she saw Chief Morris step out of his truck. Everyone went quiet.

"Son," he said to Kyle, "I'm telling you once to move that car, and I'm not asking a second time." He looked over to Claire, who was holding Amanda with her back turned to Pete. "Claire, get your ass back in that office!" he commanded.

"No!" she replied.

"Claire, go," Jim said.

"Fine," Claire finally replied. "But you suck!" she yelled back at the chief.

Chief Morris walked up to Franks. "You okay?" he asked.

"Fine," he said, wiping the dirt off his tacky suit. "I'm pressing charges, arrest her," he said, pointing imperially towards Emily.

Jim instinctively pulled Emily behind him, a snarl nearly splitting his face.

"Really, Franks?" the chief asked.

"She attacked me from behind, you saw her!" Franks insisted.

"I saw you two struggling," the chief said. "I didn't see who started it."

"Arrest her," Franks demanded.

Chief Morris walked up to Jim, who was standing in his way and showed no signs of moving.

"Nice hat," the chief said, alerting Jim to the fact he was wearing only his underwear and a cowboy hat. "I won't cuff her, and I'll have her ready to go when you show up with the bondsman," he said. "Let's not make this worse."

Emily stepped from behind Jim and gently placed her hand on his chest. "Arrange the bail, Jim," she said.

Jim hugged Emily tight, and then watched as the chief led her to his truck.

Kyle stood by the car, and Jim nodded to move the limo. He watched while Emily and Amanda where driven off.

"You suck!" Claire yelled as they passed by.

Chapter 45

Jim walked back into the room and sat on the bed. He noticed himself in the mirror and took off the cowboy hat.

"What do we do?" Kyle asked from the doorway.

Jim sat quietly, examining the hat.

Kyle sat down next to Jim, putting his hand on his shoulder. "I think we should call Reggie first, right?" Kyle asked.

A cell phone rang, and Kyle looked to Jim, who was showed no signs of moving. "Maybe that's him," Kyle said as he walked over and picked up Emily's phone. "Oh, it's a picture of an old lady," he said, turning the screen towards Jim. Jim looked up into the hollow eyes of Emily's mother, and read the caller ID: "The Death of Me." He chuckled and got up.

"Okay," he said, hugging Kyle. "Let's do this thing."

"I'm with you, whatever you want me to do," Kyle said.

"That's the gayest thing I've ever seen," Claire said from the doorway. "Pants on, now."

Jim had Kyle call Reggie to meet them at the courthouse while Jim called to arrange bail.

They pulled up to the courthouse and Reggie motioned them inside. "He's squeezing us in for five minutes to set bail for Emily, and then we're going to piss him off by arguing continuing bail for

Amanda as well," Reggie said.

Jim barely spoke as he strode toward the courtroom. As he approached, he saw Emily and Amanda sitting on a bench. They both looked to him, and he held his hand out, gesturing for them to relax.

The judge called Emily's case. "Okay," the judge said. "Somehow Ms. Perkins is now in custody. This case gets more screwed up by the day."

"Your honor, Ms. Perkins assaulted me," Franks said. "We are filing charges of assault."

"Reggie?" the judge asked. Reggie went to stand, but Jim held up his hand.

"Your honor, I'm the consulting counsel on this case," Jim said, "and I personally witnessed the district attorney assault my client. We will be seeking special accommodation to assist us in charges against Mr. Franks."

"What?" Franks shouted.

"At this time your honor, we request Ms. Perkins, being an officer of the court, having no criminal record, and being charged with a misdemeanor, be released on her on recognizance," Jim said.

"Fine," the judge agreed.

"Your honor, we have a further issue with Amanda Jeffries," Jim continued. "She was arrested on a new charge. As the new charge is related to the current crime for which she has already been arraigned, we request bail be maintained under the current order."

"Your honor, she is being charged with grand theft auto, for which she is being extradited to Florida," Franks said.

"Your honor, Mr. Franks is the one charging her with the crime, he does not have a warrant from Florida yet," Jim said.

"It's forthcoming, your honor," Franks said. "I believe it will be here within forty-eight hours."

"Forthcoming does not cut it, your honor," Jim said. "I believe Mr. Franks' disbarment and a possible criminal conviction might be forthcoming, but I still have to make it happen before he actually goes to jail."

"What the hell are you talking about?" Franks demanded.

"Franks, did you file the GTA charge or not?" the judge asked.

"Yes, your honor," Franks admitted.

"Then I'm just going to up her bail to a hundred and fifty-thousand," the judge decided. "We done?"

"Thank you, your honor," Jim said.

Franks approached Jim. "That's a lot of accusations you're making," Franks said. "I don't think you and I have been formally introduced yet." Franks held out his hand and Jim grabbed it, squeezing to the point of pain, looking Franks in the eyes.

"I'm King Kong," Jim said.

Franks pulled his hand free and backed away from Jim. "Is this the part where you offer me a crappy deal to save myself?" Franks covered with a laugh.

"No." Jim smiled coldly as he walked away.

Reggie walked out with Jim. "A little heads up next time you're planning on stealing my thunder," he said.

"Sorry," Jim said, not sounding apologetic at all.

Reggie grabbed Jim's arm to slow him down and get his attention. "I know you're pissed, and yes, Franks is an asshole. But this is the same tactic that got us here," Reggie warned. "Let me see what I can do."

"Maybe there was time for that before," Jim said. "But you're not the one going to Florida."

"I'm just trying to help," Reggie said earnestly.

"If you can give me Chad Mitchell's mobile number, that would help a lot," Jim said.

Jim walked back to the limo, where Kyle was waiting. "Well?" he asked.

"Let's go pick them up," Jim said as he got in the car.

Chapter 46

Emily sat on the bench outside the chief's office while he talked to Franks, and saw Sam burst through the front door of the station. He walked up to Emily.

"I thought this was settled?" he asked.

"I thought so, too," she said.

Sam walked back to see Amanda, and Emily strained to hear the conversation between Chief Morris and Franks.

"I'm not backing down," Franks said.

"You really going to press charges?" Morris asked. "That girl weighs what, a buck ten, maybe twenty?"

"Doesn't matter how big she is," Franks said. "Assault is assault."

"Yesterday, you were on the front page of the paper being told to man up," Morris pointed out. "Tomorrow, it's going to read you got beat up by a girl. But fine, Franks."

"She hit me," Franks whined with all the authority of a boy on a playground.

"For god's sake Franks, you provoked her," Morris said. "Let it go."

The door opened and Emily did her best to show she wasn't listening.

"Ms. Perkins, you assaulted Mr. Franks," Morris said, "but I think if you apologize, he might be willing to let it go."

She looked over at Franks, who was relishing the situation.

She stood up and took a breath. "Mr. Franks, I lost my temper and acted poorly. I apologize," she said, holding back from any admission of criminal wrong doing.

"Fine," Franks said as he stormed off.

Morris grabbed a clipboard. "Let's get this filled out so you can be on your way," he said.

"No one else I should apologize to?" she asked, mockingly.

"Well, I did happen to see a video of you singing," he said while he filled out the forms, "and I reckon you owe Kenny Rogers an apology, but I don't enforce the laws of good taste."

"Oh, I forgot how funny you are," Emily said.

Sam walked up quickly on the chief. "Why didn't you call me in on this?" he asked.

"I'm in the middle of something," the chief pointed out.

"You don't trust me to do my job?" Sam asked.

"Please excuse us a moment," the chief asked Emily as he opened the door to his office for Sam.

Emily did her best to eavesdrop on the argument.

"What are you thinking acting like this?" the chief asked.

"You intentionally kept her arrest from me," Sam said. "Why?"

"Because you have been acting like a child since you met her," the chief replied. "How do you think it looks with you spending all your off-hours with someone who grabbed your firearm and nearly killed four people?"

"What I do on my off time is my business," Sam replied.

"No, it's not," the chief scolded. "You're attitude is putting people at risk. But how I execute an arrest warrant is definitely my business, Officer Morris."

"Oh, I forgot, you're the chief, you can do no wrong!" Sam retorted.

"That's not true," the chief said.

"No, it's not," Sam agreed. "You know what I keep thinking about? Eight minutes."

"What eight minutes?" the chief asked.

"The eight minutes between the time you let her drive off, and she drunkenly blew us up," Sam said. "How did you not notice she was drunk, or on something? Answer me that, Chief Morris."

"She was fine when she left," the chief said, "complete with that sassy mouth."

"How does someone get that screwed up in eight minutes?" Sam demanded. "Ever ask yourself that question, or are you too busy ignoring anything that doesn't involve putting someone in jail?"

Sam stormed out of the office, slamming the door behind him.

Ten minutes later, the chief emerged. "I apologize for the delay," he said as he signed the last couple of sheets. "Here is your written warning against hitting people, and you are free to go."

"Thanks," Emily said.

The chief nodded, putting back his clipboard.

"Seriously," Emily said as she touched his arm. "Thank you, I know you went to bat for me."

The chief nodded. "Eavesdropping's a nasty habit, Ms. Perkins. Officer Steven's will drive you back to your motel if you need a ride."

Emily walked to the door and saw Jim enter with the bail bondsman. He looked at her and walked up to the desk.

The chief walked back out. "Ms. Jeffries, I assume."

"And Emily Perkins," Jim said.

"Ms. Perkins is free to go, there are no pending charges," the chief said.

Emily walked up behind Jim. "Go ahead and wait in the car," he said. "I'll be there in a minute."

Emily exited the building to be swept into a big hug by Kyle.

"How you doing, street fighter?" he laughed.

Emily blushed, the impropriety of her actions finally replacing the shock. "I can't believe I did that," she said. "I don't know what the hell I was thinking."

"Yeah, I know the feeling," Kyle agreed.

"Yeah, you with the limo blockade!" she laughed. "And how about little Claire?"

"Yeah, she's something," Kyle said. "How bad is this?" he asked.

"What has Jim said? He doesn't seem happy with me," Emily worried.

"He's not happy in general," Kyle said. "He's been on the phone a lot, usually out of my earshot."

Emily nodded, trying to figure out what his plan might be, if he even had one.

"I think I need to tell you something," Kyle said, "but I'm betraying someone's trust."

"Whose?" Emily asked.

Kyle was weighing what to do when the doors opened and Amanda walked out with Jim. She ran up and hugged Emily, leaving Emily feeling even guiltier. She then hugged Kyle, and he gently helped her into the car.

The car was oddly silent as Jim's clear agitation weighed everything down. He silently typed away at his phone, and once even had the car pull over while he got out and made a call. They pulled into the parking lot, where Kyle helped Amanda to her room and Jim took Emily to their door.

"Okay," Emily said. "I know I fucked up, and I know you're pissed at me, but we need to figure out how to stop this Florida warrant, because once she's there we ..."

Jim stopped her. "It's done," he said.

"What's done?" Emily asked.

"The Florida thing," Jim said. "There won't be a warrant coming out of Florida."

"Shit! That's incredible, how did you do that?" Emily asked.

"Doesn't matter," Jim said. "I'm going to have Kyle take you back to the airport in a few hours. Your flight's leaving at nine."

"What about you?" Emily asked

"I'm staying," Jim said, "at least another week to finish this thing."

Emily was getting angry, but knew she'd screwed up, and was trying to be extra reasonable. "You don't want me to stay?" she asked.

"No," Jim said. "I'll take care of it."

Emily sat trembling on the bed. "And us?" she almost whispered.

"This has nothing to do with us," he said. "This has to do with your tactics and the shit storm you caused. It would be better if I was here alone."

"But you won't be alone, will you?" she pointed out cautiously.

"I'm getting the case put to rest and I'm coming back to L.A.," he said. "That's it."

"How did you kill the Florida warrant?" she asked

"The owner of the car is taking twenty grand to say he leant her the car," Jim said. "His insurance will cover a replacement, so he's coming out ahead anyway."

Emily stood back up. "Tell me you didn't just say that. That's, that's illegal, Jim. You could be disbarred!"

"It's done," Jim said.

"That's insane!" Emily insisted.

"Yet, here we are," Jim said. "It needed to be done, so I did it."

"You just can't do that," Emily argued.

"You think this shit doesn't happen all the time?" Jim said. "You think when the firm hands you a criminal case, they haven't already tried this route?"

Emily grabbed her phone and purse. "I'm not talking to you about this," she said, and slammed the door behind her.

Chapter 47

Amanda washed up and came back into the room.

"You feeling okay?" Kyle asked.

"Yeah," Amanda said, sitting on the bed. "Just tired."

"Everything's going to be okay," Kyle said. "They're both really good lawyers. I mean, Jim somehow stopped something I thought for sure was going to destroy my life. And Emily is the toughest chick I ever met, and that's saying a lot."

Amanda smiled. "I don't want to think about it," she said.

"Okay," Kyle said. "What do you want to do?"

Amanda got up and walked to the door. "Buy me a drink?" she asked.

"You bet," Kyle said, opening the door for her.

They walked across the street to The Milky Way and grabbed a seat in back. They ordered a pitcher, and Amanda asked Kyle questions about what it was like growing up on TV.

A couple hours passed, and the bar started to get more crowded. Kyle looked down at his phone. "It's Claire," he announced.

"She has your number?" Amanda asked.

"Yeah," he said. "She wants to know what's going on. Apparently, Emily's sitting upfront and looks upset."

"Maybe we should go bring her back?" Amanda suggested.

"She feels guilty," Kyle said. "I think she thinks you're upset with her."

"That's crazy, I'm the one who screwed up," Amanda said.

"I'm going to drag her back here," Kyle said getting up.

He walked back across the street and into the lobby, where Claire was sitting on the couch talking to Emily.

"I was telling Emily about the time these bikers came and got beat up by Chief Morris. They never paid their bill, and they stole one of our TV's," she said. "And one of them exposed himself to me. His ass, not his dick. I've only seen three real penises. Plenty of assholes, though."

"Emily, come have a drink with us and relax," he said.

"Aren't we heading out soon?" Emily asked.

"What?" Kyle asked. "Oh, the flight! I told Jim we wouldn't be making that flight, so we're leaving tomorrow."

Emily tossed her hands in the air. "Nice of nobody to tell me," she huffed, getting up. "I'm just going to bed, then," she said and walked out.

Kyle sat down next to Claire and texted Amanda. "She's not coming," he wrote.

Amanda got the text and saw Jim enter. He surveyed the room, and she waived him over.

"Hi," he said, pulling out a chair. "Where are Emily and Kyle?" he asked.

"They're back at the motel," she said. "Kyle's coming back here in a few."

"Okay," Jim said. "They're going back tomorrow, but we have work to do. I took care of the warrant in Florida, but we still have to deal with the issue here."

"Well, then, won't they just do the deal?" she asked. "Like we had planned?"

"Hopefully," Jim said, "but I don't know."

Amanda watched the people around her dancing. "You don't dance anymore?" she asked.

"Not in a long time," he sighed.

Amanda nodded. "Will you dance with me, please?" she asked.

Jim shook his head. "I'm not in a dancing mood," he said.

"That's the best time to dance," she said with an insistent smile, holding out her hand. "I'm sad, and you know it makes me feel better."

He laughed and took her hand. "One dance," he said.

Jim could feel the years melting away again as they danced. For a moment, they were back at Shank Hall. It was freezing outside, and he was a student with only a C – in Spanish to worry him. He pulled her close and spun her around like the old days, but stopped when he spied Emily watching them. Their eyes locked for a moment, and she walked away.

Jim set Amanda down and chased after Emily, knowing this was bad.

"Em," he breathed as he caught up to her, grabbing her arm.

"Don't touch me," she screamed, fierce tears running down her cheeks.

"We were just dancing, it means nothing," he tried to reassure her.

"It meant something the last two and half years." She turned on him, her eyes filled with fire and glass. "You don't dance, remember?"

"I don't anymore, I always felt awkward," he tried lamely.

"You know what, you're right." She laughed a hard, bitter sound.

"Come on Em, calm down," he said

"No, you're right about everything. I'm a fool," she spat. "I'm a fool for thinking I could stop you from being with her."

"I don't want to be with her, I want to be with you," he insisted, trying to block her attempt at storming off.

"Really?" Emily said, suddenly calm. "You want to be with me?"

"Yes," he said, the relief loosening his entire body. "Of course I do." He reached out his hand, cupping her cheek.

"Still, are you sure?" she asked, searching his eyes for the answer.

"Yes!" he said again.

"Perhaps you should make a list of pros and cons, just to be sure," she suggested, her words ice against his ears.

He froze. Jim had never meant for her to see that list. "Hey, seven of those eight cons were about your crazy mother and sisters," he said.

"Yeah, and remember what eight was?" she asked.

He did remember, but was hoping she didn't. It was more than four months ago, before this whole mess with Amanda had interrupted the smooth progress of their lives. "I didn't ...." He sought for words, but they evaded him.

"You remember number eight, right?" she asked. "What was it, again?"

"Emily, I didn't know this was going to happen," he tried to explain.

Emily started laughing, hollowing out to a near-hysterical edge. "That's what makes it so fucking perfect for you, it's not even your fault!" she cried. "'#8: I'll always love Amanda.'"

Jim reached out for her again, but she slapped his hand away.

"Goodbye," she said, and took off toward the motel.

Chapter 48

Emily stopped when saw the driver leaning against the limo. "Let's go," she shouted, throwing herself into the back.

The driver hopped in. "Where to?" he asked.

"Just drive," she said, scrubbing furiously at her face. "Please."

The driver pulled away, directing the limo down the main road into town. Emily sat in back, trying to stop crying. She went to grab a bottle from the bar, but it was empty.

"Out of booze?" she asked the driver.

"Sorry," he said. "I haven't had the chance to resupply."

Emily looked out the window and noticed a small, backlit sign on a building that looked like an ice rink, or bowling alley. "Patty's," it read.

"That a bar?" she asked.

"I think so," the driver replied. "Want me to stop?"

"Yes, please," she said, opening the door before he had come to a halt. The building looked like corrugated steel on the outside, rusted and ugly. But there was music coming from within, and a couple cars and motorcycles parked in front. As she entered, the music swelled in welcome.

Southern rock played across the sound system, reverberating off the cheap wood paneling of the interior. There was a jukebox, some booths lining the wall, a few tables and chairs marked by numerous repairs, a bar on the opposite wall, and an entry to another room that looked likely to house some pool tables.

The clientele here was different from The Milky Way, she noticed right away. There were about a dozen of the rough around the edges sort, and she considered leaving. But she wanted a drink, and this was the only other bar in town.

She walked up to the bar, and could see a few people playing pool in the back.

"What can I get for you?" the large woman bartender offered.

"Let's start with a beer," she said, "then we'll take it from there."

The woman planted a bottle of Coors in front of her, and Emily took a long sip.

"Buy you a drink?" a voice asked from behind her.

"No thanks," she said without looking up.

"You sure?" the voice asked again.

Emily turned around to face the guy, a thin man with a patchy beard and flannel shirt. He looked like the after poster for meth.

"Got one, thanks," she said, turning away again.

"Maybe we can go somewhere?" he suggested.

"No thanks," she said, "just here for the beer."

"Come on, give a guy chance," he said. Emily was annoyed, but before she could say anything the bartender chimed in.

"The woman said no," the bartender said. "Don't be an ass."

"Fine," the guy huffed, holding up his hands. "Just trying to be polite."

Emily looked up at the bartender to thank her.

"Don't worry about it, have your drink and relax. Ain't no one gonna bother you again in here," she said. "I know the feeling."

Emily smiled and took a seat on one of the stools. She watched a big guy take an ill-advised shot on the pool table before realizing it was Chief Morris. He missed, sinking the eight ball.

"Haha!" his adversary laughed.

Morris stretched and shook his head. "This rounds on me, I guess."

"Thanks, Chief," the other player said. "Make mine a double."

"Now, now," the chief said, "we're playing for beers. Don't be upping the stakes on your only win of the night."

Emily watched the chief walk over. He looked different out of uniform, somehow even brawnier in jeans and a faded grey t-shirt. He had a tattoo on his left arm, but it was too faded to make it out. The one thing always easy to recognize was the cannon on his left hip. It was a big gun, but fit him fine.

"Two," the chief said, holding up two fingers for the bartender.

"You a big pool player, Chief?" Emily asked.

Morris looked at her and back at the bartender. "I'm off duty," he said. "You can call me Dan."

"He called you Chief," Emily remarked.

Morris looked over at the other player. "Him?" he said. "He's on parole, so for him I'm always on duty."

"Playing pool and buying parolees beer," Emily observed. "That's not what I expected from you."

Morris laughed. "Hell, if I couldn't socialize with folks I'd arrested, I'd be eating alone every night. Couldn't even talk to my own sister, isn't that right, Patty?" he asked the bartender as she planted two beers in front of him.

"How about you play me for a beer?" Emily asked.

Morris laughed and turned to Patty. "Can you run this over to him before he accuses me of welching?" Morris asked his sister. He then turned to Emily, and looked her in the eyes. "You want me to play pool with you for beers?" he asked.

"Why not?" she asked.

Morris considered her for a moment. "You know, I lost my first truck, a little Ford pickup, in this very bar to a man from out of town who opened with the same offer," he said. "Matter of fact, he had that very same look in his eyes."

Emily smiled, and knew he wasn't falling for it. "You think I'm hustling you?" she asked.

"I don't think you play games you can't win," he said.

"Oh Chief, I mean, Dan ... You're wrong there," she said. "I am capable of playing a long game I know I can't win. Denial is a powerful thing, you know."

"I know you had a rough day," he said. "For what it's worth, I'm sorry you got caught up in all that."

Emily nodded. "Looking back, what do you think you should have said to the guy who won your truck?"

Morris leaned his back against the bar. "It's funny you should ask," he said. "For years, I asked myself, 'Dan, why didn't you just buy that man a drink and move along?'"

Emily downed the last of her beer. "Here's your chance to rewrite history, then," she said, moseying over to an empty booth. Morris walked up with a couple beer bottles.

"I'm not certain it's appropriate for me to be buying you drinks, considering the current situation and all," he said as he slid into the booth across from her.

"But you are?" she asked.

"I suppose the wheels of justice can withstand one beer," he said.

The first beer, her second, went down quickly, and there was small talk about the history of the bar, and how he'd helped his sister buy the place from the previous owner after working there twenty years.

"Did you really arrest your sister?" she asked.

"I had to!" he said. "She took a shot at her husband."

"You're kidding?" she asked

"I am not," he insisted. "Let's ask her. Hey Patty, you miss Earl?"

he called out.

"Only because you jerked away the shot gun," she replied.

"She never get's tired of that joke," he said. "And in her defense, he was cheating on her, the scumbag."

The second beer, her third, brought them to her legal career, primarily how she went from working in the public defender's office to her current position at a prestigious law firm.

"You got one of those, 'I put him back on the street and he raped and killed again' stories?" he asked.

"Anyone in the L.A. public defenders office for over a year has one of those stories," she admitted. "But I believe in the system, you know? I just had to take it as part of the job. It's not the part I had to get away from."

"What was it you were trying to escape that brought you to defending higher class criminals?" Morris asked, somehow managing to avoid the judgmental tone that usually accompanied the question.

"Well, I really wanted to get away from the Hyundai I was driving, and the new job helped with that," she joked. "But honestly, it was the stupidity. When I defend the clients at the firm, they know they did something wrong, and they're even willing to take a certain level of accountability for it. Never the level the DA would like, of course, but some. I got sick of the people I was defending, who must have known they broke the law, acting like they're stuck in a Kafka novel when they get arrested."

Morris nodded.

"I'm sorry, Kafka was a writer," she said. "He wrote this book called ..."

"I've read *The Trial*," he interrupted, laughing. "I did go to college, Ms. Perkins."

"Sorry," she said shaking her head. "That was rude."

"Perfectly understandable," he said. "The accent's confusing for you foreigners," he smirked.

The third, Emily's fourth, beer came with a complimentary shot of tequila.

"Tell me, Dan," she said, sizing him up. "How long have you been police chief?"

"Oh, must be twelve years now," he figured.

"And was your dad chief before you?" she asked.

"No," Morris said, "this area used to be covered by the Sheriff's Department."

"So, the town made a police department?" she asked.

"Yep," he said.

"And you're the first?" she asked.

"I am," he admitted.

"Think Sam will be the chief after you?" she asked.

"I think we both know the answer to that question," he said with a sad smile.

"Yeah," she said. "There are worse things than your kid not wanting to be a cop, you know."

"Yeah," he agreed. "I've been giving that some thought."

"Married?" she asked.

"No, not anymore," he said.

"Wow, someone divorced you?" she asked.

"You find that hard to believe?" he asked, laughing.

"You just seem like one of those 'what you see is what you get' kind of guys," she mused. "I would think a woman would appreciate that."

"Yeah, but sometimes, that's referred to as 'stubborn and boring,'" he said. "Her words, of course, not mine."

"Wow," Emily said. "That's not nice."

"No, it wasn't, but you can't fault a woman for honesty," he said.

"What does she do now?" Emily asked, "Probably married a

total douche."

"She moved to Jacksonville and married a real estate agent," he said. "So, yeah," he laughed.

"Fuck marriage!" Emily said. "Overrated."

"Oh, I wouldn't say that," he disagreed slowly. "I mean, it's impossible to not feel a little bitter losing the one who you were supposed to grow old, but she gave me some of the best years of my life, and a pair of great sons."

"I guess it's hard to hate someone you used to love," she said.

"I think the everlasting part is what makes it love," he said, sipping his beer.

"Oh, Dan, are you a romantic?" she asked, smiling. "What's your other boy do? Is he also a cop?"

Morris looked down for a moment at his beer. "We lost our oldest in Iraq in '05."

For the first time, Emily saw something akin to vulnerability in the chief.

"I'm sorry," she said. "I didn't know."

"Thank you," he said. "He was awarded a bronze star for his actions," he said.

Emily sat still and silent for a moment. "You must be very proud of him," she said.

The chief nodded. "We are," he said.

Emily continued her silence until Morris realized how silent he was, too. "Sorry," he said. "It's been a rough day for me, too. What brought you out to Patty's?" he asked. "You got the Milky Way right across the street from your motel."

"Yeah, I needed a change of venue," she said.

"Didn't like the music?" he asked. "Because, we don't have a Karaoke machine here, and I'll shoot anyone who tries to hook one up."

Emily laughed. "It was the dancing that bothered me, I guess."

"Oh, I would have taken you for a dancer," he stated. "You look like the type that enjoys breaking lose every now and then."

"Yeah, I do like to dance," she said. "I would have liked to dance with my father at my wedding, but it wasn't in the cards. And evidently, the groom only dances with other women, so I'm not sure there'll be much dancing in my future."

"I guess I can see where the disenchantment with marriage is coming from," he said.

"How about you, Dan? Just supporting your sister's endeavor, or are you not a fan of the Milky Way, either?" she asked.

"I like the Milky Way," he said. "The wife and I used to go line dancing there every Friday night, back when we were married."

Emily laughed and choked on her beer. "You line dance? I would love to see that."

"What's wrong with line dancing?" Morris asked.

"Other than it's the whitest dance ever known to man?" she said.

"Oh, that's not true," Morris said. "Ask your buddy Reggie and his wife about it, they were right there with us more times than not."

Emily laughed at the image in her mind. "It's just not real dancing, a bunch of people standing in a line, doing the exact same thing at the exact same time. There's no personal expression, which is the only reason to dance," she said.

"No, you're just not getting it," Morris said. "There's more to it than that."

"Enlighten me, if you will. What's the point of line dancing?" she said, spinning her empty bottle until it pointed at the chief.

"It's about everyone getting together to blow off some steam. It's about getting dressed up with your friends and family and forgetting about all the other things for a while. And the fact you're doing it together is what makes it fun," he said. "Sometimes the moves get tricky, or sometimes you're a little off balance that day, but it's okay. Because when someone falls out of step, they have everyone they love around 'em to laugh it off and get 'em back on track. It's about being reminded that when you screw up, you're not alone. And isn't that what we all need sometimes, to be reminded we're not alone?"

Emily sat still a moment, and for some reason her mother briefly entered her mind. She straightened her bottle, drying a little spillage with her napkin.

"How'd you get so wise, Chief?" she finally asked.

Morris thought about it a moment. "My daddy used to say if you listen more than you speak, you'll grow wise," he said. "Then he'd slap me upside my head every time I spoke, so it kinda just came natural, I guess."

Emily chuckled. "And to think I didn't like you at first," she admitted.

"Unimaginable," he said smiling. "Now how about that dance?"

"There's going to be a line dance here?" she said, looking around at a rough crowd of single men.

"Nah, these guys aren't quite as into it as I am, so I guess it would just be the two of us," he said. "That's more what you had in mind, right?"

Emily thought about it a moment. She decided she was owed a dance tonight, damnit.

He took her hand and walked over to the jukebox. Surprisingly, Lionel Ritchie's "Stuck on You" filled the air, and he took her hand in his right, and placed the fingers of his left hand on the small of her back.

"I would have thought you were strictly a country guy," she said as they danced in slow, lazy circles.

"Watcha mean?" Morris asked.

"Lionel Ritchie?" she prompted.

"Oh, Lionel's a good ol' boy from up in Tuskegee," he drawled. "Anyone that don't think Lionel's singing country music ain't listening."

Emily leaned into Chief Morris, who ended up being a much better dancer than she'd predicted, and listened to the song. It was indeed a country song, she decided.

The music ended, and he gave her a light kiss on the forehead. "Thank you for making my day a little better at the end," he said. "Would you like a ride home?"

Emily looked up at Morris, and thought briefly what it might be like if she went with him.

"I mean, Patty will be happy to drive you while I lock up here," he said, smiling.

Emily smiled, liking the chief even more. "I've got a driver waiting for me out front," she said.

"Oh, yes, I forgot," the chief said, smile broadening. "You fancy city lawyers ride in style."

Emily kissed Morris on the cheek. "Thanks, Dan," she said. "Thank you for a beautiful dance."

"The pleasure was all mine," he said as he graciously escorted her to the door.

Emily rode back with the windows and sunroof open, trying to clear her head. Away from Dan's sobering presence, she could feel the alcohol kicking in with a sudden vengeance. Her mood was improved after her evening with the chief, but still felt she had to deal with the issue at hand. The limo pulled into the parking lot and she swayed cautiously to her room, stopping before she opened the door. She considered for a moment, and instead made her wobbly way to Amanda's.

Emily didn't know what she was going to say, but knew she had something to say. She knocked on the door and waited. She went to knock again, but the door opened to reveal Amanda standing in her towel again.

"Do you ever wear clothes to the door?" she asked.

"Sorry," Amanda said.

Emily stood silent for a moment. "Why are you always in that towel?" she asked, challenging Amanda with her eyes.

Amanda raised her hands to her head, letting the towel drop to her feet as she struck a pose, smiling wantonly.

Emily looked at Amanda for a moment, puzzled. "Why did you do that?" she asked.

"I felt like it," Amanda said simply.

Emily nodded gravely, and grabbed Amanda, pulling her close and kissing her. Amanda kissed her back, and they shuffled clumsily back to the bed, kicking the door closed behind them.

Chapter 49

As usual, the pain woke Amanda. She looked over and saw Emily still sleeping. She reached to the nightstand, grabbed her painkillers and a bottle of water. She had just taken a sip of water when she heard the door opening. She panicked, and tried to wake up Emily, but it was too late. Claire stood in the doorway, wide eyed and obviously jumping to a juicy conclusion.

"Wow," Claire whistled, staring.

Emily slowly started to come to, grabbing the sheet when she saw the open door, not fully remembering where she was.

"Claire, you need to knock!" Amanda insisted.

"I did!" she swore.

"Oh, shit." Emily said, glancing from her pile of clothes on the floor to Amanda's naked body. "Oh, shit," she said again, struggling to bring last night into focus. "Can you go, please?" Emily asked Claire.

"Yeah, okay," she said, "but I totally knew you were hitting on me that day," she smirked as Amanda closed the door.

Emily fell back onto the bed, covering her face with a pillow. "What time is it?" she mumbled through the fabric.

"11:38," Amanda reported.

Emily didn't know what time would be ideal, but nearly noon

seemed especially bad.

"Are you freaking out?" Amanda asked.

Emily laughed. "A little," she admitted as she was overcome with giggles.

"Sorry," Amanda said.

"Don't be," Emily said, slowly sitting up and remembering to breathe. "From what I remember, I was a very willing participant."

"Yeah," Amanda said, nodding her head and smiling. "Very! Until, of course, we got to the bed. Then you passed out on me."

Emily paused, catching her sigh of relief before it could escape. "I don't know what to say at this point," Emily admitted, worrying about hurting Amanda's feelings.

"You don't have to say anything," Amanda assured her, brushing Emily's hair from her face. "I know it wasn't anything more than fun."

Emily leaned in and kissed Amanda's forehead. "I think it was more than that," she said, "but I'm getting married."

"You think he doesn't love you, but he does," Amanda said.

"Maybe, but he will always love you more," Emily sighed. "And I understand why."

"He loves you," Amanda repeated. "Don't worry about his feelings for me, I'm a ghost from his past. You'll go home and get married and I promise, I won't be an issue."

Amanda got out of bed, kissed Emily, and headed to the bathroom.

Emily checked her phone and saw a half dozen voicemails from Jim. She was about to call him when there was a knock at the door. She considered for a moment, knowing whom it might be. She got up, covering herself with the sheet, and answered the door.

Jim looked surprised, and then noticed the sheet. "I was looking for you," he said.

"I didn't mean to worry you," she apologized.

Jim nodded and looked over her head to the rumpled bed. "This is one of those times where, 'It's not what it looks like' will work," he offered.

"No, it won't," Emily said.

"I can't believe you," he said. "What the hell are you thinking?"

"I wasn't going to be honest, but it turned out pretty good in the end," she said.

"Well, I'm sure it felt great," he snapped.

"I'm trying to figure out if you're jealous I spent the night with her, or that she slept with me, or just that you weren't invited," she said.

"I'm not jealous. I'm pissed this is your idea on how to fix things," he insisted.

"I'm not trying to fix anything," Emily said. "It just happened, and I'm not apologizing."

"Oh, why would you apologize?" Jim demanded. "Why apologize for making me worry all night that you'd been murdered, and then cheating on me with my ex-girlfriend?"

"Hey, why do you get to want her, and I don't?" she asked.

"Because I was in love with her," he said, "and it's hard to let her go. You don't have that problem."

"Maybe I am in love with her," Emily snapped back, "maybe I don't want to let her go."

"Oh, are you coming out to me, too? You're gay now, is that what you're telling me?"

"No, but I like being with her," Emily said. "And I don't know if I'm ready to say goodbye yet, either."

"Well, let me know when you are," Jim said. "I'm going to take care of this shit today, and I'm heading home. Stay as long as you like. Hell, bring her back to L.A.! I'm sure your mother is bound to like her more than me."

Jim stormed to the car.

"Shows what you know, my mother hates lesbians!" Emily yelled, standing outside in her bare feet, the sheet barely covering her ass. She was about to go in when she saw Claire watching from the next room. "What?" she snapped.

"Nothing!" Claire said, jumping back. "I just don't want you guys to go!"

Emily walked back into the room and saw Amanda standing there.

"What was that?" Amanda asked.

"I don't know," Emily said. "I just wanted him to know what it feels like, okay?" she admitted.

"You wanted to hurt him?" Amanda asked.

"Yes, and I know it's bad," Emily said, "but I can't be with someone who doesn't want to be with me."

"I told you he does," Amanda said.

"I know that's what you say, but I just don't feel it from him," Emily said. "Not anymore. And maybe I didn't really feel it before you called either, I don't know."

Emily threw her clothes on, grabbed her shoes and walked out of the room. She was about to open her door when someone called her name.

"Ms. Perkins," Morris called again.

Emily turned around and smiled. "Hey, Chief!" she said, genuinely glad to see him again.

Morris got out of his truck and walked over.

"Miss me already?" Emily quipped, but Morris was even more glum than usual. "What's up?" Emily said, concern now creasing her brow.

Morris bowed his head and looked uncomfortable. "Sam was riding me on the timeline between Ms. Jeffries' traffic stop and her ... event," he began.

"Yeah?" Emily asked.

"After her arrest, we sent the blood from our DUI test to a lab in Birmingham ..."

"You had no right," Emily interrupted. "Whatever you found cannot be admitted into evidence, that's a blatant overreach of your right to ..."

Morris stopped her with an upheld hand. "It was to double check our results, because we didn't show enough alcohol in her system to trigger ... well, what she did. I think you need to read this," Morris said, holding up a folder.

Emily looked at it, afraid to touch it. "The report? What does it say?" she asked. "I'll argue against its admissibility, anyhow."

Morris handed her the folder. "Know when to stop fighting," he sighed. "Sometimes, it's better to trust people."

Emily watched Morris leave, then walked into her room and set the unopened file on the table. She started the shower, deciding to wash up first and clear her head, but soon found herself back in front of the table, considering the folder. She sat down and flipped to the first page.

Chapter 50

Jim stopped at the light and checked his phone.

"So, she was at Amanda's the whole night?" Kyle asked.

"Yep," Jim said.

"Okay," Kyle said. "Girls do that all the time, have sleepovers and shit, right?"

Jim quietly looked out his window.

"They … were together, you think?" Kyle asked.

Jim didn't respond.

"See, this is what's confusing," Kyle said, "because that really does it for me."

Jim turned and glared at Kyle.

"Sorry," Kyle said. "That was insensitive."

The light turned green and Jim hit the gas. He drove to the library and walked in with Kyle.

"Jim, Kyle, how's it going?" Reggie greeted them.

"It's been a rare day, Reggie," Kyle said before Jim could answer.

"Well, hopefully this goes as planned, and we help some people today," Reggie offered. "I got the mayor coming in, as well as at least a dozen homeowners in immediate need."

"Where do we set up?" Jim asked.

"We're over in this little room here," Reggie said, pointing to the same room that held his clinic.

"Where are we on Amanda's case?" Jim asked walking to the room. "Franks discover yet there's no warrant coming?"

"Yeah, and he's pissed," Reggie said. "Going on about how you must have done something illegal. But he's having to drop the GTA charge."

"And the rest?" Jim asked.

"He's going to keep going," Reggie sighed. "He thinks the only way to redeem himself is to put Amanda in jail."

"Well, he's an idiot," Jim said. "You still comfortable being the go between on this?"

"Yeah, I think it's better for all concerned," Reggie said.

"Good. Tell him I'm cutting a check to Chad Mitchell's campaign fund every day this case drags on," Jim said. "And I've got a colleague coming down who used to work for the ABA, and she's going to go through the last five years of his cases, looking for any inconsistencies. And when she finds something, and I have no doubt she will, we're going after him personally."

"That's a lot to say," Reggie said. "But I'll relay the message."

"I want him to see me coming, and know what his little stunt has earned him. How much was spent for the last DA election in this county?" Jim asked.

"Maybe ten grand," Reggie said.

"Let Franks know I've already put Chad's account in the black, then." Jim said. "You invited him, right?

"Of course. He's a big part of the legal team in this town, it would have be strange to not invite him, anyway." Reggie said. "But you sure there's nothing he can do to trip us up?" The concern spread itself across Reggie's face. "You've done some fine work here, Jim. I don't want this to fall apart because of a personal vendetta."

"It won't," Jim said. "I just want to see his face. But you better keep him away from me, or he won't be leaving with his teeth," he growled, failing to reassure Reggie.

Jim looked around the room and set up his laptop, plugging it into the projector. A group of men called Reggie over, and Kyle came over to help.

"Need me to do anything?" Kyle asked.

Jim looked at Kyle and suddenly felt lightheaded. The stress from earlier, now combined with a case of mild stage freight, was getting to him. "I need some air," he said as he walked to the door. Kyle opened it for him, and Jim stepped outside, taking deep breaths.

"Dude, you okay?" Kyle asked.

"I'll be fine," Jim said, sitting on a bench. "Just dealing with a lot of shit."

"I know," Kyle said, "but it's going to work out. That Franks guy is a pussy, and he's going to back down, and Emily's not gay, she's just having cold feet or something. And this thing here, well, you're doing them a favor. They'll be thankful."

Jim leaned back and steadied his breathing. "I don't know if she wants to be with me," he said. "I was never certain."

"We're talking about Emily, right?" Kyle clarified.

"Yeah," Jim said with a cynic's smile. "I'm talking about my fiancée, who I don't think really loves me."

"I know what you mean," Kyle said.

"What?" Jim said. "What does that mean?"

"I mean, I would feel the same way if I were you," Kyle explained. "Amanda's easy to love. She's a puppy dog everyone wants to hold and take care of. She's a wreck. I bet when you met her, she was already in some kind of trouble."

Jim laughed. "Did she tell you about that?" he asked.

"No, I just know her now," Kyle said. "It's not her fault, she's just one of those people. Emily, on the other hand ... that woman scares me. She should be an agent or something, she's mean."

Jim laughed again. "She can be brutal," he agreed, "but she's really only like that for her clients."

"Yeah, but she's not someone you take care of," Kyle explained. "She doesn't need you, and that's scary."

Jim thought about it and realized Kyle was on to something. He'd always wanted to take care of Amanda, but Emily was the person with whom he wanted to spend his life.

Jim stood up and took a breath. "You're a smart kid, Kyle," he said. "I'm glad you came."

"Thanks," Kyle said, "but can I ask you a question?"

"Yeah, shoot," Jim said as he walked back to the door.

"You really spank it while you're asleep?" Kyle asked. "Emily claims you're like totally dead to the world when you do it."

"Don't believe a word that woman says," Jim said, "she's a lawyer."

"Yeah, I didn't," Kyle said as they walked inside, "until Amanda confirmed it. You're seriously weird, you know that?"

*

People started to arrive within the hour. Jim recognized Clint Nelson, the owner of what had been the only gas station in town, and shook his hand.

"You're having a foreclosure issue?" Jim asked.

"Yeah," Clint admitted. "We were having trouble before the explosion, and now with the insurance holding things up, I don't think we'll make it."

Jim, feeling bad for Clint, promised he would make things right.

"So, your name is Clint?" Kyle asked. "And you own Eastwood's?"

Jim moved on. He'd already heard the story, and there were many faces with stories to share. The room slowly filled to capacity, and Jim was introduced to the mayor, as well as several members of the city council. Chief Morris arrived and took a seat next to the mayor, where they seemed to be discussing an issue with a road closing.

The room was nearly full, and Reggie decided to start the meeting.

Chapter 51

Emily closed the folder and leaned back in the chair. The shower was still running and the room had turned steamy, adding to the surreal feeling in her head. She got up to turn the shower off, and had to sit on the toilet seat for a moment while she tried to absorb the news. Somehow, even in the confusion and shock of it all, things suddenly made more sense.

Emily, who had been half undressed for her shower, put on some pants and the sweatshirt she bought a couple days before, then walked over to Amanda's room. She knocked, and tried to think about what to say. She knocked a second time and the door opened, again with Amanda in a towel.

"It's like you know when I'm going to shower," she said. "No hot water anyway, though."

Emily stood there, waiting for the words to come that could convey what she felt, but all that came were the three words that must have shaken Amanda's life months ago. "You have cancer," she said.

Amanda stood motionless in the doorway, until her posture fell into the shape of utter defeat.

A thousand questions, a need for precision and details were grinding Emily's mind to a halt. She didn't know how to proceed.

"Six months," Amanda said, "eight, maybe." She turned and

walked back into the room.

"That's how long you've known, or how long you ... think," Emily fumbled. She wasn't prepared to be tactful. Not many were in this situation, she remembered. God, how she missed her father.

Amanda thought for a moment. "Both, actually," she said. "But I've known it was a possibility since my mother died. I've always had problems down there," she added, "so it was just a matter of time."

"Why didn't you tell me?" Emily asked, "Why didn't you tell either of us, we could have taken care of this right away!"

Amanda sat on the edge of the bed, "I don't know," she said.

"Well, you must have had a reason," Emily demanded. "You intentionally kept this from me, or us. You must have known this would have made a difference!"

"Well, now you know," Amanda said, "so I guess I can just plead crazy from grief, or on drugs to help deal with the constant pain, or whatever. Then you can move on and feel like you've done your good deed."

"That's not what would happen," Emily insisted.

"I wanted him back." Amanda turned her face away from Emily. "I wanted him back, but not out of pity. I wanted him to want me again. I didn't want to be alone, and he was the only person I could think of being with. But he's gone, and that's my fault. Now he's yours. Help me not spend the rest of my life in a prison, and I'll leave you two alone forever. I promise."

"That's not going to happen," Emily declared, planting herself with all the flexibility of an oak in front of Amanda. "He loves you, has never stopped loving you, never will. And, as weird as it sounds, I love you, too." Emily bent down and stroked Amanda's hair, in the sweet way she'd seen her do to Jim. "And, if you think either of us are the type of people to let someone we love run off to die alone, and without a fight, than you have badly misjudged me. You've misjudged both of us."

Amanda's fight against tears was failing, and was lost all together as she felt Emily's lips on forehead. She wrapped her arms around her. Emily whispered in her ear, "You're not alone, Amanda. We love you, and you're coming home with us."

Chapter 52

"The plan is simple, really," Jim explained, projecting his voice through the swollen gathering of locals. "You're going to agree with the bank on what your homes are worth, and you're going to buy them at that price."

Jim projected the first slide of his presentation. "This is an actual house here in town, and its appraised value back in 2006. It was a healthy hundred and seventy-five grand. The owner was encouraged by his bank to take out a home loan at a really low interest rate, which would be adjusted over time. It was good deal, and the bank offered him a total package of one hundred and fifty-five."

Jim moved to the next slide, showing the same home. "Six years later, this same house is worth only eighty-five," he said. "The house is the same, the town is the same, the owners are the same. Only the economy is different."

Jim clicked to the next slide, revealing an upward graph. "Of course, the other thing that somehow changed is the standard interest rate. In spite of everything else, the rate has gone up and up, increasing the monthly payments on the owner's home loan."

The next slide showed a large foreclosure sign. "You've seen the result in almost every street of this community. People can't afford to make the increased payments on their homes, homes that are now worth far less than their loans, and the bank forecloses on the property. It's happening all over this town, and across the nation, really," he said.

"Reggie has met with some of you and told you how to push back against the banks to buy yourselves more time, but this doesn't fix the problem," Jim continued. "We need a solution, and I think that solution is to let the banks foreclose, and then sell the homes."

The slide flipped, now displaying a picture of a big 'For Sale' sign. "The banks don't expect more than eighty-five for this home, and comparable prices for most the homes being foreclosed. When all the homes start to sell for these low prices, they will drop further, bringing down all the home values in the area."

"Doesn't sound like much of a plan yet," heckled someone in the audience.

"You're right," Jim said. "But what if the owner turned around and bought his home back?" he asked. "What if you could sign a piece of paper and own your home for the price the bank says it's now worth?" The audience seemed to like the idea, but Jim knew they didn't yet understand its complexity.

"The problem is, you can't do that," Jim continued. "If you default on your payments, your credit will be no good for years, as far as home loans go. No bank will grant you a mortgage. But it's possible for someone else, someone with an excellent credit rating and demonstrable ability to pay, to buy your home, and essentially, sell it back to you for the price they paid to the bank."

Jim clicked on a slide, presenting an aerial view of Ashford. "The town. The city of Ashford can buy up all the houses currently scheduled for foreclosure, and essentially resell them back to the owners." Jim said. "We do this by creating what's called a real estate investment trust, a REIT, owned by the city. The city-owned REIT will buy the homes at current, fair market value. You will then sign a lease-to-own option with the city, giving you back ownership of your home, except at a monthly payment and a total amount much lower than you were previously paying."

The audience seemed confused, but Jim continued. "You won't even have to pretend to move out, you just keep living in your home, and pay less money."

"Excuse me," Franks broke in, "but this is ridiculous. Explain to me how this is not defrauding the banks?"

"Mr. Franks, I knew you would have a question like that," Jim said tightly, imagining alligator teeth closing around Franks' arm. "I'm not going to be around town much longer, and Reggie can't do this alone, so I asked someone local to help us out. Chad, can you come up here?"

Chad Mitchell, the young man running against Franks, came up on stage. "Chad, can you help Mr. Franks understand the law?" Jim asked, stepping back.

"Sure thing," Chad said, only slightly smug. "See Charlie, what you don't get about criminal law is the idea of intent. No one here signed these mortgage with the knowledge this would happen. Did the banks know when they encouraged people to sign? Well, that's a good question, and one I would've investigated, if I was you. But if the good people here entered those agreements in good faith, and now choose to let the banks do what they are threatening to do, then that's all legal."

Franks squirmed in his seat, agitated over the staged mocking.

"There is nothing illegal, or unethical, about letting the banks take the property," Jim reiterated.

The mayor, showing more respect than Franks had, raised his hand. "Yes, Mr. Mayor?" Jim asked.

"This all sounds very progressive, has anyone done this before?" he asked.

Jim thought about the question, and knew this was it. "No," he said. "There is no town I know of that has ever attempted this." He held his breath.

"Then why do you think we should?" the mayor asked.

Jim looked at Reggie, who knew the answer, and could probably have explained it better, but Jim was going to attempt it anyway.

"You have something here we don't have in L.A.," he said. "New York doesn't have it, Chicago doesn't have it, just about every city in this country doesn't have it. You're a small town. You trust each other. You look out for one another. You've got community."

"I see the people volunteering to fix up Eastwood's, not for money, but because Clint's their neighbor. I see the people doing grocery runs for the elderly and those without cars. I see Reggie going door to door, and bringing in students to help those who have legal questions. These aren't volunteer groups, or organizations; these are people who don't need any call to action. You all just look out for one another."

Jim looked up and saw Emily and Amanda walk in, hand in hand. "This town is facing a huge problem. Nearly one out of five families are facing a threat to their homes," Jim said. "If you all decide to work together, you can do something the rest of the country can't: stay the course and maintain the line. 'You look out for your own' is something I used to hear about the South, quite a bit, and to be honest, I used to think it sounded selfish, maybe even racist. But meeting you people in person, and watching how you do things, I understand it's something else. You're at your best when you're working together, for each other."

"Are you saying there are some here who would be helping to pay for another's home?" Franks demanded. "You'd expect me to help pay for someone else's bad decision making? This isn't new; it's called socialism!" he finished.

"Everyone's going to pay their part, Franks," Jim sighed. "It's just that some may have to pay on a different timeline than others. It's about helping your neighbor when they're struggling. By the way, are you the Franks we should be speaking to? Don't you live with your mother, in the house your father paid for?"

Reggie got up and spent thirty minutes explaining the specifics of the plan, and then Chad Mitchell announced his intent to file suit against four major banks on behalf of the town. If the town elected him, he said, he would go after those banks criminally, too. Because, as Jim helped him write, "Our DA shouldn't be the one who we're afraid of; he should be the one that protects us."

Chapter 53

Jim approached Amanda and Emily at the far end of the room, where he was greeted with hugs. "That was amazing," she gushed. "I had no idea what you were working on. It's brilliant."

"If they can do it," Jim said.

"They can," Emily said. "They're big on that whole we-take-care-of-our-own thing."

Jim looked over at Amanda, who was doing her best impersonation of being happy. "You okay?" Jim asked.

Amanda nodded and quickly looked down. Emily tugged Jim's hand. "We need to talk to Reggie, can you grab him?"

"Why?" Jim asked. "About the case?"

"Please?" Emily asked, "Can you grab him?"

Jim looked over at Amanda, who nodded in soft agreement. He motioned to Reggie, and Emily insisted Amanda and Reggie talk privately.

"What the hell is happening?" Jim asked once they were alone.

"What should have happened from the beginning," Emily said.

"I can handle this," Jim said. "I'm kicking Franks' ass in every way possible. The warrant's quashed, and once Chad's in office, he'll back the original deal for no jail time."

"I saw, and I'm totally proud of how vicious you can be," she glowed with pride. "But this isn't the way it needs to be."

"It's a little late for that," Jim said. "Just let me finish this, so we can go back to the way we were. Sweetheart, please."

Emily looked around the room, needing to get Jim away. "Baby, we need to talk," she said.

"About what?" Jim said, getting agitated. Suddenly, he didn't want to let go of her arm.

"Let's go to the limo; we need to go somewhere private," she said.

"I'm in the middle of this thing," Jim said, "and so was Reggie."

"Yeah, but this is important, and I need to speak to you privately, right now," she insisted.

"Right this minute?" he asked, his voice beginning to quaver. He could feel disaster looming in her determination.

"Yes," Emily said, "I'm sorry, but yes. You need to know this right now."

She pulled him outside and he stopped her once out the door.

"Just tell me what's going on," Jim pleaded.

"We have to go," Emily said. "We have to get back to L.A. soon, like tonight, if possible, or tomorrow morning at the latest."

"I told you, I'll be back in a few days," Jim said, relieved to hear her say 'we,' at least.

Emily was starting to get emotional and put her hands on his shoulders, although she didn't know if she was preparing him or herself.

"What's going on?" he asked again.

"We have to get Amanda to a hospital," she said. "A good one, the best."

"What's wrong with her?" he asked, his worry changing direction. "Why did you bring her here if she's sick?"

"She's dying, baby," Emily whispered. "She's dying."

"What?" Jim asked. "What does that mean?"

"Ovarian cancer," she said, "she should be getting treatment, and that's what she was doing in Florida. We need to get her somewhere right away."

Jim pushed Emily off him. "She's not dying," he said. "She's always a wreck of some sort, but she's fine. She would have told me. She would have told me, if she had cancer."

Emily tried to reach out, but Jim slapped her hand away. "Bullshit," he said, letting his anger carry him back into the building.

He strode to the room holding Reggie and Amanda, prepared to call bullshit again on the whole matter. Looking into the glass, though, he saw Reggie hugging Amanda as she cried. He knew. He backed away from the door and felt his insides go numb.

Emily was just a few steps behind him, and pushed him into the next room, closing the door. "We have to trust Reggie to get this thing put aside so we can take her home," she insisted. Jim leaned against the wall, his chest feeling the impact of a cannon ball.

"Why didn't she tell me?" he asked. "She told you?"

"She didn't," Emily said. "I found it in a toxicology report. Well, Morris found it and gave it to me. The drugs listed were all for treating cancer. Except for the Oxy, although I guess in a way it is. At least she doesn't need rehab," Emily tried to joke.

"We need to find a doctor," Jim said, beginning to find comfort in control. "Who do we know in oncology? Is Cedars-Sinai any good with this shit?"

"We will," Emily agreed, "but we need to get her back home first."

Jim's head was starting to clear, and he looked up at Emily. His sweet, fight to the death, fiancée. "You're okay with this?" he asked.

"Of course," she said, hugging him. "We're going to do everything we can."

Jim and Emily sat together for a few minutes before deciding it was time to check on Amanda. Reggie was sitting with her, holding her hands and talking soothingly.

Emily nudged Jim when she saw Chief Morris approaching with the judge.

"I was very impressed with all that," the judge said to Jim. "I have some questions about some specifics, but overall I think you may have helped save some folks' homes. Not to mention win that Mitchell boy the election."

"Thank you, your honor," Jim said. "Reggie is on top of things and should be able to answer any questions you have. And I'm available whenever you need me."

"Right," the judge said, peering into the room where Amanda and Reggie were talking. "I have another matter to discuss with him as well," he explained, knocking on the glass.

Reggie got up and opened the door.

"Reggie, I was just telling Jim here I learned a lot today," the judge said.

"Oh, thank you, your honor," Reggie said.

"Oh yeah, I'm learning all sort of things today," the judge said. "What was it you were telling me, Chief, about the way bail works?"

"Well, I was looking at some of the finer print on our bail docs, and saw something mighty interesting," the chief drawled. "The defendant is not allowed to leave the state, unless they have an emergency medical need, documented by a doctor."

"Oh, so something like a toxicology report would be fine then," the judge said, looking at Reggie. "I'd accept something like that, if I was a judge on such a case, that is. Of course, once the patient was better, they'd have to come stand trial."

"Are you going to be around for about twenty more minutes, your honor?" Reggie asked.

"Oh, I would imagine so," the judge said. "My granddaughter's trying her hardest to impress that good Christian boy from the TV. Gonna break her heart when she figures out he's gay, you know."

Reggie grabbed his phone and started arranging the paperwork.

Amanda got up and hugged the judge. "Thank you," she said.

"No reason to thank me, dear," he said. "When you're feeling better, you're gonna come back here, and don't think you're getting any special favors."

"I won't," she promised.

"Good," the judge said. "Because I really miss my damn coffee in the mornings."

"Sorry," Amanda said. It was the last time she would have to apologize in Ashford, Alabama.

The judge headed off to corral his granddaughter, who was in the process of fondling Kyle's left arm.

Within ten minutes, Reggie had the paperwork ready, and in another ten, Amanda was free to go.

They headed back to the motel and began packing. For Amanda, this meant throwing her few clothes into a thick garbage bag pilfered from the motel's supplies, and she was done in less time than she knew it would take Jim to pack up his toiletries. Leaving her bag outside Emily's door, she headed to the Milky Way, where she'd seen Sam's cruiser parked in the lot. He was sitting alone at a table, and stood upon seeing her.

"I don't know what to say," Sam said, pulling out a chair for her at his table. "I'm sorry."

"It's okay," Amanda consoled him, albeit weakly.

"You're going to get treatment in California, right?" Sam asked. "They have the best doctors, and I'm sure they can help you."

Amanda smiled. "I'm not sure that's possible."

"But you're going to try, right?" Sam insisted. "I mean, you can't just quit. People love you, and you can't just quit on them."

"I promise, I won't just quit," Amanda said.

"I'm sorry you got caught up here," Sam said. "You should have been getting help all this time."

"None of this is your fault, Sam." Amanda grasped his hand in both of hers. "And, I'm glad I got stuck here. I met you."

Sam blushed into a smile. "Can I come see you in California, after you get settled?"

"Of course," Amanda said, "but don't go missing work or anything. I don't want you getting in any more trouble for me."

"I'm not a very good cop anyway," Sam said. "I'm going to leave the job, I've decided."

"Didn't you just tell me I can't quit?" Amanda asked. "Why would you quit?"

"I'm not cut out to be a cop," Sam said. "My dad is, my brother was. I'm just not the hero type, I guess."

"Listen to me," Amanda said, reaching to include his other hand in her grasp. "I don't remember the explosion, but Emily read me the report. You pulled me out of that fire, saving my life. Then, you helped the truck driver, who was on fire, saving his life. And, Clint said without you, the entire building would have been lost. So you kind of saved his life, too."

"But if I had been paying attention, none of that would have happened," Sam reminded her.

"You weren't paying attention because you were helping me off my ass," Amanda said, smiling. "You're not the type of hero who looks for villains; you're the type who rescues damsels in distress. You're my favorite kind of hero."

Sam smiled and blushed.

"I have to go," Amanda said as she slowly stood, Sam mirroring her gesture and speed. The sad expression on Sam's face urged her in to a passionate kiss. Sam gently pulled her in closer, and they were both lost to thoughts of the great romance that might have been.

As Amanda broke away, she opened her eyes a mere inch from Sam's, a flash of the life they could have shared reflected between them.

In that life, she didn't have cancer, she hadn't blown up a gas station, and she'd never propositioned the chief. She'd strolled into Eastwood's and spied a dashing policeman. They talked, went out for dinner and dancing, and her pass through the town became an extended stay. After a few months, he'd proposed. She became part of the community, living a long life with a sweet, handsome, courageous man who loved her for all the quirks that sent most guys running.

"You're going to make some girl so happy," she whispered, tears now streaming down her face.

Sam tried to dry her cheeks, but she pulled away. "Come see me if you can," she said, pressing her lips to his one last time before making her final exit from the Milky Way.

*

While Amanda met with Sam, and Jim and Emily packed their bags, Kyle was busy working on a surprise. One of the unexpected benefits of befriending a film star was access to luxuries that eluded most civilians. After a fifteen minute phone call, Kyle had arranged for a private jet to meet them at a local airport within three hours.

Of all the good-byes they made, the most emotional one came from Claire.

"Please take me with you!" she pleaded. "There's nothing for me here! I know I seem like a local, but I'm one of you!"

Kyle offered her his email, and told her she should write, but that wasn't good enough for little Claire. He finally gave in and swept her up for a kiss.

Together, they watched the plane land on the small strip of asphalt, and the driver exchanged luggage with the flight crew. They were getting ready to board when Morris pulled up.

"Making as big an exit as you do an entrance," he said to Amanda, nodding at the plane.

"Come to see me off?" Amanda asked.

"Came to say goodbye to my dance partner," he said, bowing to Emily.

Emily walked over and hugged Morris. "Thank you," she whispered in his ear.

"The pleasure was all mine," he said as he kissed her lips, making Jim pout just a little.

Morris shook hands with Jim and Kyle, and finally Amanda.

"I seem to remember you saying you didn't have any people," Morris said.

"I seem to remember you agreeing," she said.

"I'm glad to see we were both wrong," Morris said. "Try not to blow up L.A.; they're not as nice as us folks down here about little things like that, you know."

The four of them sat, comfortable and quiet, in the aircraft's big leather seats. Kyle finally called his agent, and his parents, which made Emily feel guilty about not calling her mother.

Amanda looked out the window and Jim took the seat next to her.

"Cool plane," he said.

"Yeah, comfy," she said, stretching out.

Jim struggled with the right thing to say. "I'm going to start looking for the best doctor in the world tomorrow," he said.

"I know you will," she said. "And I know when they tell you there's nothing else they can do, you'll look for more. But I've had months to deal with this. I can accept my fate, Jim. I just didn't want to be alone," she explained.

"You won't be," he said. "I promise."

Emily watched as Jim took Amanda's hand, and for a moment felt a twinge of jealousy. But she knew what she'd committed to, and she knew she had a lifetime ahead of her with Jim.

Chapter 54

Emily woke up in her own bed for the first time in nearly a week. She could feel Jim's weight next to her, and rolled in closer to his warmth. She slowly got out of bed and did her best to not wake him.

Emily checked her phone. It was 8:35, and she had no messages. She pulled on a pair of clean jeans and an old Stanford sweatshirt. Tiptoeing passed the guest room, she peaked in on Amanda, who was fast asleep. Emily slipped silently down the stairs and out the front door.

She checked her phone again as she pulled into her mother's driveway. It was 9:05, and she knew her mother would be well out of bed and likely on to her routine of reading the paper and haranguing whatever public official made the news. Her sister, as usual, wouldn't rise until nearly noon.

Katherine looked up as Emily walked into the kitchen. "Well, I don't know what I've done to deserve such a visit!" Katherine said grandly as Emily walked over to the ever-present pot of hot coffee.

"No returned calls for nearly a week," she said. "I would have been worried if I wasn't certain you simply like putting me through these things."

Emily remained silent and sat down across her mother, sipping the coffee.

"Well?" Katherine demanded. "Say something!"

"I missed good coffee," Emily sighed pleasantly. "I've been drinking the worst coffee from a Day's Inn motel lobby."

"That's it?" Katherine said, "No 'hello,' no 'I'm sorry for making you worry,' nothing?"

Emily savored another sip of the coffee, holding the moment. "Hi, mom. I'm sorry I made you worry."

Katherine got up and walked to the pantry. "I have some of these mini coffeecakes, we should eat them before they go bad."

That was her mother's standard way of offering food. She liked to act as if she was offering scraps, or something slightly off and about to be thrown out, but in reality she probably had bought them yesterday, hoping someone would share them with her.

"Well, how did it go?" Katherine asked. "Did you get the girl off?"

"Yes," Emily confirmed.

"And what was she like?" Katherine asked.

"She's nice," Emily said, "sweet. You'll like her."

"Why, am I going to meet her?" Katherine asked. "Oh my god, did he have the gall to invite her to the wedding? That dumb ass!"

Emily carefully laid her hands over her mother's. "Don't call him that, Mom," she said gently.

"Well, I don't understand," Katherine said, her hands trembling like soft birds under Emily's touch.

"Her name is Amanda, and she's going to be staying with us for a while," Emily explained.

"What do you mean, staying with you?" Katherine asked. "At your home? Right now?"

"Yes," Emily said.

"How the hell did that happen?" her mother asked. "Is he going to marry the two of you? Because if we're going to move this wedding to Utah, I'll have to update the invitations."

Emily took another sip of her coffee and began sharing the events of their trip with her mother. She kept to the more important details, the exploding gas station, the police chief and his cute son, the even cuter TV star, the smart and decent local public defender, the precocious desk clerk, the mistake Emily made in being too aggressive with the racist prosecutor, and, finally, Amanda's illness.

Her mother listened to every word. Emily had never seen her more attentive, or heard her more quiet, but then again, Emily couldn't recall ever speaking to her mother as a friend. It was a change from their usual, adversarial exchanges. It took her back to a time before her father had died, before their relationship had become fraught with unrelenting reminders of what they both had lost. Suddenly, Emily remembered being a little girl, a preschooler, maybe, running off the bus, bursting to share her day with her mother, who always watched her come and go through the glass of the kitchen window.

"So, you're just going to let this woman live with you, knowing she has her eyes on your fiancé?" Katherine asked.

"I am," Emily said. "We're going to find her the best medical attention we can."

"And if they say there is nothing they can do?" Katherine asked.

"Then we'll make sure she's comfortable, and not alone," Emily said.

Katherine got up to get another cup of coffee. "Well, we still have a lot to accomplish before the wedding," she said. "I hope we can get back on that this week, we only have a few weeks."

"I know," Emily said as she got up. She paused. "I'm sorry Dad's not here," she said to her mother.

"Well, yes, I'm sure he would have loved to see you in that wedding dress," Katherine said as she poured her coffee.

"No, Mom," Emily said. "I'm sorry Dad's not here for you."

Her mother stopped pouring. "What do you mean?" she asked.

Emily finally had the words. Maybe not the right words, but

they would have to do. "I'm sorry you lost him," she said. "I don't think I ever told you that. I've always been so preoccupied with my own loss that I never acknowledged yours."

"Don't be daft," her mother said. "I'm a grown woman, you were just a child, of course it hurt you more."

"Not more," Emily said, "just different." She steadied herself, ready to ask the question that had brought her to her mother's table. "I was hoping you would walk me down the aisle, Mom."

Emily could see she'd caught Katherine off-guard. "I thought we'd ask your uncle Larry to do that," she said, "I know he would be honored."

Emily nodded, "Uncle Larry's great, but he's not the one I want to walk me down the aisle, because I know I'm going to be scared. It's going to be really scary for me, and when I get frightened, I want to look next to me and see the person who gave me my courage."

"Don't be silly," Katherine said, fidgeting with her coffee cup.

"It's true, Mom," Emily said. "I got my desire to stand up for people from my father, but I got the courage to do it from you. And I want you next to me when I take the biggest leap of my life."

Katherine put her coffee cup down and tried to look away.

"I love you, Mom," Emily said. "I'm sorry if you sometimes feel like I don't acknowledge or appreciate you. I do, and I promise you're not ever going to be alone, okay?"

Emily didn't remember the last time she saw her mother smile, or cry, but it had been long enough that the effect was contagious. They stood together in the kitchen for sometime, and when Emily finally told her she had to go, her mother gave her a parting gift. "I am so proud of you," she said.

Chapter 55

Amanda woke up and felt oddly comfortable. She sat up and looked around, seeing the room for the first time in the daylight. There was a treadmill in the corner, and boxes stacked in the closet. And she laughed when she saw the old BMW poster.

She began down the stairs and found Jim in the kitchen. He looked adorable, she thought, in his ratty pajama bottoms and faded UWM t-shirt. She stood still for a moment, taking the image in and allowing herself the momentary fantasy this was her life, not Emily's.

"Oh, morning," Jim said when he noticed Amanda standing there. "Coffee?"

"God, yes!" Amanda said.

Jim poured her a cup and brought her the cream he knew she liked.

"Emily still asleep?" Amanda asked.

"No, she left a note she was going to see her mother," he said. "So, look out when she comes back. Bad time to hit her up for sex, by the way."

"I'll try to control myself," Amanda laughed, and then paused, appraising Jim. "But, I don't want there to be secrets between us, Jim. You know we didn't have sex that night, right? Emily and I, we, well, it never got that far."

Jim smiled his cockiest grin. "I know," he said. "If it had, I doubt I'd still be in the picture," he winked. "I know exactly how good you can be, remember?" He turned to the sink, feeling an unknown weight drop from his shoulders and resisting the urge to throw his fists into the air, champion-style. "We probably shouldn't let Emily know that I know, you know?" he asked. "I think maybe it helps her to think we're even, which I could definitely use."

Amanda laughed. "You are never going to be even with that woman, Jim. She is far too good for you."

"Don't I know it," he agreed. "Anyway, I got some names back for doctors I want you to see," Jim said. "I'm going to get appointments set today."

"Okay," Amanda said, having decided in the air not to fight them on doctors, and to agree with any treatments they wanted. "Thank you," she said. Her consent was a small price to pay for something that would make them happier, at least for as long as it continued to give them hope.

"How was the room?" Jim asked.

"Great," Amanda said, savoring her coffee.

"You're the first guest in it," Jim said. "I'll get some of the stuff cleared away so you have more room for your things."

"I don't have stuff," Amanda laughed. "Stuff went boom, remember?"

"Oh, Emily's taking you shopping today, so trust me, you're going to have stuff," he said.

"She's really great, Jim," Amanda said. "I am happy for you, I hope you know that."

Jim stopped and looked at Amanda, and for a moment he let his mind wander to the life he was certain he would have, back when he was in college.

"Thank you," he said. "I think she's incredible, too."

The front door opened and Emily strolled into the kitchen. "I got bagels, if you're hungry," she said.

As Amanda watched Emily and Jim walk about the kitchen, engaged in the domestic dance of their regular life, she felt at home for the first time. She wondered if this was what a family felt like.

Chapter 56

Jim returned to work the next day and began catching up on the past week. After assuring everyone his mother had soldiered through her illness, Jim was able to save the excuse for another day, or for his mother's actual demise, whichever came first.

He made it a priority to spend more time at home and helped get Amanda to her doctor appointments and tests. The frustration of not finding a treatment plan that offered any real hope took its toll on Jim, and more often than not his telephone exchanges with highly respected doctors had to be followed up with emails apologizing for his behavior and language. They were all understanding, and Jim realized oncologists must have even thicker skin than lawyers.

It was helpful Kyle remained a big part of Jim's life both personally and professionally. After some soul-searching, Kyle decided to forgo the movie franchise and sat down with the producers of his show to come up with a new vehicle for him, the story of a young gay man in law school. The networks turned it down, but it was finally bought by a cable channel.

Kyle embraced being who he was, and in a major PR coup, landed an hour long interview with Oprah, where he came out nationally. The highlight of the hour for Jim was when Oprah asked whom he had trusted enough to come out to, and Kyle told the world it was his lawyer and best friend, Jim Morgan.

Jim received phone calls from several well-known celebrities that week, and picked up two big clients.

Reggie kept in touch, and not only did Ashford move forward on the plan, saving hundreds of people in the community from losing their homes, but Reggie was also asked to consult with several other towns to help them with their own strategy. Jim was also pleased to hear Chad Mitchell won the election in a landslide victory, and immediately filed a criminal complaint against the banks, as promised.

As time went on, Jim couldn't ignore the evidence proving Amanda, the most alive person he'd ever met, was dying. As the wedding approached, Amanda was at Emily's side through all the preparations, but he could see even simple activities taking their toll on her. And, when Emily decided that after the wedding she would take some time off work, Jim was grateful.

The awkwardness between Jim and Amanda faded over time, until their relationship was better, stronger, purer than before. However, it paled in comparison to the bond Amanda had formed with Emily. Thus, when he wasn't worried about Amanda, he found himself worried for Emily.

Chapter 57

Emily had already handed off most of her caseload before the wedding, so it wasn't an issue to extend her leave. Amanda ended up being a big help with the wedding, even acting as a moderator between Emily and her mother when they would disagree.

Emily was better able than Jim to deal with the news from the doctors. It was in both their natures to want to fix everything, but he was taking the lack of options much harder. Emily scoured the web for new cancer treatments, but in the end, the real experts all had the same advice: try to make her as comfortable as you can. This was accomplished through pain medications, and they seemed effective, at least at first.

The decision to make Amanda her maid of honor was a simple one, as it ended the argument between her sisters as to who it should be, and no one had the lack of taste to question giving the honor to the beautiful but terminally ill cancer patient.

The wedding itself was a grand success. Emily knew it, because even her mother agreed. Her dress fit perfectly, her husband behaved himself, and when she looked over the line of women that included her mother, Amanda, and her two sisters, the hole her father had left closed a little for the first time.

Her wedding dance was the highlight, as her new husband swept her effortlessly across the floor, clearly having put in some practice before the big day. Amanda's surprise partner, Sam, looked dashing, and even helped Emily put together what was certainly the first line dance held at the Beverly Wilshire Hotel, although most of the guests were too uptight to actively take part.

Sam, who had resigned from the Ashford police department as soon as the investigation had cleared him, was now a firefighter training to be a paramedic. He promised to visit often, and kept to his word.

Jim and Emily had talked about surprising Amanda by taking her with them on a honeymoon to Paris, but by the time the wedding came, travel was out of the question.

Emily didn't mark the first day she could tell Amanda was sick just by looking at her, but it was clear on the faces of those who would come to visit. It seemed like each week came with its own, fresh reminder the end was approaching. Emily spent many hours in the bathroom crying to keep a positive attitude in front of Amanda and Jim.

After a few months, the doctors' appointments became less about helping Amanda than checking in to have her prescriptions renewed. When the primary oncologist suggested to Emily it was time to consider a hospice nurse, she spent nearly an hour crying, alone in her car.

Chapter 58

Nearly nine months had passed since Amanda had flown to Los Angeles on a fancy, private plane. In that time, she had become closer to Jim and Emily than she'd ever thought possible. She routinely felt bad about how out of their way they went for her, but instead of apologizing, she tried to express the appreciation she carried in her heart.

She loved California. The weather was always beautiful, and there was always something to do. She visited Disneyland and Sea World, she tried surfing for the first time, and she loved just driving down the coastline in Jim's BMW.

The wedding was beautiful, and not once did she need to pretend it was hers; she was just happy for them. Sam showing up was a great surprise. It was nice to have someone else to talk to, so Jim and Emily could enjoy their day. Even Jim's parents were nice to her, although she was certain it was mostly guilt.

She was excited to see Kyle talk with Oprah, and even more touched to see Jim pretending not to cry when Kyle called him out by name as his best friend.

The time had gone by quickly, though each day seemed to bring some new pain or problem. Although the doctors in Los Angeles weren't any better at curing cancer than doctors anywhere else in the world, they did seem pretty liberal with the drugs, which

Amanda appreciated. The feeling of legally getting high in a convertible on PCH was nothing short of liberating.

Jim kept his word and cleared out the room for her, and she and Emily had a lot of fun decorating it, but it was only a matter of six months before she had to admit the stairs had become too much for her. The delivery of the hospital bed to the living room was an awkward event, but they made the best of it by all three piling in to watch movies and eat popcorn.

Sooner than she liked, the bed became her primary station. Amanda had to enjoy the beautiful Los Angeles days through the window, which Emily kept open for her. She began to sleep most of the day as the drugs that worked to keep the pain at bay took her energy away as payment.

She thought it was sweet for Jim to lie and tell her he had taken a few days off work because they were redecorating the offices. She felt bad for keeping them both away from their jobs, but enjoyed the attention anyway. As her grandmother had always said, she didn't do well alone.

Everyone kept speaking in hushed tones, trying not to wake her, but she loved to hear them talk. She felt bad about falling asleep during conversations. Sometimes, she would look up during a conversion with Emily and see Jim, realizing she must have dozed off. She didn't remember who was talking to her and holding her hand when she closed her eyes, but she knew she wasn't alone.

*

The horizon settled and the earth steadied, gently coming to a rest. The sky seeped in as she closed her eyes, filling her with a peaceful glow. She felt warm hands on hers, and knew she was loved. She fell still, and the pain faded away.

Chapter 59

Emily sat on the bench in the cemetery. Three years had passed since Jim and Emily said goodbye to Amanda. She noticed the beautiful bouquet of flowers Jim obviously sent, and set her own next to his. Jim didn't like cemeteries, but Emily found them peaceful.

She sat and talked to Amanda, catching her up on all the events in the lives of those she had loved. Kyle had earned his second Emmy and was in a serious relationship. Emily's oldest sister had finally gotten engaged and moved out, allowing her mother to buy a smaller place closer to Emily and Jim. Sam had also gotten engaged, and wanted her and Jim to come out for the wedding. Claire had come out to Los Angeles the month she turned eighteen, looking for a job. She was now working for Kyle as the world's weirdest personal assistant, and had even been approached about doing a reality TV show.

Reggie was on TV last week, discussing the plan Jim put together for small towns to pull together and save their homes. He kept trying to give the credit to Jim, but Jim insisted it was all Reggie's for doing the heavy lifting.

Some of the people in Ashford had a different take on things, and didn't credit Jim or Reggie. They say everything got better when that crazy lady blew up the gas station. There's even a tree, planted in Amanda's honor, where she parked her stolen car before blowing it up.

Amanda's death was hard on Emily, and she had fallen into a depression for the first few months. Eventually, her friends and family had brought her back around, especially her mother.

She had become closer to Katherine in the past couple of years, and when the baby came, she'd seen a whole new side of her. They now spent at least one day a week together.

Jim and Emily's relationship wasn't always perfect, but she no longer had any doubts they loved each other. Losing Amanda seemed to have made Jim sensitive to the idea of losing Emily, and that made him more appreciative of every moment.

Jim was busier than ever with work, being one of the most sought after entertainment lawyers in Los Angeles, and Emily was dealing with the struggle of getting back to work while being a mother. It was hard sometimes, and occasionally she would fall out of step or lose her balance, but the people she loved were always there to remind her she wasn't alone. And that, she had come to learn, was all anyone truly needs.

About The Author

The Benefits of Line Dancing is Edward's first book. He is currently the CEO of USWeb, and splits his time between Las Vegas and Baja, Mexico. For more information about Edward, visit edshull.com.

www.ingramcontent.com/pod-product-compliance
Lightning Source LLC
Chambersburg PA
CBHW060518180626

46817CB00002B/394